The Book of Not

Tsitsi Dangarembga is the author of three novels, including *Nervous Conditions*, winner of the Commonwealth Writers' Prize, and *This Mournable Body*, which was shortlisted for the Booker Prize. She is also a film-maker, playwright and the director of the Institute of Creative Arts for Progress in Africa Trust. She lives in Harare, Zimbabwe.

by the same author

NERVOUS CONDITIONS
THIS MOURNABLE BODY

TSITSI DANGAREMBGA

The Book of Not

faber

This paperback edition first published in 2021
by Faber & Faber Limited
Bloomsbury House, 74–77 Great Russell Street
London WC1B 3DA

First published in the UK
by Ayebia Clarke Publishing Limited
7 Syringa Walk
Banbury
OX16 1FR
Oxfordshire

Typeset by Typo•glyphix, Burton-on-Trent, DE14 3HE
Printed and bound by CPI Group (UK) Ltd, Croydon, CRO 4YY

A CIP record for this book
is available from the British Library

ISBN 978–0–571–36814–3

London Borough of Hackney	
91300001157381	
Askews & Holts	
AF	£8.99
	6628981

To Mami and Baba and Mukoma Gwin for being there;
also to Rudo and Munewenyu, to Olaf, Tonderai,
Chadamoyo and Masimba.

The Book of Not

Who's Who

Tambudzai Sigauke (Tambu) – the narrator

Mai – mother, usually Tambu's mother

Mainini – a young aunt, also a term of respect applied to any young woman, or young relative

Baba – father, usually Tambudzai's father

Jeremiah – Tambudzai's father

Netsai – Tambu's sister

Rambanai – Tambu's youngest sister

Dambudzo – Tambu's younger brother

Babamukuru – Tambu's uncle

Maiguru (sometimes known as **Mai**) – Tambu's aunt, wife of Babamukuru

Nyasha – Tambu's cousin, daughter of Babamukuru and Maiguru

Nyari – Netsai's friend

Sylvester – the gardener at the Mission

Sister Emmanuel – headmistress of the Young Ladies' College of the Sacred Heart

Sister Catherine – Latin teacher at the Young Ladies' College of the Sacred Heart

Miss Plato – matron at the Young Ladies' College of the Sacred Heart

Ntombizethu (Ntombi), Irene, Anastasia, Benhilda, Patience, Cynthia – members of the 'African dormitory' at the Young Ladies' College of the Sacred Heart

3

Tracey Stevenson – pupil at the Young Ladies' College of the Sacred Heart and later advertising executive at Steers, D'Arcy and MacPedius Advertising Agency

Bougainvillea (Bo), Linda, Josephine, Deidre, Angela – some of the pupils at the Young Ladies' College of the Sacred Heart

Mrs May – matron at Twiss Hostel

Mark May – son of Mrs May

Mr Steers – managing director of Steers, D'Arcy and MacPedius Advertising Agency

Dick Lawson – senior copywriter at Steers, D'Arcy and MacPedius Advertising Agency

Belinda – typist at Steers, D'Arcy and MacPedius Advertising Agency

Pedzi – receptionist at Steers, D'Arcy and MacPedius Advertising Agency

I

Up, up, up, the leg spun. A piece of person, up there in the sky. Earth and acrid vapours coated my tongue. Silence surged out to die away at the ragged shriek of a cricket in the bushes at the edge of the village clearing.

You could not see her anymore, the figure who, a few moments ago, had padded out of the *musasa* shrub after a man in combat canvas, rippled green like a Chinese jungle. I knew this, the lack of wisdom of it. All the villagers at the meeting knew. Everyone saw the folly, except Netsai, my sister. Now, in the seconds after the boom, like a funereal drumbeat, sounded by Netsai's step, mothers groaned in relief as the babies upon their backs wailed and twisted their arms. The village mothers jiggled the infants wrapped in thin coarse towels, shock and relief carved into their exhausted faces, crescents of white teeth gleaming in the moonlight.

In the darkness, Netsai's leg arced up. Something was required of me! I was her sister, her elder sister. I was, by that position, required to perform the act that would protect her. How miserable I was, for nothing lay in my power, so that both the powerlessness and the misery frustrated. And in my quiet misery my chest quaked, bones vibrated in and out as though the strings of my heart strained and tore, and I felt as though I jumped on to the spinning limb and rode it as it rotated, moving up to somewhere out of it.

What I wanted was to get away. But the moon was too far beyond, and there were white bits under me, where the flesh was shredded off and the bone gleamed that famed ivory, and those below cowered and, if they were not quick enough, were spattered in blood. Then came the jolt, as of a fall, and I saw the leg was caught in an ungainly way in the smaller branches of a *mutamba* tree, the foot hooked, long like that infamous fruit.

Mai, our mother, fell down. She did not get up. Thus again something was required of me. I was the eldest girl, the eldest child now two brothers had died. I was expected to perform an appropriate action. So I rose from the Zambia cloth spread out on the grit which my mother had reminded me to bring, moving slowly, first rolling onto my knees and hands like an old woman, and holding my head down to summon the peace that comes with not seeing, the kind of peace I possessed in war time. Then, when I had removed myself further from the group I had been brought to be a part of, I pushed up to standing.

Mai was still on the ground. Again, at sixteen, I had nothing that Mai wanted. It was all too much for me, so I just stood watching her, arms folded, rigid and taking care to be aloof, and I didn't look up at the *mutamba* tree anymore. It was too dark to see anything now; there was only glistening, the leg glistening, and the woman on the ground. They were an axis that fixed me like poles of a force that bound, prevented me from jumping up and rotating towards I did not know what – some more terrible agony. Mai pushed her tongue into shiny patches where blood was mixed with earth. Mai groaned, 'Netsai! Netsai!' She clawed at the ground, slithering forward like a snake.

The axis, with Mai one moving apex, evolved into a shifting triangle as a man came towards her. It was the man Netsai should not have followed, whose combat suit rippled green like a Chinese jungle. He was the Comrade, the guerrilla, the Big Brother, the *Mukoma,* who had come later, after we had all gathered for the *morari,* and the meeting had started and the villagers were becoming intoxicated – innocently, as they said, for they were compelled to watch – with the presence of blood.

I didn't want to look at him either, so I still didn't have anywhere to look. Behind came the girl. She was the one everyone noticed, with a shaking of envious disapproval, because she moved like a purr, as though she was just fed, that one, just washed and her skin shining with oil. She had come first to the meeting, after we were all seated, but before the beating which was the purpose of the *morari.* The man who rippled green and the girl of ripe flesh stood in Mai's path and remained so when she gripped their calves with her hands in order to pull herself past them. The man and the girl stopped Mai from touching her daughter. So Mai sprang up, as though to reach the swaying leg, and they pulled her, this time more roughly.

Holding Mai, the man looked from Netsai on the ground in the grass and bushes beyond my vision, to the girl next to him with tortured helplessness. So Mai didn't touch Netsai, did not feel her daughter, which they said later was good, as it could have changed Netsai's position in such a way as to accelerate the bleeding. The man had a rifle slung over his back, melting into the jungle of the cloth, the weapon a shrug away, doing nothing for him now, unable to intimidate his grief. I was afraid at any moment he would change

7

his mind, fire with anger at his helplessness. They said later . . . you never heard it properly, as though love was not a respectable topic to talk of but mere lust enclosed in other clothing.

They said . . . and I heard it here and there much later, from Nyari and Mai Sagonda and other people in the village, and certainly when Mai spoke of it, love was never mentioned . . . they said he said, when he drank too much after the war, he was in love with both of them. Netsai was his first war love, picked as she brought *sadza* to this freedom fighter's hideaway. Soon she decided she had to leave and cross over the mountains to Mozambique because her activities had been discovered by the security forces. But everyone knew even if there was this war outside that called her, there was another inside which was the way she made the air about her shimmer and sparkle with joy when she spoke of this Big Brother. That was when the Big Brother took this young girl, Dudziro, and loved both of them, a comrade indeterminate and undecided. Now he and Dudziro prevented Mai from reaching her daughter. The *Mukoma* did not tell us what to do, as we expected, and so we stood around waiting. No one could ask Babamukuru, as Babamukuru wasn't talking.

Babamukuru couldn't say anything for he was barely alive. And it was hard to look at the man in green and his helplessness, as we all knew Babamukuru would have been dead if the man contained in cloth the colour of a Chinese jungle hadn't saved him.

In fact, Babamukuru's disciplining with the *sjamboks* of war was why our feet had shuffled over the grey earth that night, with only a sickle moon to taunt with the absence of

8

light, I amongst the nervous girls that the comrades had insisted witness the pulverising of a person, the mincing of a man, all of us jumping at everything, the movement of the wind, the swirling of a companion's skirt, the variegations of night beneath the shadowed bushes.

We had been summoned to Babamukuru's trial. He was, the charges went, not exactly a collaborator, but one whose soul hankered to be at one with the occupying Rhodesian forces. *Mutengesi.* The people in the village said Babamukuru was one who'd sell every ounce of his own blood for a drop of someone else's. As a student at the Young Ladies' College of the Sacred Heart, a school Babamukuru had decided to enrol me at against my mother's wishes, I was proof of my uncle's dubious spirit. For why would a man select a school for his child where the education was superior to the education given to the children of other people? A school that would not, unlike other schools in areas where guerrillas battled for independence, be closed? A school peopled not by those who looked like us, but by Europeans? I was to watch the decimation of my uncle in order to instill loyalty in me.

I had not been aware of all of this when Babamukuru had driven me and my aunt, Maiguru, to the village. My uncle had spoken to me evasively, saying only that he had been called, had thought I should accompany him as the destination was my home, and there was to be a meeting. I remember how I had not dared to break my aunt's silence with a question.

It was the end of the May holiday in my second year at the Young Ladies' College of the Sacred Heart. I spent the holidays at the mission, using as an excuse the intensifying of war, when in reality I did not have the heart to return three times a year to fetching water from the river, the juddering paraffin lamp light and *sadza* with only one, extremely small, portion of relish.

There was, in addition to that, my mother's constant innuendo, 'Oh, you, *wekuchirungu*! Do you still like *matumbu*, Tambudzai! Can you white people eat *mufushwa* with peanut butter?' Finally, there was the constant strain of not asking and not being told about Netsai's movements. If you went to school with white people and sat next to them in class, wouldn't you end up telling them something? One day the white people would discover my sister's activities.

'Look at how terrible he is with us,' Mai had whispered in low grumbles in the afternoon, in the bedroom in the house where I was to sleep, referring to Babamukuru. I had just arrived and was shown up to my quarters like a guest. 'And that aunt of yours,' my mother gloated with anticipation, 'coming here like that with him. Does she think she's coming to one of his European meetings! Today she will see it, how things are moving here in the village.'

Garbled accounts. You ask and that's what you get. 'Terrible, Mai? What has Babamukuru done?' I tried, even though reluctantly, to probe.

'Look at the way Samhungu has put a fence round his place!' she exclaimed enviously about our neighbours. 'Don't think the working Samhungus, the ones with jobs, haven't helped their poor relatives! They have helped! They have made the Samhungus here in the village safer with that fence because of all these things that are going on around us! But we, your mother and father here, we are left to the mercy of the open like that by Babamukuru as if we are forest animals. In spite of all that money of his! Don't think people don't see it, Tambudzai! People see it. They ask where people put all the things they have if no one sees it coming home to other people!'

'What did *Mukoma* say?' my father wanted to know, when he joined my mother and I to greet me more formally. I repeated the little information I had, that Babamukuru was expected at a meeting at which he thought I should be present. Mai's eyes gleamed with suppressed satisfaction. 'Yes, we have our own meetings!' she chanted. 'Here in Mambo Mutasa's land in Sabhuku Sigauke's village, we know how to have them! And the Big Brothers know us,' she went on, sounding excited and boastful. 'We are known, remember that, Tambudzai, and we have meetings!'

'Your uncle!' reproved Baba, to silence Mai and prevent her from talking too much in front of me. 'How could he travel with all this going on? What hole would he push through with every side waiting and thinking, there's meat, we'll get it! *Yave nyama yekugocha, baya wabaya!*' He began to sing an old war song, bawled these days in the cities at football matches, uneasily eyeing Mai, in an attempt at humour.

I was loose-limbed. I remember that, wandering around the homestead. I came down from the old four-roomed house which Babamukuru had constructed at his wedding, and had subsequently bequeathed to my mother and father before building his newer and more imposing one. My old bedroom was my mother's round kitchen but I was grown too old and too fine to be placed there. All afternoon Babamukuru and my father sat in my uncle's new living room, and Maiguru brewed tea for them in her kitchen with the tea leaves she had brought, and buttered and served the bread she had packed from the mission. My mother was preparing our evening meal so she did not fall in Maiguru's line of vision, consequently was not offered tea and did not drink it.

I touched this – a broken upturned wheelbarrow beaten to lace by wind and rain – examined that – the twisted axel of a scotch cart – the things that break and cannot be fixed because the force of wholeness has abdicated. It was surprising to see how little there was to remind me that I had lived here for twelve years of my childhood. In this absence of anchoring, I shuffled around picking up a half-seeded maize cob and throwing the grain to the chickens, as though nothing had happened, doing my best to pretend when family elders met and talked like this in war time – then it was the same as in peace time: a wedding, a new water tank, bream in the dam down at the fields – an event to improve the family was in the planning.

'*Zviunganidze*! Pull yourself together!' Mai had advised when she came out with a dish of *sadza* and a cup of sour-milk shortly before sunset. 'Maybe it would have been better if you weren't here, Tambudzai, but *vana Mukoma*, the Big Brothers, those Comrades of ours, they said that one has to be there.' She did not look at me, but into the cup as though she were handing it to some older person whose eyes she was prevented by decorum from meeting. 'They wanted Babamukuru to bring you back from school so that they know you know it!' I took small pieces of *sadza* and sips of sourmilk, while Mai eyed me derisively, remarking, 'It's difficult, isn't it, the eating's difficult!'

I took a large sour gulp so as not to answer. I could not tell her what was difficult. It was not the food. It was her. It was the awful covetous emptiness in her eyes, and then the gleaming when she paired Babamukuru's name with the mention of a fence. It was the nothingness upon which she stood as upon the summit of her life, from which she clawed about for gleanings from other women's husbands, such as Babamukuru. I shuddered, spilling the sourmilk. What could make a woman so avaricious and hollow? Oh, how to become more of a person!

'Pull yourself together, and know what's outside. That's what will help,' my mother said, her voice as dry as maize husks.

'Take a Zambia,' she instructed later when the sun set. She took the hand of Dambudzo, my little brother, and ordered me to stay close to Rambanai, my other sister. 'Your father's gone on before with Babamukuru.' *'Baba wenyu'*, she said, 'your father', making it clear it was our parent and not her husband who had decided to proceed with his brother, our uncle. Her eyes gleamed again and she pulled at Dambudzo's hand unnecessarily. 'And of course that woman, Maiguru, who thinks she is as much as them decided not to wait for us, just go on with them. Mm! We'll see what she says when it's finished. Now, children, we don't want any crying, not for anything! Not because you are hungry, or because you're tired! We don't want any crying for anything.'

The pale sand gleamed eerily in the slight moonlight as we set off. The candles were out at the Samhungus' homestead. 'People who eat and sleep before the sun sinks! Those are sellouts, such people,' snorted Mai softly. 'Scurrying into the dark when the soldiers say curfew, frightened of anything, just like cockroaches!' She pulled at Dambudzo to make him hurry. The neighbour's cattle were in their kraal, and mooing in distress, not having been out long enough to take sufficient pasture. Otherwise the homestead was silent as though inhabited by ghostly people. Beyond us and around the foot of the hill on the other side of the road, a red glow flickered as the last *sadza* was cooked, or a faint orange shaft told of a paraffin lamp still alight: perhaps a school child was reading. Soon even these faded away, one by one. Only the sliver of moon sent out its watery light, but Mai was walking fast, not needing light to show her the direction.

'Today, Tambudzai,' she breathed almost gently, 'don't be frightened. If you show anybody any fear at all, you will be asked what you are afraid of. Then, Tambudzai, I hope you are listening, it will be finished for you! They will say you are afraid because you have been sent here not by your own free wish, but by someone who cannot come himself, someone who dares not be seen! They will say you are afraid because the oppressors sent you!'

I believe she would have spoken differently if she had thought I was more of an ally. But Mai was probably frightened of this girl who was growing beyond her into the European world. At times like this, it is a case of muscles and blood and contractions and pain, a case of out of whose stomach a person came that makes one woman to another a mother or daughter?

How does a daughter know that she feels appropriately towards the woman who is her mother? Yes, it was difficult to know what to do with Mai, how to conceive her.

I thought I hated her fawning, but what I see I hated is the degree of it. If she was fawning, she was not fawning enough. She diluted it with her spitefulness, the hopeless clawing of a small cornered spirit towards what was beyond it. And if she had spirit, it was not great enough, being shrunk by the bitterness of her temper. In any case, I was a teenager, an intelligent one, who had been given a scholarship by the nuns of the Young Ladies' College of the Sacred Heart. I was thereby being transformed into a young woman with a future. What I was most interested in was myself and what I would become. You don't see the contradiction, when the front of your uniform has plumped out and you have been brought the three sensible elastic bras stipulated by the senior school's clothes list; when you go to the moon each month and know you carry inside you for future development the mysteries of life and of woman; when you yearn to say to your mother, 'I'll give you a book' so that she can sit first her grade seven and then her form two and then her O-Level certificate, so that where there is the profound job of growing life to be done, the garden of it can be tended together. No, you don't see the contradiction of being astonished at being oneself so plenipotentiary and begging God to make you not like your mother.

'Whatever you see,' Mai warned again as we passed the buildings at Rutivi School and went on to the playing fields, speaking more gently now as if nearing our destination reassured her. 'Whatever it is, do not say anything. Just sing, whatever the song, sing it. And answer as everyone else does. Otherwise, be silent.'

Behind the playing fields was an area where tall *musasas* were left standing and were not chopped down for building or firewood. These formed a ring which provided shade for visiting school buses. The ground to the north was worn bare by football elevens and athletics teams warming up. Then the *musasa* shrub began. Short squat bushes splayed out from the stumps of adult trees that the village had harvested in their entirety; and the crippled wood, interspersed with sharp undernourished grass and occasionally a stalwart tree of wild fruits, straggled half-way up the dark lumbering form of Rutivi Mountain. There were shapes in the clearing between the tall trees and the shrubs. Some were sitting. It was difficult to tell whether they were men or women. Others padded silently to empty spots as we did.

'*Pamberi nerusununguko! Pamberi nechimurenga! Pasi nevadzvinyiriri!*' I did not want to see whose voice was chanting so passionately. I sat now in the depths of the machine that brought death to people, and I was intolerably petrified to be in the belly of the beast that belched war.

'Forward with freedom! Forward with the war of liberation! Down with oppressors!'

This fighting, and the limbs and the fluids and the excreta that it scattered over the land, intoxicated the men and women and youth and children who had come to be told we were all, together with the guerrillas, the sacrifice of whose blood justice was purchased.

'Forward with freedom! Forward with the war of liberation! Down with them!' Clenched fists rose misshapenly large upon malnourished arms where the body had eaten its own meat in order to survive. The villagers echoed each slogan with such force that the earth on which we sat shivered. I tried not to look, so I would not make the mistake of saying I had seen anything when I returned to school. I tried not to hear so I would never repeat the words of war anywhere. Mai's voice was shrill and her eyes gleamed.

'*Sisi* Tambu! *Sisi* Tambu!'

Receiving no response, Rambanai edged closer to me and whispered more loudly, '*Sisi* Tambu, look!'

'Shh! You, be quiet!' Mai hissed.

'I am just telling *Sisi* Tambu that *Mukoma*, the one over there, who is giving the slogans, he came to our home two days ago. Remember, Mai, you killed a cock. The *Vakoma*, they only eat meat, *Sisi* Tambu, so they can be strong. But before him, we had the one who always talked to *Sisi* Netsai. That *Mukoma*, Mai,' a thought struck her, 'the one who talked to *Sisi* Netsai, didn't he eat beans, Mai! Yes, he was given beans! Isn't he strong, Mai? Is that why he stopped coming?'

'I said be quiet! Or else he'll come to you!' hissed Mai. 'Look at that one, he's stopped the slogans. Rambanai, he's looking at you!' Rambanai shrunk against her mother who had put the fear of the *Mukoma* into her. I looked around now, at the mention of Netsai. Perhaps I would see my sister.

I could not make her out. I had not seen her since she left some months ago, and before that, because of school, I had seen her rarely. What did a woman who fought look like? Did she look the same as before, now as one who bore the arms of death, who planted landmines in the roads that connected vast farms so that farmers' wives in their jeeps exploded?

'Do we hate oppressors?' The village's education commenced. The Comrade glared round the gathering, defying anyone to so much as dream a wrong answer. In reality everyone knew the correct response except me. I was the only one who had not before taken part at a *morari* gathering.

'No!' the village affirmed the righteousness of the struggle.

'If a person takes your land, what is he?'

'An oppressor!' the call and answer crescendoed.

'If a person does not give you half of what you have helped him to obtain, what he could not have made without you, what is he?' the Comrade roared, tearing his rifle from his back like an extra limb and waving it aloft.

'An oppressor!' the women exulted in their naming. Mai spoke throatily and stretched her neck to see a shadowy group of men who were seated half-way up the circle of villagers beyond us.

'Babamukuru!' breathed Rambanai, fearless now that the Big Brother was bellowing doctrine. 'And Baba.' She nudged me in the ribs, pointing with her chin.

'Do we hate oppressors!' raged the Big Brother.

'No!' everyone denied.

'What do we hate?' the Comrade demanded, his voice cracking into sharp, explosive particles.

'We hate oppression!' all the people exhaled with such relief it was as if they rejoiced. So our morale was raised to a pitch where the Big Brother burst into song. From behind Babamukuru and Baba, a group of armed combatants rose. '*Bhunu, rowa musoro rigomhanya*! The white man, hit it on the head to make it run!' Dhi dhi-dhi, dhi dhi-dhi, the Comrade's feet danced, stirring up the smell of dust faintly. The young girls pierced the night with the thin, thin notes of the soprano; it cut painfully to hear such beautiful music carry such instructions into the rustling shrubbery. 'To make it run . . . to teach it a lesson,' the basses rumbled.

The tenors, overpowered by ecstasy, out-sung the sopranos, holding their notes longer and longer as if possessed by a spirit so intent on avenging it did not require breath in the body that received it, and the basses and altos struck their lines again and again, round and round, like a canon; and it was in this passion that a Comrade struck Babamukuru with the butt of his rifle.

That's how it started and went on with all of us watching and doing nothing, keeping quiet in a quiet watch, and Mai breathing in catches of satisfaction like a woman who has not been gratified for too long, caressed upon untouched places. And so it went on, until the girl who was washed, the girl of the plump shining skin arrived and a little later the Big Brother in the green that rippled across his frame like a jungle followed. Mai, my mother, does not tell me. She knows his name, but she's like that, she has never told me; she says, yes, our *Mukuwasha*, our son-in-law, your *Babamunini*, your brother-in-law! And I now know there is no sense in asking. Nor in asking Netsai, to whom other questions must first be posed, the sort that embarrass in the asking: my sister, how can you with one limb less than me, unlike me, keep your motion and its direction?

'Is this the man?' the Big Brother concealed by a jungle demanded. He took in, in a moment, as he strode up, what was going on and being done to Babamukuru.

'It's him!' the political instructor replied in an accent of the north of the country like Mai's. 'That's him! The one we were warned of.' He swung his A-K high, like a mortar to pound down into a pestle. His boot ground into

Babamukuru's neck to steady the target. The Big Brother calmly held up his hand. The passion in the younger soldier's limbs transferred to his face as he obeyed. It was then that my sister Netsai walked forward, out of the bush where she had been waiting. Loping with a joyful stride, her gun belt rolling around her hip like a string of beads, the young woman of war moved to reach the Big Brother's side, and the earth beneath her exploded.

Later, although Babamukuru had the only vehicle around, we all knew Babamukuru would have been as dead as any example if it hadn't been for this *Mukoma*. How could you expect someone who'd nearly died himself to prevent the death of someone whose leg had spun and hooked and continued bleeding? And nobody else had anything. The doctor was kilometres away on her farm. And what Mai had now was froth at the mouth. Her neck had sinews that shivered and trembled as she lifted her head and strained and heaved with sounds that no one heard. So there was an end to that awful moment, of being suspended at a point between the balancing forces that form the apices of a triangle, but this was not better. I sat down finally when people started moving forward.

Everyone sat down around Mai. They were silent in the faint white flicker of moonlight. No one did anything immediately that I could discern to help her, and so I sat there silently, deliberately not feeling too many hates and rages and despairs to enumerate.

'Netsai, *iwe*! You are my Netsai! And I will not let you go! I will not take you down off the sling on my back, I won't take you down, never, never!' Mai shuddered in a shrill that was worse than her silence.

Sekuru Benjamin had the grace of age, so that none but the most vicious human beings touched him. So the war had not gripped him personally beyond frightening him and forcing him to see that which cannot be remembered and therefore cannot be spoken of. With his walking stick, already dusty with the kilometres he had walked that evening, *Sekuru* took up a position half-way between my mother and her neighbours from the village, one knee down in the blood my mother had licked. Bo-bo! Bo-bo-bo! Bo-bo-bo! He began the ceremonial clap. Then everyone joined in, bo-bo-bo-bo, a steady sustained beat above the noises from Mai, who had given up calling the daughter who did not answer but was shaking her head and grunting with her eyes rolling from side to side in her head.

'Arrive, our dear grandmother! You who are in the winds, come to your home!' intoned *Sekuru* Benjamin.

'No!' said my mother, in an offended man's voice. Our stomachs turned cold and we knew that the death that hovered over us that night had invited unknown patently evil spirits. 'I shall not arrive!' my mother refused in the same strange voice. Then Mai fell back in a faint, Mai Samhungu went to hold her with another neighbour, and others ran almost silently here and there, to those who were helping them and to the other victims.

Villagers picked up Mai, who came to almost immediately and did not know what was happening. Mai Samhungu gently put a hand over Mai's mouth, as though to wipe away the remains of wet earth, and then moved it to her eyes so that she would not see again either the form of her daughter that no one yet attended, nor the dangling leg.

Netsai moaned softly on the ground. Her throat knotted

21

as Mai's had. Sweat glistened pale on her upper lip in the slivers of moonlight that came through the trees, and in one drop hung the reflection of the limb in the branches. She dragged in too little air to keep her alive, but too much to allow her to die. What I knew then is that I did not know anything and never would anymore, and I saw that no one knew anything either as no one was doing anything.

Finally, some put their heads together and whispered and then turned covertly, almost guiltily but also brazenly to look at Babamukuru. It was Nyari, Netsai's old school friend, who stripped off her petticoat. Nyari's teeth rent a rip in the cloth. The other girl, whose skin was too shiny and whose air was too satisfied, backed into the bushes as Nyari knelt. Our Big Brother in green looked after her muttering, 'Careful!' The girl nodded. Nyari did not even look at them but tugged at the nylon. Our Big Brother knelt beside her, and twisted the strips above Netsai's thigh as soon as they were ready.

Meanwhile, Babamukuru was heaving himself up, groaning. His bruises were as thick as livers, but he strained up to sit unaided. He nodded as my father joined the villagers who were looking at him. I could see Baba gesturing and nodding. Babamukuru looked up although his eyes were slightly glazed. Finally, he focused on the villagers, who were now all observing him patiently, and realised he was expected to act.

What was he going to do? Was he going to fall back, like Mai, or walk to the brink of his life, like Netsai? What he did was turn onto his hands and knees and push himself up further. Babamukuru knew what had happened, and he walked like a dancer. Half weaving, half floating, he arrived at his car. His bloody hands rummaged for his car keys as he did, and then the men around the tree where he had sat called him back, for they had recognised a problem: should the doctor be begged to come, or should Babamukuru take Netsai – and himself for that matter – to the white woman's surgery. Now, in the dead of night, they began to debate: could anyone risk that with the curfew raging?

The discussion went on for minutes during which blood seeped from my sister's leg, but was prevented from flowing by Nyari's petticoat. I watched Nyari's cloth stain as it threaded her friend's life in. Nyari had Netsai's head in her lap and threw desperate, lidded eyes at my father and village elders who were wasting the drops of the girl. The delegation looked at Babamukuru who bowed his head and whispered in some confusion, 'You said I should drive her, isn't it. You said the best thing to do is to drive.'

In the end *Mukoma* Chiko, the child of a cousin of Babamukuru's, took charge even beyond Babamukuru, and it was decided Netsai should be given what first aid was available while Babamukuru would drive away first thing in the morning. If asked why he was out so early he would indicate the wounded girl. If that led to his being asked why he had waited so long with someone so injured he would reply he was afraid of the curfew. They said I had to go in the car with her, so that I could speak in my English accent if I was asked, proving allegiance and providing camouflage, also so that I would know. In any case, I was to return to school.

'Go!' said Mai. She spoke as Babamukuru was revving the car and the cocks from closeby homesteads beat their wings and stretched upon their perches and crowed to announce a dawn that had not yet arrived. She was speaking in a whisper to make sure her voice lay under the noise of the engine. 'Go, Tambudzai! To those people who are killing your sister!'

I had one leg in the car. I kept on moving. When the car crept and crunched over the sand, I gritted my teeth, put my head out of the window and hissed, 'Yes! You know I'm going, don't you! So that's what I'm doing, I'm going!'

'Tambudzai,' said Babamukuru automatically, still dazed and drunken with pain and grief. 'Tambudzai, what are you saying to your mother!'

Mai wasn't waving. Her gaze was trained on the side of the car where my sister lay. I didn't wave. Nobody did.

'Leave them, Baba,' said Maiguru in a voice that encompassed me, my mother, what had happened that night, and Nyari and the few who remained, Mai Samhungu and Mai Mutasa, besides my father. Maiguru didn't want to face anymore anything that had to do with how Babamukuru had been denounced.

The rim above the hill brightened, as we bumped over the last bit of dirt road before we turned into the Nyanga Highway. I sat at the far side of my seat, behind my aunt. She was quiet and motionless; she also seemed to be wedging herself invisibly into marginal spaces. I pressed myself up against the opposite door to where they placed Netsai's head. I was folding my arms and squeezing in to make myself as small as possible, as not there as I could under the vividness of the past hours' facts.

There were children on the road, with books under their arms and cheekbones jutting like precipices that

Maiguru and I turned round from at the same moment, in order not to see. The children scuttled away at the judder of the engine which they feared could only belong to a Rhodesian. Besides the children to focus on were the bare fields that no one had the strength to tend, or the patches of bush where anything that desperate flight could take as cover was burnt. It was only when we were past all this, when we were beyond the village and approaching antibiotics and morphine, that I looked out of the window at the red earth and stalks of harvested maize on the farms where men in overalls moved like languid dark dots. The doctor's farm was one of these. We were approaching the drugs and sutures my sister and uncle needed. It was difficult to think of so much of it, need. I forced myself into an emptiness; and yes, it is better where there is nothing so there is nothing to tell.

Patched up by the doctor on the farm, Netsai was admitted at Umtali General Hospital and rushed into surgery. Babamukuru was given pain killers, x-rays and stitches. None of the staff who attended asked any questions that could not be answered. They accepted Babamukuru's explanations without comment. Maiguru wanted me to walk the last few kilometres to the Young Ladies' College of the Sacred Heart, but Babamukuru said he could take me to school before my sister woke up.

School too seemed empty because now, after these holidays, it was impossible to relate to anything. Empty rooms, empty desks, empty books, empty air between us, the second form whose classroom was also on the second floor, and the mountain with the cross on top, down which plantations, dark, of wattle and pine crept like dispirited armies.

2

So, sitting in class you could see the mountains where your sister still talks about walking, back and forth, back and forth, forth and back, that perseverating path towards that exploding off of a leg.

That was in the second year; a deterioration of hope. The first year was better because I knew what I wanted. My desires in that initial year were positive: to achieve, achieve, achieve some more, and I knew how to realise them. I was going to learn until I had more learning than anyone about me, first in the classroom, then in the school and finally in the community. The form one classroom was on the ground floor, and I sat proudly in front when I first arrived at the Young Ladies' College of the Sacred Heart. It was a large classroom. The one at Rutivi School would have seated three times as many students. In this great space I selected each time a place up close to the teacher, in order to be a good student. The front wall and the blackboard – which latter was not a slab of truculent grey where nastily disposed children chiselled holes with nails and stones, in order to confound sadistic teachers, as was the case at Rutivi School and to a lesser extent at the mission – the front wall and blackboard were very close, and the teacher hovered closer still, so that being an outstanding student, I was obliged to and contentedly maintained a tight focus. Windows open as eyes, with ten astoundingly complete panes each, were set in the side wall so that they stared at the mountains. But these openings were situated at the napes of our necks as we sat attentively at the front. If you were stifled, either for want of knowledge or due to too much of it, you had to twist your neck through at least a hundred and twenty degrees to feel on the cheek the freshness of mountain air. But we were little girls with a mission to improve ourselves by excelling, and few of our first row necks were sufficiently flexible. Then even when this manoeuvre was achieved, in the college grounds swayed a range of pompously pointed and creaking cedars, which prohibited a view of the mountains.

I did not think anything of this barrier in my first year. It shielded me propitiously from imponderables beyond, and the college grounds were idyllically beautiful. I now cannot conceive that human beings created such beauty. Those dark conifers were like a distant shore to green lakes of tranquil lawns upon which peace from too many tenses and conjugations glided and where we stretched at break in the too crisp days of June with our jerseys off and our skirts rolled up, like chilly mermaids sunning. The college building, luminous and white, sprawled languidly at the garden's upper margins, as a charming resort may rest at the edge of Lake Kariba's waters. How beautiful the aesthetic of my secondary school was, demonstrating beyond any doubt I could muster, how languor was related to lethargy as elegance was to squalor.

There were, too, other lessons to be picked out by an eager mind in the lie of the Sacred Heart territory. The Young Ladies' College of the Sacred Heart delivered a formidable education, and its standards were set kilometres before the school gate was arrived at. The college was located on the opposite side of Umtali, as it was called then, from the mission, occupying a tract of land that rises up to meet fragile sparkling skies between the town and our eastern border. The winds blow across that sky from the Indian Ocean, over the Mozambique mountains where the drops from the sea glide together like frightened girls. The rain falls gently. There is the general hospital on the right of the first approach, the one that leads into town from the mission. Then come the government schools and a choice of the post office or fast food outlet depending on which avenue is turned into. But there was not much to choose from between the routes then, because the post office ordered segregated queues, and the fast food place sold you cool drinks and dry buns from the back window only, but not hamburgers; so, no, there was not much to have driving into town on the way to school, nothing in the way of an ambitious girl's lessons.

On the other side, however, in the suburb close to the college, my forehead resting on the window of Babamukuru's car, I observed how the inhabitants did not stroll out in what clothes came to hand as we did, but in gorgeously designed garments and fabulous shoes whose chunky heels required from the city authorities, and obtained by dint of slow moving men in green overalls, perfectly even paving stones. Thus I, and many other students, established a code of dress which we affected in later life, along with the sense that an efficient city council combined with a willing if lethargic workforce was mandatory to make anything happen. Nor did Baba and Maiguru ever comment on these matters as they drove me to school. I believe Maiguru was already depressed that the fine garments she brought with her from her studies in England had begun to be eaten by moths, and there was no hope of replacing them with the austerity war-quality goods presently in the shops, a quality that reduced the standards of everything. Babamukuru I know now, although I did not know then, was listening to other music. Yet it is strange that the parents I had adopted were silent on this. How similar their reticence seemed, when I came to consider the matter, to the villager's silence at my uncle's beating. It was as though our ancestors had placed a curse on passing observations which would bring to percipient souls vicious retribution. So we were quiet in the car, while in the shady avenues approaching school, pedigreed Alsatians dribbled silver saliva at the green-overalled working men from behind iron fences. They even howled and threw themselves up the enclosures in a fury to fall on Babamukuru as we drove by on the tarmac. The residents served aces down the centres of their tennis courts, or dived splash bombs into their swimming pools, and gardeners clad in orange overalls looked over at us, the intermediates, lethargically. Not even then did Babamukuru comment, nor did I speak, so unlike the lessons at school, there was no test for these lessons learnt in transit.

Entering the school you passed through a great wrought iron gate as imposing as St Peter's portal. Up, you drove, along the road between the hockey fields and tennis courts to the boundary set by the cedars. Here you turned left about the broad roundabout, over whose centre the peaceful lawns lay. At the top you progressed parallel to the school buildings for all of half a kilometre, passing on to the southern end of those lawns as evergreen as conifers.

Here grew a copse of jacarandas that poured purple shade on parking bays. Pace, pace, pace. Pace, pace, pace. Six or seven steps were needed to traverse these parking spaces whose white painted boundaries accommodated the large and long vehicles of elite Rhodesians. Since in those days the size of the cars of the elite raised respect rather than questions, I quickly identified and stored the principles of aesthetics exhibited at my school, which informed relationships between design and form and purpose so opulently, without reference to material resources.

At the opposite end of the school were the dormitory buildings. Behind the form two accommodation block shimmered the swimming pool. This was secluded away behind a hibiscus hedge that in season bloomed lusciously scarlet, the pool set here so that visitors would not surprise us and we would not parade before them when clad in little clothing. The car park and swimming pool signified visitors and rest and thus were of paramount importance to most of the pupils. But for me the most significant building was the classroom block. Gleaming long and white in the sun like a beatified building, the block presided over the school grounds from above the gardens, as if to bless all our activities. Down opposite this block, beyond the cedars, were the playing fields, and between all four rolled the tranquil green lawns seen from the classrooms. Ah, those lawns, studded here and there with indigenous and exotic flowering trees alight as though hung with embers: the scarlet poinsettia that in later nightmares bore buds of crystals of blood, and the clear yellow flare of the mimosa!

It is true, even in the form one classroom, to obtain the learning and distinction my ambition was set upon, I needed to work harder at Sacred Heart than at either Rutivi School or the mission. I was not a girl who could giggle and write notes to boyfriends in class, and still attain the honour roll. Slips of moments cost me marks. Whenever I thought of something that was not on the syllabus during lessons, the same slip repeated in my marks so that I was no longer one of the best. However, this did not matter for I could work as hard as necessary when I was attending. As I liked to be good at what I did, I was not afraid of hard work. I would put in what was required to reach the peak I aspired to. It was especially important to be at the top, as it was quite clear to me and to everyone I had to be one of the best. Average simply did not apply; I had to be absolutely outstanding or nothing. So I worked hard from my very first year at the Young Ladies' College of the Sacred Heart, devising exercises and strategies to make me good at paying attention, at remembering every word from the teacher's mouth, and not just the words but the inflections too, so that I knew what was important and reproduced each teacher's peculiar inflection at examinations. Attending was having your mind open to everything all the time, and being able to bond it there, so that what came into the mind could not run out as from a sponge that is squeezed and uselessly relinquishes moisture. There was a lot of work to bind in the bits of knowledge that added up to what you would become; you had to expend a lot, positioning for as long as it took those stepping stones of information to your future.

Learning how to attend like that took a lot of concentration. It was exhausting, so although my first year at the Young Ladies' College of the Sacred Heart was gentler than the second year, due to the circumscribing of vision and the blocked view of the mountains I have described, I was more often than not exhausted even in that first year. To keep us attending, there were three sets of examinations, one every term, plus monthly gradings. I found these assessments useful as through them I measured myself against my classmates, assessing my progress. I did not succeed in coming first in either the first year or the second. That position was held by a girl called Seema Patel. Ntombizethu Mhlanga, who slept in the same dormitory as I did, whose skin was as peaceful as midnight, invariably came second. Third place was taken by a girl called Tracey Stevenson. By the middle of the first year, I had crammed my way to fourth. In order to encourage more hard work in myself, I set myself a goal. I then set my sights, as a sort of landmark for my progress, on beating the girl immediately before me, this Tracey Stevenson. She was nondescript looking apart from toned muscles and large hands and feet as a result of which she excelled at swimming. Streaky brown hair flopped flat and formless upon her head, while her eyes shifted across colour borders, as though they were small pale chameleons, so that I was constantly confused as to whether they were grey or green or blue or turquoise.

No, I did not overtake this classmate, as I wished to, in the first year. However, at the mid-term evaluation, Tracey surprised everyone by dropping to fifth. Nevertheless, she was a fighter. The spirit that took her to the end of the swimming pool in record time served her now. Determinedly she sat in class after her fall, which she put down to too much concentration on swimming. In her seat in the front, she listened to the teacher with a smile on her face while her eyes remained large and serious. At the end of the term, she succeeded in leap-frogging both another classmate, Angela, and myself, to return to the third position.

I was depressed at my inability to excel, to do what was clearly possible as other human beings managed it. Therefore, in order to keep myself interested in prowess, I adjusted my vision somewhat to one that was more readily attainable. Rather than seek a position I could not have, I opted for certainty. It is true, I hankered still to see high ninety per cents strewn over my report card, averages that figured my future and confirmed my place today, with a scholarship, at Sacred Heart. It was difficult to adjust this measure of myself downwards. Nevertheless, in order not to deflate myself after Tracey had catapulted beyond me again, I set a secondary standard of marks over sixty per cent, in order to qualify for the college's honour roll. Sometimes I wished I was not aware of it so keenly, but with my uncle's training in the importance of education, my awareness was razor sharp. I lived and breathed and learnt by rote now for a place on the school's roll of honour. This, although not as good as being at the top, had its own rewards. You were awarded a copper plate, laced at the edges and patterned with dots on the rim. Your name was in it, your very own name, Tambudzai Sigauke. Like a miracle, that name that you hardly ever read anywhere else appeared in the centre of the plate, as though it was something special. Tambudzai Sigauke! Something special! You kept on looking, and your name in the middle of the plate all the time kept on attracting. Beneath was the name of the school, the Young Ladies' College of the Sacred Heart, and the year. It was a contract, that coupling of appellations, of good intent, as I saw it. If I learnt what was required, my name would be placed together thus, with the institution that offered the most prestigious education to young women in the country, and so I would drop into my pocket, from where it could not be taken away, the key to my future. No, I could not tolerate the idea of failure. So I went on planning my life while life was planning an insurgence.

So all changed after the meeting I went to, the one I was brought to, both to be exhibited at Babamukuru's trial for treason to the soul of the people and to be instructed. It all was different after this *morari* where fear paralysed the heart. Indeed, having returned to school, I renewed my contract with myself to overtake Tracey Stevenson, or at the very least obtain the honour roll in all the school's gradings. Now, being there on a copper plate was even more necessary: it was as if that name so perfectly inscribed couldn't be blown off so jaggedly, just like that, not in the middle of a night, nor in the middle of anything. But now, after a leg was blown off, she came walking backwards over those stones of learning and concentration, hopping, going hop-hop-hopla because she had only one leg. I could see her clearly as I sat in class, my mind opening to the teacher. It was a woman. It was my sister. Would the honour roll hold its promise? I could not concentrate. Whenever I focused, the woman stepped back, groaning too many questions. Besides, I suffered secretly a sense of inferiority that came from having been at the primitive scene. Being a student at the Young Ladies' College of the Sacred Heart, I possessed images from the school's films and library: cavemen dragging their women where they wanted them by the hair or bludgeoning their prey. And in the final analysis there was everyone, sitting mesmerised and agreeing about the

34

appropriateness of this behaviour. What about the one who wasn't a woman, who was my sister, holding the means of someone else's death strapped to her back, rolling her hips towards a man in a gesture of life, so she was after all not a girl but already a woman? Sometimes a tear trickled towards my nose and I had to rub, pretending something had fallen into my eye to prevent a drip on my textbook. I had trouble, in fact started to dread, attending. It was as if a vital part had been exploded away and in the absence that was left I was cracked and defective, as though indispensable parts leaked, and I could not gather energy.

On this particular day, a few weeks after school recommenced, I tried once more to concentrate. I particularly wished to as it was Latin class. This subject was taken by Sister Catherine who was my favourite teacher. I just felt something about her, not knowing what. In Sister Catherine's hour there was a special edge to my cramming and recitations of conjugations and declensions. I wanted to do well to make both of us happy, rather than because of my perceptions of my situation. Sister Catherine never displayed any of the unbearable, prejudged attitudes towards Ntombizethu and me that emanated from some of the other teachers. She had a gentle voice. She used it as if she was always making music, but tentatively so. She pushed every note out on a breath, like a woman surprised by the beautiful notes she struck, and that astonishment tied up her lungs so that she had to fight to keep air flowing. Yet the impression you obtained from her was that she was determined in spite of everything to put out her melodies. 'Tah-mboo-dzah-ee,' she called me. I was obliged to smirk. You had to do that about a *murungu* attempting Shona. So I turned down the corners of my mouth and rolled my eyes at Sister's accent; but I only turned and rolled them a little bit, as I liked the way she tried to express the tonality correctly, and how she looked with a warm brown gaze at whomever she spoke to, including me. That smile didn't question either: it covered me.

This morning, towards the end of class, Sister paused. I wasn't looking at anything or anyone in the classroom. I was preventing the appearance of the hopping woman who was a girl. By not paying attention I was making her not come down the mountain. So I felt, rather than saw, there was not a murmur of movement from the classroom, no lifting of hands that knew, no rustling of pages by fingers that hoped still to find out the answers. This meant Sister was waiting facing the chosen one; she had already decided who should be given the honour of showing off knowledge. In silence, the class also waited for this girl to reply.

Very vaguely, I could feel it was I who was chosen. Yes, I was the one for whom everyone was waiting. Panic prickled at each of my pores, raising shiny goosebumps on my skin, and webs flickered out from the textbook page like treacherous tightropes to lead me back to learning, but they were cords upon which I did not want to walk. I could tell I was too tired to keep my balance sufficiently to make sense of the Latin phrases, as I was enervated from forcing, for the better part of the morning, everything out of mind, in case that woman who was my sister came hopping down on the stepping stones of attention. The silence went on for a long time while I vacillated between being in the class and not being there, and Sister and the rest of the girls waited.

I hesitated too long. Another girl jumped in with answers.

'The. . . um. . . the lords . . . thanked the. . . the. . . faithful servants . . . with a great feast!' volunteered a soft voice that wavered in the middle syllables, as if it was requesting approbation yet was not sure this would be given. I immediately became more miserable as the speaker was the girl I wanted to out-learn, Tracey Stevenson.

Sister was pleased with the response. As I was, Tracey was also one of the Latin teacher's favourites. 'Yes!' The nun hesitated for a minute in which I sensed she turned from me. When she spoke her voice was more distant, as though she had her back to me, but she was as usual wonderfully enthusiastic. Pat-pat, her hands clapped. 'That's a fine translation. Well done, Tracey!'

When the warmth in Sister's voice slid out over the class, like the thick, sweet, creamy-brown caramel mixtures we made down on the ground floor in the domestic science kitchen, you felt it was a terrible thing not to know. Sister made you want to do well, to put your best out there, not at all in order to please her but to show you had it in you. Me! Her voice made you think even now you still had it in you! And how she smiled when you did it!

Now Sister read the next sentence of the exercise. I was sufficiently part of the class once more to realise the translation to that was easy. 'The soldiers have laid waste the city and the women and children are weeping.' This time I wanted to put my hand up even before Sister asked me. But that would mean I had to open my eyes. They were closed against the dark green pine and wattle plantations on the mountain slopes, and the great tracts of burnt bush beside them, green growth oxidised to ash the better to see those

37

people whose legs were to be blown off. If I opened my eyes, I would end up turning my head. Mesmerised I might forget and the tear might fall. If I kept the eyes closed, I would not do well, rather face a lifetime of being nothing, like Mai. This because of my sister. Because of my young sister, Netsai! *Iwe*, Netsai, oh you wild and irresponsible girl! This is what I thought and it was a relief to do so as this perspective released me from being transfixed by what I could not, on any account, remember and made moving forward possible. Oh, Netsai, how-I-wish-you-were-not my sister, who informed you a woman's business is aiming communist rifles at people like kind and gentle Sister Catherine! And didn't my sister see how able such people were, which meant her own leg was in danger of being blown off. Oh, who could be blamed, if Netsai didn't know!

Ha! Those thoughts crept up on you just like that, even when you weren't thinking them. You just couldn't flee far enough; they always insinuated. My eyes flew open.

The classroom was very silent. Sister Catherine was bending over me calling, 'Tah-mboo-dzah-ee!' Ntombizethu, from the dormitory, put both hands to her mouth and narrowed her eyes at me, reminding me to smirk, but this time I was not able. Sister was regarding me much too kindly. Her hand moved out. How I jumped when hers touched mine! She rubbed my hand. I saw the movement pale upon dark but did not feel it. 'Let go!' I heard the teacher's words, yet I did not understand them. All that was happening was very confusing, but she was my favourite nun. I felt something was terribly wrong, but I smiled up at her tentatively, hopefully. The silence continued in the class. More and more girls twisted round to discover what was going on. Ntombizethu took her hand from her mouth. Her eyes widened with apprehension. Only now did I realise from the soft warmth upon my skin that Sister and I were in physical contact. 'Let go,' Sister repeated. Now shame came crushing down on me. I was appalled at having let my skin and this white person's touch. A dentist could see a person tremble in agony and not touch. A doctor could watch a person dissolve into death and not touch. This could happen because it was taboo: this person and that one could not touch. The army did its work asceptically, with grenades and landmines and bullets. So my first impression was I had soiled my teacher in some way. I liked her and I did not want to do that. Sister should not touch me. I started with all my muscles to pull away. I was horrified to see my hand disobedient and motionless.

'Please, Tam-boo-dzah-ee!' The nun sounded worried. 'Please, let go!' Sister repeated. Only then did I see my fist was clenched not around the teacher's wrist but about the formica desk top. Once more I flung my hand back. The chair tipped. There was something soothing in the motion that released relief. Sister put out her free arm to prevent an accident. Back and forth, back and forth, forth and back, I was rocking without realising it.

'Are you all right, Tah-mboo-dzah-ee?' Sister Catherine stopped the motion.

I looked down in embarrassment at my desk, took time to wipe away with my beige uniform blouse smears of sweat that were spread where I had gripped.

'What is the matter?' Sister was very anxious.

'I'm fine,' I told her. My favourite teacher was anxious. But my sister lay first in the sand and then in a hospital bed without a leg. What would Sister do if I told her? What would the other girls do if they heard? They all had their little boxes tight in their chests for their memories of war. There was too much grief here for a room of girls. Thinking this, I did let go. I forgot about not letting anything out. I kept on wiping so that my tears fell on the cloth sleeve. It was like that when people were kind to you. Sometimes you forgot.

'Let's continue with the exercise, please,' Sister began again. 'Who can translate the next sentence?' There was a rustle of hands being raised. We were in the A stream, and could conjugate any -o, -are, -avi, -atum verb Sister drew out of the textbook. She kept standing beside me hopefully, but I kept my head down, over where the tears dripped, wanting to close my eyes so there wasn't any chance of looking at the mountains, but being afraid if I did that I would squeeze the tears out again.

'The large fierce armies have marched into the city.' It was Tracey once more, and Sister turned away without noticing any sniffing.

'Last one, please,' went on Sister, 'quickly, if you please, girls, before the bell rings.' Even when she was talking to us, Sister used 'please' in almost every sentence. Tap-tap-tap, her heels moved off over the grey linoleum. The tiles were milkily misty, like early mornings on the mountain tops that tied up your joy, those ragged peaks a view of which, like views of women with snakes for tresses, turned watchers to stone. The floor in the whole school was a difficult-to-dirty transmutation of black and white to grey, soft as the sacred heart after which our college was named. It made you think of the divine breast of a sanctified dove.

'Yes, please!' said Sister to the classroom. Tap-tap-tap, she moved on again. A modern nun, she wore high heels in sexless colours like dull black, dull brown, dull navy.

'The mothers are carrying the crying children away from the market!' came an obedient reply.

'Good!' said Sister, in her happy, caramel voice. 'Well done, Ntombizethu!'

So the lesson ended with Ntombizethu being picked, as if to confirm I had little value because I was not able!

I tried to think of something tasty we had made in the domestic science class to take my mind from this last minute humiliation. I could not bear to think of my dormitory mate basking in the praise that should have been mine! That nascent little Zimbabwean soul of mine that the war was fighting for became seriously disgruntled at someone who was close enough to live in the same dormitory as I did receiving, rather than I, Sister's approbation. Oh, Ntombizethu! I allowed, or perhaps urged, myself to grow crosser and crosser with the girl, no longer recalling I had not been prepared with an answer. Nor did I remind myself that others too had been praised, and I had not been indignant. I simply wallowed quite luxuriously in ill-feeling towards the girl from the dormitory, whose name we shortened to Ntombi. 'Girl!' we sometimes called her, 'Hey, Our Girl!' we said, translating the Zulu phrase with which she was named. How voluptuous the anger felt against Girl. Yes, my roommate had stolen my praise! Ko-ko-kongolo! Kongolo-kongoko-kongolo! The bell went, as I wafted, as on a sea of soothing waves, on animosity.

Sister gathered up her books. We didn't have a homework exercise to hand in, so she did not have much to carry and there was no need for me to hurry forward to help her as I usually did. Our teacher walked out while the rest of us scraped back our chairs and opened our desks to put textbooks away. I avoided looking at the mountains, even though standing up brought me in full view of the window. In went the Latin texts and exercise books; out came the Maths material, for we were expecting Mrs Hall who loved her Logarithms. And all the while I enjoyed a great indignation against Ntombi.

3

Maths was the last lesson before lunch. After Mrs Hall meted out homework with satisfaction, as though it were a punishment, we walked down corridors to the right, then downstairs and straight ahead to reach the dining room. The corridors telescoped in and out before me, so that I swayed as though I were sailing on a sea, even though I was merely walking, moving along corridors with arches that framed all of us students into the school on one side, framed the mountains outside on the other – the mountains with menace in their existing there where they did, on the border to Mozambique, so that they were mountains that could not be looked at. I also passed the honours board on my way to eat, another point I preferred not to encounter.

The dining room had long thin windows framed in dark wood, to catch the little light that trickled in from beyond the arches. It was always dim inside and the lights required to be switched on at five in the evening. We lined up outside and then filed into the hall according to seniority. Tingili, tingili! Ti-ti-tingili! a silver tone rang out when we had taken our places, while the prefects stood tall as pillars in the spaces between the tables to stare impassively or frown as necessary at our behaviour. Sister Emmanuel, our headmistress, took meals with us at the top table, except for three or four occasions a week when, it occurs to me now, she absented herself for the sake of her digestion. It was the headmistress who prepared us for grace by striking with a slender rod a small silver triangle. Sister waited until the last little first former stopped shuffling before she intoned 'Benedictus, benedicte!' in a voice of much sterner metal than the triangle. She was tall and had a somewhat beige-coloured face, a few shades lighter than our uniform blouses. As well, this face was massive and long like the barrel of a cannon. Ngili-ngili-tingili! Sister tapped the bell into shorter tones after grace, indicating we should be seated.

It was a sombre and imposing hall. The ceiling was high above us. The walls were panelled in planks of dark wood which drank light as drains suck away water. The floor was made of smaller slabs measuring three inches by nine of the same material. As if to compensate, a large mirror stretched across the far side, where the first formers were positioned. The mirror was decorated with bunches of grapes and leaves that twined in and out around its margins. An imperative script at the top declared, 'I saw them eat and I knew who they were'. Being known – Tambudzai of the village who went to a meeting! The thought of it made me shudder. Bougainvillea though, who sat at my table, was a girl who didn't mind being known. Her body swelled all over the place in a way that made me anxious and embarrassed just to look at it, and made other girls jealous. But it was not simply that. Bougainvillea could flutter a little finger, if she wished, in a way that compelled everybody to observe it. At meals Bougainvillea sat next to Tracey, who was her special friend, although in the form room Tracey occupied a seat at the front, and Bougainvillea one towards the back, at the side where she could bring the pine-scented breeze onto her face by raising her chin. There were individual chairs at the thick heavy tables, and napkin rings, although you had to bring your own napkin. We sat six to a table according to form. Deidre and her friend, Angela, were another couple at our table. Ntombi and I made up the remaining two. The friendship pattern between the other four meant that I sat next to Ntombi. That was the same as our sleeping arrangement in the dormitory as there, too, we organised ourselves according to form.

I was still seething as everyone pulled back chairs and the bang of knives on plates, as we started on bread and margarine, clattered to the ceiling, so that sitting next to Girl was unbearably aggravating. We had managed to put some distance between ourselves in class, but on the whole whenever you saw one of us – lining up before the dining hall or at assembly, in the biology lab when you needed a dissection partner or in chemistry where we burnt our gases – wherever there was one of us, you saw the other. It was an assumption on the part of our schoolmates, a sort of pre-ordained bonding. People took it for granted we would love each other and prefer to do everything together. How false that was! Each year the nuns went out into the surrounding areas, away from the well-fenced suburb in which the school was situated. To these outlying places the nuns delivered a beacon of hope, by inviting girls to attend an entrance examination to the convent. Two girls were chosen each year from amongst the hundreds tested. Once we arrived at the school, the two of us found out we were five per cent. Or rather, we did not exceed this figure as that was the quota set by the Rhodesian government on difference, and the nuns were obliged to respect it.

45

'Look at them,' said Bougainvillea, gazing first at my hand as it hovered over the butter dish, and then at Ntombizethu's. What Tracey had and what she, Bougainvillea, lacked in brain power, Bougainvillea made up for with sheer world weariness and accomplished ennui. She gave a half smile, and wiggled a compelling finger, as though had she not been so tired the observation would have cheered her up sufficiently to give her life some meaning. 'See what I mean,' she turned to Tracey. 'They've both got such fine hands. Look at those amazing fingers!' As I saw it, she looked more pointedly at Ntombizethu's than at my extremities. This did not do me any good at all, bringing on another slash of jealousy. 'You know what, Trace!' There was a ripple of energy in Bougainvillea's voice at the idea. 'It's not just those two! Have you noticed? It's all of them!' She kept her gaze on Ntombizethu's hands, which were now holding a slice of bread beneath her knife in order to spread the margarine. 'Let's have a look!' she raised an eyebrow with a practised investigatory motion as she inclined her head forward. Ntombizethu stretched her hands out. 'See!' Bougainvillea stretched out her own as if she would touch her classmate's, but did not quite. 'Just look at the shape of that nail, and that crescent, it's a perfect half moon! Isn't it wonderful!'

Tracey was blushing by now, and Ntombizethu looked self-conscious, but Bougainvillea looked very pleased with herself. Ntombizethu wiggled her fingers. 'Thanks, Bo!' she used the diminutive easily. 'Thanks. Hey! Do you mind? Can I have some Nesquik?' I know she's striving to be cool, like we imagine Marie Osmond might be, or Karen Carpenter, under the circumstances. I know she's striving hard, because I would be too in that situation.

Only I don't have to, because I usually have some; she never does because her father is a cleaning hand, and she hasn't, as I do – although my father is a peasant as well – have a well-off uncle. Poor idiot, having to behave like that, I think with a mixture of annoyance at her for being an idiot and superiority at sometimes having my own chocolate powder. This disdainful mixture of emotion compensated me somewhat for the Latin translation. Oh, Netsai! If it weren't for you, this very day I'd have my own carton of chocolate powder on the table! I could *offer* my roommate some, and humiliate her with generosity. Tracey was looking into her milk mug with embarrassment. I decided this was a good way to distance myself from what was going on and imitated my other classmate's concentration.

'Do you think I could,' Ntombizethu asked Bougainvillea tentatively, but with a flash in her eye, playing tit for tat, 'have a little bit of your Nesquik?' She stretched out her hand once more, so that I almost forgot to breathe, afraid Ntombi was about to touch Bougainvillea's chocolate container. Practically everything affected me like this in those days, making me terribly fearful.

We were allowed to bring our oral habits to table. The college provided the basics: bread and milk with every meal, plus a more solid stodge to keep us pelting over the hockey pitch. We ate the occasional freshwater fish in the faith that this would do our brain cells as much good as the sea variety, and the proverbial distressed vegetables. But we had to look to ourselves, or rather our parents, to indulge addiction to chillies or pickled onions, a sweet tooth and other gastronomic fixations.

47

The girls took great pride in telling each other how far they'd gone to propitiate their gustatory fetishes. Diverse fish and meat pastes, yeast extracts, the powders of beans and grains, whose consumption proved the consumer was a better being compared with others, were stacked in the centre of every table. You had to cross a border, most usually the southern one, to obtain most of the necessary items, for our country was at war, with the result that almost everything within it, edible or not, naturally with the exception of explosives, was of what the authorities called 'a temporary austerity quality'. So Bougainvillea liked everyone to know she had brought the Nesquik with her from the last family holiday in South Africa. Now above this sign of her classmate's superiority, Ntombizethu's hand hovered as though she would touch the icon. It was terrible to observe, Ntombizethu being on the brink like that, of touching the white girl's carton. I was not sure what was going on. Did Ntombizethu really have the stamina to pull that tin over and serve herself from it? Or was she in the end going to give in and sell something fundamental for the taste of chocolate?

Bougainvillea's more mobile eyebrow quivered, per-haps with mirth, while the other remained languid at Ntombizethu's temerity. My roommate was a girl who never brought anything to table that a fashionable person would be seen eating. Now she was threatening to put her hand, so recently declared beautiful, upon Bougainvillea's tin of taste, as it were, the mouth-watering powdered chocolate. Here the question for Bougainvillea, and all the other white girls there was, after Ntombizethu had touched it, would the chocolate be still edible? Under our circumstances, poor

Bougainvillea's options were limited. If she dragged the container out of Ntombi's reach she could be blamed for being stingy, or even worse, a racist. So Ntombi thought she had tied Bougainvillea up in a knot. I could see she was about to begin laughing, and I wondered how it could be that Ntombi had outmanoeuvred one of the white girls. But for all her triumph over it, my roommate could not claim her victory and put her hand on the tin of powder.

Poor Ntombi. It was difficult for her to find the courage for consolidation. My roommate's father was a cleaner at the Umtali Boys Secondary School, responsible for the toilets, and he lived in the school compound. You couldn't think of what he earned because it was too unpleasant, or your mind just couldn't conceive of such cosmic absences of dollars. As I was, Ntombi was on a scholarship that provided much education, but fewer books, yet less uniform and failed completely to encompass the pleasures contained in bottles of Bovril or Oxo and jars of Robertson's or Chiver's marmalade, whether lime or orange. I see now this deficit affected us severely, since our comparative skills were not developed in making fine judgements, living as we did lives of either/or, not called upon to decide which of several fine varieties was most worthy. True, Maiguru managed to slip a bottle of Tomango tomato sauce or Willards peanut butter into my tuck. One term she even splashed out on a bottle of Mrs Ball's chutney! It was so audacious and such a great joke that we giggled like two schoolgirls instead of one with her aunt, as Maiguru laid out the biscuits and ordinary jam she had brought for me, and I packed the metal box I carried my provisions in. We couldn't stop laughing because the missionary who lived next to Babamukuru had the same name as the chutney, Mrs Ball. I lay in bed that night, the eve before school, thinking, imagine that, putting your name. . . detaching your label that you were given and putting it to something that isn't you! Imagine!

The kind of tuck Ntombizethu brought, by the school's norms, never came to table. Irene, the little first former in the dormitory Ntombi and I occupied, was the only one of all the room's inhabitants who was able to afford those pastes. But the little first year, who was small in years only, insisted – too stridently, I thought, for who wouldn't want to be seen spreading anchovy paste or Camembert spread, whatever the taste, since the act of spreading, a prelude to consumption, declared you a better breed than those who did not consume such delicacies upon their carbohydrates – that she'd eaten these foreign items and couldn't see what the fuss was about. 'Foodstuffs' she called them disdainfully, those nourishments stuffed with food content and class. Even the way she spoke the word, with a great hiss on the 'f' showed it was not her mouth that dictated her taste, but another agenda.

The dormitory that Ntombi and I occupied together with Irene was situated in the first form block, on St Ignatius, the most junior corridor. In this room, besides Irene and Ntombi and I, lived Anastasia, Benhilda and Patience. Anastasia was in form five, Benhilda in form four. They were two other girls who never brought to school tuck that could be carried decently to the dining hall table. They returned at each beginning of term with squashed parcels of brown paper stained with fetid smelling oil, as though it had been used many times to carry bread from the *magrosa*. In the fatty wrappings were mouth watering *mbambaira*, boiled cobs of mealies bearing full glistening rows of seeds, round *nyimo* beans winking with the eyes on top, and *nzungu* nestled close together. However delicious, the food could not be taken to table, indeed could not be carried from the dormitory. The last girl in our room was Patience. Being in form three, she was, like Benhilda, a middle former. Patience liked to reflect many sides of a matter in her behaviour so as to avoid conflict. In this mode, she brought to school items that no one could remark upon. She offered around roast peanuts in a packet from the store rather than a pod, and never unwrapped lengths of brown paper to reveal the delicious if demoralising *mbambaira*. The bottles she brought were always those available at reputable supermarkets like OKs and Checkers. Besides, if she had to decide on what sauce to purchase, Patience invariably chose the one in a plastic pack which was cheaper, rather than the glass bottle that was more expensive. Poor Ntombi! Because she lived in the city, she could not even bring the garden produce Benhilda and Anastasia enjoyed; she unwrapped ruefully a cluster of mangoes, some mouldy-looking *madhumbe* and a plastic bag of *musoni* so desiccated it was dry as bark. That made everyone laugh, asking where she would cook it. 'What kind of place is this?' she retorted, doing her best to hold her own, but not able to prevent her voice trembling. 'Isn't there wood outside? Are you saying there isn't a cooking hearth here? Those women who clean here, are you saying they have electricity? If it has to be cooked, I'll find the fire for it!' she declared with a great deal of bravado, but it was just bravado. There was somewhere, in spite of everything, an unspeakable desire for chocolate.

Now, at lunch, Bougainvillea dealt with her dilemma in a masterly fashion. She leant over and dipped her teaspoon into her jar of chocolate flavouring. The small spoon came up heaped and Bougainvillea tapped her finger against the stem. When the round mound which rose above the spoon's bowl was shaken down to half, she pulled Ntombi's milk glass towards her and dolloped the contents of the spoon into it.

'Isn't it funny,' she mused, pushing the glass back to Ntombi and turning to Tracey with another raise of a nearly fatigued eyebrow, 'the way they just sit there, hey?' Bougainvillea's chest lifted, her nostrils flared slightly, but she did not possess the energy a proper snort demanded. 'My mum does that all the time with the guys on the farm! They stand around while you dish out their rations!'

Blood welled up into Tracey's cheeks a second time. It was quite horrible to see her darken. Meanwhile, Ntombi – at least as far as we could tell from her demeanour – calmly lifted her own spoon and beat at the clumps of chocolate which floated on her milk so that they combined with the rest of the liquid. I could not look anywhere because it was so shaming. How I admired Bougainvillea who had avoided acquiring the label of 'mean', and at the same time had protected the edibility of her chocolate. In one languid move by Bougainvillea, Ntombi's resistance was laid waste as if by a force from our textbook, a Roman army. What a mess that Ntombi was! I barely succeeded in not shaking my head. If she could not bring to table the tuck she wanted, why on earth did she have to go and embarrass everybody else by begging! A sentence spoken with conviction: 'I really enjoy that milk supplement. Well, I don't happen to have any at the moment and don't see that I'll be getting any right now. Do you mind if I have a bit of yours?' Then a purposeful grip upon the yellow cardboard of the carton; if she had to plead for something she didn't have, I wanted it done with a bit more distinction. For surely – I was convinced – Bougainvillea would treat the girl in a more dignified way if she put some self-respect into her query. Bending over my plate, I looked up at my roommate sourly. Now that her face was concealed over glass, Ntombi looked tired if you looked at her properly. The meal was toad in the hole, a good stodgy distraction from such upsets. I piled the doughy mixture high upon my platter.

'Go on, have some, too,' Bougainvillea offered me. She was looking, as she spoke, upon the Nesquik carton which no one was now touching, as we were all digging into what we knew would be the most edible meal of the day. The convent menu stretched to an appetising offering but once in three repasts. My classmate who had just spoken was looking at me with some urgency and pleading of her own. You didn't really play with white girls, but you had these moments of interaction. I debated whether to pull the tin over. I was still preoccupied with the issue of dignity. Upon considering this command to consume, though, I could not make up my mind what in this case constituted a proper sort of personhood. There were so many angles to it. Bougainvillea wanted me now to take the powder; I would be doing her a favour, but why did she want me to have it and so was she to be trusted? Then again, there were reasons to obey such directives, for upon a taste, I would work hard to ensure more portions in any way I could, thus preparing for my success in the future. On the other hand, by taking in what was offered that I could not provide for myself, I might become seriously outraged, or could fall into the habit of believing I deserved as much as they had, without having earned it. How could anyone solve that riddle? Outrage drove you over mountainous plantations of pine and wattle. I could not and did not want to think of such things, so I just gave what I believed was a dignified smile, first at Tracey, then at Bougainvillea without reaching for the Nesquik. By now everyone at the table had re-engaged with the movement of chocolate powder from Bougainvillea's tin to Ntombi's glass; its possible passage into mine. So everyone needed relief.

'The eyes too. Just like a cow's!' Tracey tried to copy Bougainvillea's kind of gallantry, although her friend's way was not at all how Tracey did things. Now that she had begun, Tracey gave an uncomfortable, uncharacteristic giggle, for Bougainvillea was the one who behaved like that when she was not being languid or dry, and instead was practising being flirtatious. But now Tracey giggled and gazed at Ntombi who, after a prolonged sip that hid her features, raised her eyes to survey the rest of the table. No one could think of anything to say at this, and so there was silence.

The talk all around in the dining hall was reaching midmeal crescendo.

'I hate,' insisted Linda, the girl who was also class monitor all the time, speaking despondently but clearly at the next table, 'I hate writing to my mum on austerity quality. You know how there's always so much to tell, especially if you're homesick. I get carried away and my nib goes right through the paper!'

'I love South Africa,' Josephine, our junior tennis star who whipped the seniors as she was Manicaland champion, declared in response. 'It's not like here! Down there absolutely every sports shop's got Slazenger racquets.'

'I got felt tips,' the girl opposite Josephine offered. I forget her name. 'It's ages since any shop here had any.'

'Maybe there's a reason for that, maybe there just might be a war on,' called Bougainvillea to the nondescript girl at the neighbouring table; Bougainvillea, named for a beautiful plant that hedged in homes, the girl whose parents farmed out close to the Mozambican border.

'War!' Tracey shook her head, half in alarm. 'Come off it, Bo. . .'

'Bougainvillea!' her friend corrected Tracey shortly.

'Sorry, Bo, I mean Bougainvillea, I just mean, what're you talking about, war! OK, a security problem, but war, Bougainvillea, come off it! War! Honestly!'

'Well, perhaps there won't be,' Bougainvillea stared at Tracey, whose parents lived in the town of Umtali. After that she glanced first at me, then at Ntombi. I was feeling terrible by now, experiencing myself as an inhuman and treacherous person, so I was very relieved when the farmer's daughter changed the subject, removed the sharpness from her voice and returned to being only mildly interested in everything. 'Guess what I've got, in the dormie, a whole tin of MacIntoshes, that's something else you can get there.'

'Yah,' Tracey sighed longingly. 'Isn't it lovely; you can get everything you want in South Africa.'

'Rye-Vita,' romanticised Angela.

'Roquefort!' breathed Deidre, and they went on listing all the items stacked upon shop shelves in the neighbouring land that could not be bought here and consequently made South Africa a much more desirable country than Rhodesia.

While this talk goes on, the nannies, dressed in pink, unlike the green cleaning nannies, pop out of the swing doors to the kitchen. Large wooden trays bearing our food in their hands, they back in and out, never banging knees or jolting elbows. They move fluidly, but when they set a jug or a plate before Ntombi or me, they smack it down with a jut of the chin and spills, as though slapping a hard, crushing thing down on obnoxious crawling objects. As this happens and our classmates, these girls with preferences that count, talk about which is better, Johannesburg, Port Elizabeth or Durban, Ntombi's cheeks sag until you think they will melt right off her bones like chocolate left out in the sun. I don't look at her because I don't want to see her melting, but Tracey looks and flushes once more. A particularly belligerent pink-clad woman practically throws a plate of bread at Ntombi. In the silence following the clattering of the stainless steel platter on which this second helping of soft fresh bread comes, Tracey, referring to her earlier comment, cried a bit too shrilly, 'It's a compliment, hey Ntombi!'

Bougainvillea assured the table, with the authority of her farm origins, 'You know what their eyes are like, hey! And those eyelashes! Whoever's caught a cow putting on mascara?'

She laughed again dryly at the thought of a cow peering into its magnifying mirror. 'Who would mind! I wouldn't mind having eyes like a cow's. When someone has a gorgeous wide-eyed gaze,' she turned to Ntombi, 'we say they've got eyes like a cow's.'

'Ha-ha-ha' laughed everyone, including Ntombi and I.

Dessert was banana custard. Bougainvillea offered Ntombi and me more chocolate to shake over the sweet. As I did not want anything else to happen but for peace to prevail, I pushed my bowl forward to have the powder sprinkled onto the sauce. This time, the gleam gone out of her eye, Ntombi ignored the proffered spoon. Languidly, Bougainvillea tipped the contents back into the tin.

Ti-ti-tingili! Sister Emmanuel rang the bell again and said grace.

We went to the dormitories after lunch, to rest and get ready for the afternoon. I couldn't face the four other girls, whom Ntombi would immediately inform about the lunchtime events. I returned upstairs and sat in the empty classroom. With my back to the window I went over the Latin lesson.

Finally, the day was over. We had supper, followed by prep and recreation, then we went back to the dormitories to change. We said prayers out on Saint Ignatius' corridor. We lined up and knelt in our nightclothes in the long grey tiled hall, where the night lights shone with a soft orange glow, having been turned down to low. I changed quickly, so as not to have to talk to Ntombi, or any of the girls, as that would surely remind Ntombi of Latin class and then of the events that followed.

Ko-ko-ko-ko-kongolo! Kongolo! The bell chimed as I emerged into St Ignatius' corridor. There was a wooden table and chair at the end where the staff member on duty sat if it was not yet time for the girls to emerge. Upon a high window ledge behind this place stood a large brass bell. Now this bell was in Sister Catherine's hands. Girls streamed from the dozen rooms which opened off the junior corridor, doing up last buttons and groping at dressing gown sashes. The other girls from my dormitory, which was the last one on the corridor, straggled out last. We knelt, with our whispers fading away, in two straight rows, our shoulders brushing the walls.

'Oh my God,' Sister Catherine began once there was neither motion nor noise.

'I am heartily sorry for having offended thee,' we all joined in, heads bowed. 'And I detest all my sins because I dread the loss of heaven and the pains of hell, but most of all because I have offended thee my God who art all goodness deserving of all my love.

'I firmly resolve with the help of thy Grace to do penance and to mend my ways, Amen.' We all murmured, each with her own petition, through the missive.

4

Zigzag, zigzag, I crossed the crazy paving, never looking up because the sky was too blisteringly blue for this early time of day, and I knew this meant too much was wrong. You could tell by the signs, if you looked, what was right and what wasn't in what was happening. Zigzag, zigzag, zigzag, I went, carefully picking up and placing my feet. You couldn't step on the cracks either, so you had to look at the ground. You had to be careful of the cracks or you'd fall in, straight into the caves of your heart. It was after breakfast, following a night of listening to the convent cats scream like demented banshees, and a night of trying to move the icebergs that built in the blood as I imagined how Bougainvillea Edwards negotiated her holidays. Was my sister or one of Netsai's friends going to creep up and kill her? No wonder she had to go to Cape Town! Tracey's parents worked in the town where all you saw of the war were truckloads of troops in fatigues and security guards who searched your bags at the entrance to Checkers and OK supermarkets. I was glad at least this classmate, whom I cared about in that distant way that we cared about each other, was so lucky, and I wanted to tie up my own luck about me this morning.

On school day mornings we had assembly. The sixth formers congregated nearest to the dormitories. They were next to the fifth years, and so the forms descended, filling up the patio between the lawns and the headmistress' office with beige and burgundy uniformed pupils, until the first form lined up beside the domestic science classroom. That patio was a glaring space, many square yards in area, and every inch was carefully laid, like a giant twinkling jigsaw puzzle, with glitterstone crazy paving. Wink-wink the stones went, like a lecherous person weighing up what to do with one of the pupils. In front a flight of steps, fat with authority as a pregnant woman, swept up to the college's main entrance and this entrance was guarded by Sister Emmanuel's office, a large edifice which gleamed at the front of the foyer like a potent empress' fortress. To the left and right of this awe-inspiring heart of the college lay the halls which led to the dining room and classrooms. I liked to stand at assembly and look up at the library. Stepping into the library was as exciting as stepping into a winnow basket, the first transport choice of local magical people, as others board a flying saucer or a magic carpet. Away, away you whisked in that place, into the pictures of other people's imaginations, the pages of other people's histories. And how warming it was to be not here but somewhere else, over there, between this and that, where you could become anything at all and where anything, including good things, could happen! Yes, the library ran above the domestic science classroom. Aromas of sugar, butter, lemon and cinnamon wafted up while you sat in your cubicle concentrating acutely, book in hand, but not really there, somewhere else. It was a small ecstasy of being.

At this time, since it was around twenty to eight, the assembly area was filling up. Already a dozen girls loitered in the second form line. I slowed down, risking stepping on one of those cavernous cracks that were there to engulf you. Monstrous caution was required before you joined the form. If you mistakenly placed yourself behind the wrong person, you could end up suffering quite savagely. The person who joined the line after you did not present such a problem, as she could determine for herself which classmate happened to be ahead, and could make her own decisions concerning the desirability of that girl's proximity. But if she was ahead of you, a white girl could pitch peremptorily further forward, when you stood too close, prompting the classmate before her to do the same, and the next one too, until you were a lonely figure afloat on a sea of scorn as matter of fact as the clouds above us. And even if she remained stationary, there was agony in not knowing whether she would move from your presence or not, whether you had judged the distance correctly or not, for there was an imperative, broken by Sister Catherine only to reinforce it in all of us: your skin and theirs should not come in contact.

The necessary care to avoid such situations meant coming down to assembly with a girl from the dormitory as a sort of insulation. Sometimes I even came out with Ntombi herself. But my dorm-mates were often late. I didn't want to be part of that tardiness. What I wanted for myself was to make a good impression. In fact, that is not true; what I wanted was to make a better impression.

The unfortunate matter was that lateness was now endemic in our dormitory. Nobody, least of all we, could, it seemed, do anything about it. Ko-ko-kongolo! The wake up call rang in the early hours. In contrast to evenings in the corridor, though, at this hour the bell described its great clanging arcs in the hands of our matron. Her name was Miss Plato, this appellation having been brought, along with a guttural growling accent, from some middle, unmentionable part of the European continent. She was a stern and implacable woman. She was infamous throughout the school for demanding to keep everything where she grunted it belonged. Be it shoelaces above the tongues of shoes, clothes in cupboards or students in dormitories, Miss Plato relentlessly desired each and every item to be in order. Miss Plato wore white, of a particularly antiseptic unsulliable sort, over every clothable part of her body. She increased the sense of not wanting anything unsanctioned or disordered to touch her by wearing, even in the horrible heat of October, long white sleeves sewn tightly into cuffs that fitted precisely, without a centimetre to spare, about her wrists where flesh hung loosely. From her head soared a winged cap like a nurse's. Its edges were so sharp, whatever the temperature or humidity, you pressed yourself up against the corridor walls whenever you saw the matron approach. We put our hands to our midriffs when she was gone, because a sharp sensation thereabouts persuaded us she had gored us.

Now we six that I have spoken of, Anastasia, Benhilda, Patience, Ntombi, Irene and myself, occupied the last room on the junior corridor. Miss Plato did not like us, the girls in the final dormitory on St Ignatius'. The other girls on the corridor never commented, but everyone knew the matron took up the bell at the top of the corridor, near the large, shiny jasmine-perfumed St Ignatius' bathrooms. Yet she not once entered a dormitory before she had walked past every door and reached the room which was called, by the members of the school who did not live in it, the African dormitory. Down she charged, brandishing the brass bell, to the end of St Ignatius' corridor. That final dormitory was allocated its end position in order to allow a drain to run outside, down beside the fire escape, from a small bathroom and laundry which opened off the bedroom. This dormitory, which was the only one to have its own ablution section, was called the African dormitory because we six young women slept there.

The arrangement pleased Miss Plato immensely. Kongolo! She battered the tongue of the bell against its shell at six a.m., striding on her rubber heels towards the African dormitory. That first bell was a wake up call. It always took me some moments to get out of bed. Sleep, when it came, wrapped me up in an airless, clinging cocoon. I heard everything distantly while I had the impression that I was burrowing through the asphyxiating fabric of a blanket, and I believe now I did not want to surface and face the day's offerings. 'Ask father! Ask father!' the doves in the pine trees that separated the dormitories from the nuns' cloister demanded loudly. Ko-ko-ko-ko-kongolo! the tolling bell insisted. Up and down the corridor now, at five minutes past the hour, crept the muffled morning sounds of schoolgirls waking. In the African dormitory too the soft bumping of cupboard doors and opening of others, whispered commands from one girl to another to get out of the way became more frequent and more nervous as the matron neared us.

This morning Benhilda, our fourth former, was looking for her black veil, in order to depart for mass. Patience was standing in the bathroom doorway with a towel held up before her chest. She was looking awfully stricken for so early in the morning, the tension very probably a source of the high blood pressure from which she suffered later. Strong green smells of pure soap gushed out of the toilet, where the tap was running, and the water was cut with the blue of the morning that splintered in through a small window of frosted glass under the ceiling.

'Get in!' warned Patience impatiently. This instruction was to Ntombi, Irene and me, the three juniors who slept in beds along the inside wall. 'What's this?' The third former's voice buzzed with apprehension so that she sounded like a bee. 'Someone get in there! Chop-chop, hey!' With this she blundered into the corner of my bed in her hurry to reach her cupboard, for I slept at the end, next to the entrance from the corridor. Technically, that position should have been Irene's as she was the most junior and should have occupied the least preferred point, but she said she was afraid to sleep in a position so exposed; what if, in the middle of the night, a being crept down the corridor and committed an awful violation upon us? Then wouldn't she be the first victim?

Finally finding her cupboard door and flinging it open, Patience whipped a Vaseline jar from the middle shelf. Her movements were executed so quickly and with such wild distraction that a pile of games shirts fell onto the floor. Back into the cupboard she stuffed the clothes feverishly. In the next moment her leg was up on the edge of her bed and she looked back at us juniors as we slowly ascended out of our blankets. 'Has the bell rung?' she demanded. 'Tell me! Or hasn't it, hey! And even if it hasn't, one of you still has to get in there right now! Come on, get on with it and do

64

it!' Vigorously she rubbed the emollient in over the cracks of stressed flaky skin.

'Uh-uh!' Ntombi yawned as she hauled herself to sitting, at the same time rubbing her eyes.

'Uh-uh!' reprimanded Patience sharply. 'Now what's this uh-uh supposed to mean! Get out of bed! Can't you hear? Please!' Patience had a problem with sharpness and could not keep it up for long. 'Please! There, there's the bell! Miss Plato's coming!'

'Let her!' Irene sprawled on her mattress. 'That's the waking up call. There's half an hour. We've still got thirty whole minutes!' With this our first former rolled over and stretched her body like a cat. Taking great pleasure in her lassitude, she purred. 'Come on, Pat! Take it easy, just this once!'

Anastasia, though – who was in the fifth form, and technically should have had a room all to herself with a washbasin up on St Sophie's corridor, but because of the systems that Miss Plato loved was still in the African dormitory – wasn't about to take anything easy. As a senior she knew she ought to be responsible, and knew that others held her responsible too for the events that went on in our dormitory. Wasn't that why she was not a prefect? Clearly she could keep neither a timetable nor order in this room with too many people; the rooms on the junior corridor were meant to accommodate four pupils each, but we were six girls in the dormitory. 'It's twenty past six,' our fifth former now warned us, and insisted doubtfully, 'You three! Come on; just listen to what Patience said! She said chop-chop! Hey, Tambudzai, Ntombi, and you too, Irene! You juniors had better get moving, and don't think you don't have to listen to us! We're still your seniors!'

I made a slit out of one eye. Through it I watched Anastasia pack her thirty-eight inch bosom into frayed thirty-six inch cups she had been given at discount from the convent's thrift shop. Bang! Miss Plato surprised us all, including the hapless fifth former, who had one breast cupped in its cotton case and the other one hanging.

'Shit, man!' breathed Anastasia, as the matron burst through the door which she, Miss Plato, had hurled open.

'Can you not hear? Can you not hear?' Miss Plato bawled. As though to test this premise she held the brass bell at arm's length and shook it madly. As I was still on my bed beside the door and so right beside it, the peals ricocheted everywhere inside my skull wildly. The sight of the matron in such a menacing passion, plus, it appears, the fact that the sense of motion is connected to the sense of hearing, so that malfunction in auditory processes can result in malfunction of movement, paralysed me completely. I did not dare put my hands up to cover my ears, nor move away from the cacophony. The bell-ringer stood at the doorway like the bringer of an awful, powerful prophecy and cried, 'Can you not hear the ring of the bell that says up you must be standing!'

Indeed, that bell could be heard all over the northern block of the school. So up I tried to stand, but this only brought me closer to the awful clanging. Miss Plato refused to give way. I collapsed back onto the blankets. Ntombi, who had the bed next to mine, took advantage of my unpleasant circumstance to saunter into the washroom.

'I vill not have it!' the bell-ringing matron shrieked. Now she was shaking the bell almost in front of me.

'Vy have I everyday in this vay to talk, when it should be enough vonce to tell you! If you in this vay vant,' the matron charged, 'I must tell Sister Emmanuel!' Her face mottled to red beneath her jutting cap. Ntombi accelerated over the last few steps and banged the door to the bathroom. Anastasia now had both breasts covered and stood almost at attention. Benhilda, who was at the little mirror above the wash-basin opposite Patience's bed, managed to fix the hair grips which kept her black lace veil in place more or less calmly. Patience stood as though transfixed, her leg up on the bed, a blob of Vaseline in her palm. Meanwhile Irene buried her face in her pillow. I could hear the little movements that meant her shoulders were shaking.

'You are thinking it is funny!' Miss Plato cried. 'Over vhat are you laughing!'

I personally do not remember smiling. I remember my mouth twisting in surprise, my eyes popping large at the harshness of it and at the awful clanging as she was still shaking the bell at intervals. In fact, I recall doing everything I could to find an expression that made it clear I agreed with the matron about the unacceptability of our poor time keeping. Therefore I was very surprised when, ko-ko-kongolo, the bell was given a last furious shake and Miss Plato bent over, reaching out to grab and tug at my bedding.

'And all the time you are just sitting there!' she raged, 'vhen I say you are late! Bad girl! Vhy are you not moving! Up, up!' She pulled again at the blankets. So infuriated was she, the hand that gripped the bedclothes was shivering.

Anastasia gave me a satisfied look of well-you-thought-you-were-so-clever. I swung my legs up and over my bed to stand up on the other side from Miss Plato. But the look from Anastasia and the shouting, Ntombi sauntering away like that, and the clanging of metal – it all enraged me.

'Tambu!' Anastasia groaned between clenched teeth, looking at me now in a stricken way. 'What are you doing, Tambu!' I looked down to see the other end of the sheet in my hands, which were pulling like a tug-of-war with Miss Plato. Immediately I let go, and it was very lucky that our room was so overcrowded, otherwise Miss Plato would have fallen. As it was, she staggered back to Patience's bed but a hand stretched down spared her the ignominy of sitting upon it.

The idea of Miss Plato sitting on one of our beds had very much the effect of a slap in my face so that it brought me back to my senses. The understanding demeanour I had previously displayed towards Miss Plato concerning our bad habit of lateness came to the fore once more and I hung my head in a flood of contrition. Oh, how could I have been so unafraid! Where had the fear gone for that mad moment, the fright that would have made me behave properly towards the matron? It was difficult for me to believe that I, who had been brought up so well by Babamukuru, and who wanted so much to please, could have behaved in that brash, undisciplined and defiant fashion, and play tug-of-war over the sheets with the matron.

'I'm sorry, Miss Plato!' a small voice trembled. I became yet more upset thinking one of the other girls had beaten me to the act of apology.

'I'm really sorry, matron! I don't know what came over me!' the rather flat and monotonous voice continued. In a few seconds I recognised the words as mine so that I became proud of my voice again and accepted it once more as an important part of my person.

At the same time, Miss Plato was still fuming. 'Now you are sorry!' You could tell the matron begrudged us this slight measure of her good grace for her tone remained exceedingly belligerent. Oh, it was terribly difficult! I hung my head as far as I could in an effort to mollify her somewhat. It seems I had a little success. 'All right!' she went on at a slightly softer volume. 'I see you are sorry. But that you should be also! I have to tell you, you vill come nowhere in this vorld vhen you yourselves alvays late are making! How many from you must yet to vash?' she enquired, suspiciously, while her nostrils flared to a quiver as though the little flaps of flesh endeavoured to determine the answer.

'Hardly any from us!' declared Irene, unable to suppress a giggle, as Anastasia, who had by now dressed herself quickly, squeezed her way past the matron with Benhilda, deciding it was more sensible to be at mass than remain in Miss Plato's vicinity. This left four of us to face the matron. At some point our plump little first former had divested herself of her nightdress and now swept over to the towel rack by the wash basin in her bikini cut panties. She turned back to Miss Plato with the towel in hand. 'Benhilda and Anastasia to mass are gone!' exclaimed the child. 'One from us, Ntombi, is cleaning herself. Another, Patience, is already clean. There are only we two who are remaining!'

However, Miss Plato, being of German extraction, was not perturbed by this nudity, and simply advised the youngest girl in the dormitory, 'Vash yourself quickly indeed, vithin half an hour! But think of it, in this time you must also your uniforms on be putting! Tambudzai, see that you are into any more trouble not getting.'

Ko-ko-kongolo! the bell rang as she proceeded back up the corridor.

Ntombi took an awfully long time in the bathroom. Growing nervous, I began to consider how nefariously Ntombi was scheming to ensure my lateness so that I ended up in more trouble with the matron. Maybe Miss Plato would act on her word, report me to Sister Emmanuel! How angry I became with Ntombi. With an effort, although my impulse was to bang on the bathroom door while uttering insulting words, I managed to lay out my uniform calmly, and picked balls of fluff off my socks, then I started on my face, not because there were any spots but to take my mind off the idea of another encounter with Miss Plato, or indeed, with any other authority. I was just as worried about another encounter with myself. What if I did something else I didn't know I could do, like pull the sheets! What would it be, and wouldn't it be awful?

'Squash,' Ntombi shot nastily, when she finally came out from her washing, a towel around her waist. She darted laughing and triumphant glances towards the bed upon which I had collapsed as I waited despondently for her to vacate the room I needed to enter as soon as possible. 'Hey,' my classmate stood blocking my way to the washroom and enjoying the situation tremendously. 'Man, Miss Plato just flattened you! Hey, everybody, didn't Miss Plato squash Tambu!' Grunts of agreement came from Irene and Patience. Swelled with the victory she had won over me, Ntombi proceeded to the cupboard we shared. This sharing of cupboards, the putting people in close proximity to each other, was a necessity arising from charity. As the dormitories on our corridor were built to accommodate a regulation four pupils, each room possessed four built-in units, but as the nuns' compassion towards us caused them to wish to educate as many of us as possible, there were now six of us at the Young Ladies' College of the Sacred Heart, housed in this four-person room on St Ignatius' corridor. This meant we first and second formers had to share cupboards. Ntombi remained immersed in the joy of my having been crushed. 'Didn't Miss Plato really show her!' she turned to the other girls, a sanitary pad in hand. 'Those people who think they are a wonder, who think they can do whatever they want! *Fototo*! Squash! Just like that! There are people there who will show them!' Patience and Irene grunted again, much to my disappointment. They didn't want to look at me either, so I could see that by what I had done to Miss Plato, I had shamed the dormitory more than usual.

So it was after this deflating, or 'squashing' beginning to the day for everyone that I stepped out onto our assembly area and looked about nervously. I could distinguish Linda Browning, the monitor from the opposite table in the dining hall, shifting from one foot to the other at the back of the queue, and so I stood for a while considering. Could a person stand behind Linda? She was known for her clumsiness which meant she had little sense of the proximity of other persons. This lack of sense made her back into you without notice. If you backed away you ran the risk of bumping into the girl behind you. There was something they – a particular kind of girl – did when that happened. This was a pulling back of their very aura from contact with you, in a way that said not even your shadows that blocked the sun should intermingle. And looks of such horror flooded their faces at this accidental contact that you often looked around to see what horrendous monster caused the expression, before you realised it was your person. The girls put up with going to school with us because the nuns gave them a prestigious education. But this did not at all mean these particular white girls could bear the idea or the reality of touching us. Linda was not one of these; she was not easily dismayed by contact with us herself. But her clumsiness could force you into someone who couldn't bear it.

'I still think Cape Town's more fun than Durban!' Bougainvillea and Tracey swept by. 'You've only got the beach in Durban. Cape Town's got much more! In Cape Town you've got culture!'

I watched them carefully, sizing up who was where and estimating who would stand where in the form. Bougainvillea was the leader. Tracey would take her place behind Bo. Tracey didn't mind touching me. That meant even if she moved unexpectedly, I would not have to lurch to the rear. I sidled up behind her. It was now up to whoever stood behind me to decide whether she could risk contact or not. We began assembly with the Lord's Prayer, led by Sister Emmanuel. But even before our headmistress appeared, I was praying Ntombi would come quickly from the dormitories and stand behind me. That way the agony of fear of bumping into a white girl who stood behind you if anyone moved suddenly would be hers, not mine. We spent a lot of time consumed by this kind of terror. We didn't speak of it amongst ourselves. It was all too humiliating, but the horror of it gnawed within us.

'Good morning, girls!'

Soon Sister Emmanuel stood before us at a lectern on a little platform. This platform was really an apron set half-way up the flight of steps, and which so broke the climb to the headmistress' office into two portions, as though it was necessary for a visitor to pause and contain herself before she approached the fortress. We always knew when Sister was in her office, since being set at the top of the main steps, the office commanded a complete view of the school grounds and main approach, so that when she was in it we could also see her and tamed our behaviour to make it circumspect.

Our headmistress glanced at the too-blue sky and smiled, not being intimidated by its merciless shining. 'It's a pity,' came the remark in her casual way, whose informality was magnified by her American accent that made you think of bank robbers, ragged beauties in bordello bars, prim pioneers and cowboys, 'a pity to send you in on a day like this,' she continued, as she often did on these drought-stricken days. She seemed to enjoy this little joke of hers immensely. 'There must be a hundred things you'd rather be doing! Like cool-ing down in the swimming pool!' There was a pause, then Sister began again. 'In the name of the Father and of the Son and of the Holy Ghost.' We touched our foreheads, hearts, right and left shoulders. 'Our Father, which art in heaven. . .' led Sister.

After prayers Sister made announcements. This morn-ing we were informed that training for the Manicaland inter-schools gala was to begin that week, that our physical health was as important as our mental and spiritual robust-ness, moreover we had always excelled at this competition and so would we please take it seriously. Tracey was excited and shifted her weight from one leg to the other. Tracey was the backstroke and medley school junior champion. We were expecting national colours from her that season, and her excitement extended to the whole form. We all shifted our weight from one foot to the other, for we all saw ourselves as Tracey and Tracey as us in her quest for glory, and we all wished her well in her endeavour. Josephine crossed her arms in satisfaction at the next announcement, which was about tennis. They were to send a school team on tour to other girls' schools in southern Africa during the holidays. Would the girls involved please obtain forms from Miss Whitley, the games mistress, for the parents to sign, indicating their sponsorship of the journey? Bougainvillea, who was already Manicaland junior runner up, smiled too. She shot a glance back at Tracey. 'Great, hey!' she mouths. 'I told you about him! That sweet guy in Cape Town!' A prefect frowned. Bougainvillea grinned at her disarmingly.

Next Sister Emmanuel informed us about the choir which would not meet that Friday as usual because Mrs Dupont, the choir mistress, had undergone minor surgery. Benhilda, beyond in the fourth form line, shrunk a bit with disappointment. She was a strong alto in the choir, being one of those who got her lungs pumping in the rhythm of her heart to bring out her music. As a result, the guitar club, continued the headmistress, would sing in church this Sunday, and was to sit with Sister Catherine after dinner and homework, while the rest of us were at recreation. Benhilda was in the guitar club too. Sister Catherine let her use her own guitar to practise on, as Benhilda didn't have one of her own. It meant Benhilda could only practise and never perform. All the same, at the latter part of the announcement, my dorm-mate brightened up immediately.

Sister went on to inform us that the social at the Catholic Hall was finalised for a fortnight on Friday. Those of us from the lower fifth form up who wished to go were to give their names to their class mistresses. Anastasia, who was the only one from the dormitory who was eligible, as she was a fifth former, crossed her arms and looked at her feet. It went without saying there wasn't anyone for her to socialise with at the town Catholic Hall, so no matter how much she wanted an evening of fun, she wouldn't be going. Sister told us that this item about the social brought her to her last announcement, which was as exasperating as it was unpleasant.

'It is,' Sister regretfully shook her head, 'quite unspeakable.' The furrow between her brows indicated the gravity of the occasion, and instead of speaking she pressed her gaze against us. A shiver trekked through the school. The pupils of Sister's eyes shrunk as she considered what she had to say, to glint in the morning sun like the tips of a surgeon's scalpels. Then she drew those sharp scalpel points down the line of tall girls who stood to her right, like a surgeon preparing excision. Behind me Ntombi drew a breath that did not come out again. I held mine too. What was to be cut out! What excision was Sister preparing!

It was the sixth formers who were squirming under the razor-like gaze. We had two columns of these seniors. There was the line consisting of the intelligent young women who wrote their A-Levels after two years, and another line for the less intelligent girls who made do with an M-level qualification, which was accepted in South Africa but not in England.

The thing these girls had in common, if not their intellect, was roughly their ages, and the development of their bodies. Contours that must be strapped in were a serious consideration at the Young Ladies' College. The three bra limit the uniform list stipulated applied most pertinently here, and was strictly enforced through precision at cupboard checking time on the part of Miss Plato. The matron's meticulousness put doting mothers on a leash and made them turn a deaf ear to daughterly persuasion concerning both the number and sexiness of these undergarments. On the other hand, our seniors progressed from socks to pumps with heels and sheer clinging nylons every day if they could afford them. Sister's attention to such detail taught us the permutations and limits of decorum. Now, with Sister staring at the senior forms so acutely, we imagined a terrible biologically-based indiscretion amongst them. A senior had been caught with a joint, bunking out at the very least, if not eloping! But Sister's gaze swept down across the fourth form, to the third formers, where it alighted on Patience after Benhilda. The staff, who with the prefects placed themselves around the margins of the assembly area to nip bad behaviour in the bud, stood up more sternly, the straightening of their backbones seeming to be in proportion to the severity of the infringement we were on the brink of being informed of. Sister's sharpened pupils moved again. A tremor flapped through the school. 'It is,' said Sister Emmanuel furiously, 'it is the African dormitory.'

A sigh seeped out of the young ladies. Shoulders drooped, knees bent, easing weight that was grown suddenly irrelevant. Cheeks puffed out, blowing fringes in relief from moist foreheads.

'It has been brought to my attention,' seethed the head-mistress. Pink patterned her chin and forehead. 'It has been brought to my attention,' she repeated, with such a strain of emotion tightening her voice that for her own sake, quite forgetting your own distress, you wished there was some way for her to relax it.

'It has,' she began a third time, 'been brought to my attention that the Africandormitory!' she ran her words together in her outrage, 'the Africandormitory has once more caused a clog up of the college's sewerage system! The entire drainage will have to be over-hauled. And we are going to have to do this because,' – here Sister paused in disbelief at our great irresponsibility – 'because in spite of repeated warnings about the very serious consequences of their actions, the young ladies in that dormitory insist on throwing their used feminine hygiene pads into their toilet.'

Sister picked us out one by one, each after the other, impaling us on that scalpel gaze. 'I regret to say this is not the first time this has occurred, and I have explained repeatedly why this must not be so. I am aware the girls in the African dormitory may not be cognisant of the reasons why such articles should not be deposited in toilet bowls, but this is one of the reasons you are brought here. I am sure, young ladies, you are aware you are brought here to polish your behaviour! Let me repeat once again, a sewerage system is expensive. It is not, is that clear, to be clogged up with your personal hygiene items!'

The dots of us, Anastasia over in the fifth form column, Benhilda and Patience in middle school, the juniors, Ntombi, Irene and I, all drooped and contracted and cringed. I saw myself as though from far above, in a place where there were no toilet drains to clog, as one of those, that Tambudzai. There wasn't any question, especially not after that disobedient tug-of-war with Miss Plato, of my having the energy to own myself. How all of us pined and yearned during that assembly not to be ourselves, but someone else!

Sister seemed to notice this great yearning we had. Either she felt she had made her point, or she did not want to distress us further. So she quickly concluded, 'You are causing the whole school great expense that we should not be carrying at this moment. I am extremely annoyed. In the name of the Father and of the Son and of the Holy Spirit, Amen.' We were blessed and form by form we trudged to our classrooms. I looked down again, so as not to step on the cracks and fall into them. Where would I go, fall into that self I wouldn't be? For the same reason, I didn't want to look at anyone who looked more like me than the majority of girls, so I didn't want to observe Ntombi. Looking down, I bumped into Tracey. She smiled at me. I smiled back and felt relief. We moved on to the classroom.

The situation was this: I was in two aspects a biologically blasphemous person. This became increasingly clear as I walked, my head low, to the first lesson. My corporeal crime indicted me on two counts. First were the secretions that dripped crimson into the toilet bowl, or, stopped with cotton wool, clogged the school's waste system. Then there was the other type of gene that made me look different from the majority of pupils. Even if these others ran the risk, as I did, of rendering waste removal systems dysfunctional, at least they were different in appearance. How was I going to redeem myself, I wondered miserably? It was at times like this that the thought of Netsai practically took away all my strength. Well, what was I going to do? I asked myself. What was within my reach? In answer, trudging up the steps to the second form classroom, looking at the tips of my shoes, I resolved I would not ever again 'time out'. I would pay minute attention, memorising every word the teacher said in every subject, every page in every book. This was something I could do to convince anyone who needed it of my worth. Sports were no good, because the competitions were mostly at government schools, and you weren't allowed to go to them. I did an extended long jump, but what was the use if you couldn't compete with the best to show that you too were excellent? I felt strengthened by this resolve, so I put it into practice immediately. Sister Catherine in Latin commented contentedly on how alert I had become. But it was only a few days later that my bodily aberrations, as I increasingly thought of them, once more got me into trouble.

It was after breakfast. I needed to relieve myself. We were walking, coming out of the dining hall on our way back to the dormitories. We had forty minutes after our great aluminium jugs of milk and platters of bread in which to brush our teeth before Miss Plato shook the assembly bell. You had to calculate these matters precisely to make sure all remained correct. You had, for example, the option of going to the bathrooms at the end of the first form classroom, but if you did, would you get back in time to make your bed and put clothes flung all over in haste to get dressed before the breakfast bell, neatly into your cupboard?

The cupboards did not have locks. Miss Plato inspected them at will, in order to mete out tidiness points. If your cupboard was too untidy too often, she gave you a mark, a small black blot against your name on the board beside the library. Library hours were compulsory for all, and so everybody saw it. The idea of the mark was bad enough, but what made it worse was everybody could see you had one. That meant everybody could see what kind of person other people thought you were. *Tiripo, kana makadini wo!* I am well if you are all right too! That was the greeting we gave to each other, first heard on Mai's back when it was nothing more than a great buzzing booming confusion of utterance. That greeting went round the land like a blanket that covered and kept warm, a fabulous protection from fate. Everything was reciprocal and so were we; we all knew it, so said it every day in our greetings. This meant that what people saw you as being was a large part of what you were! Added to this basic existential truth, was the particular truth of the convent. Four of those disapproving blobs meant you did not qualify for the honour roll, regardless of how well you performed at classwork. We had been told not a single girl from our dormitory had ever achieved the honour roll. A roll of honour! I was determined to attain it. Nor did my determination waver even though I subscribed, as a result of all my upbringing, to the 'I am well if you are well too' view of the universe.

All this meant that now, when I needed to open my bowels but also wanted to tidy up in order to remain on the honour roll, and so did not want to walk all the way to the first form classrooms, I did not know what to do. The junior hostel bathrooms opened off St Ignatius' corridor, at the top as you entered the dormitory hall from the dining room. Usually Miss Plato or a prefect stood at the corner to make sure nothing prohibited happened. I generally took it for granted that these authority figures were on the lookout, but today, in my pressed circumstances, I quickly realised none were in sight. A few girls from the other dormitories, I remember Deidre Brophy and Barbara Arnott, ducked off into the bathrooms before me. All at once, I ducked in after them.

The toilets had swing doors. You saw them, as you walked to and fro, to the classrooms and the dining hall, swinging, shuttering away from you a forbidden world of fragrant bodily necessities. It was my first time in those toilets. Ablution blocks were like that in those days: sanctified places. There were rows of showers with shiny curtains, bathtubs that gleamed like mother of pearl in pale coral colours; along one wall were plump-bellied washbasins so deep as to be splashproof, never leaving a puddle beneath, and the smell of jasmine seeped out from everything. I frowned to think of how careless you'd have to be when you washed in this fine bathroom to leave the floor slippery with splashes. But I could not look around as much as I wanted to enjoy the shininess of the taps, the frosting of the windows. On I moved, tense and quick, past a row of enigmatic looking machines that we knew were incinerators although we did not have one in our bathroom. Sometimes, when it grew too much, Anastasia or Benhilda wrapped a pad in toilet paper and kept it until there was time to deposit it in an incinerator in one of the classroom bathrooms, which the regulations allowed us to visit. I pulled the door to a cubicle violently behind me in my haste to make sure I was not seen by a white girl.

'Hey! Do you mind!' Deidre complained two doors up. I held my breath and sat down. Now, I felt a tremor of triumph as I exposed my buttocks, imagining all the white girls doing the same. But I immediately felt guilty for having aspirations above my station. I was where I was not supposed to be. I was breaking the law, I castigated myself. This tension made my performance at the matter I had come to resolve unsatisfactory, then the situation worsened as I reached for tissue. Two white *takkies*, the round-shaped rubber of the toes resembling nastily smiling lips, were glaring at me from under the door.

'I have you seen!' It was the matron. Her voice trembled with the triumph of having caught me. 'It is in this toilet you are meant not to be sitting!' she cried. 'Open!' she continued shrilly and loudly, so that Deidre and Barbara and all the girls who had come into the ablution block heard. Brown school sandals gathered around the *takkies*. Miss Plato could not help it now with the audience around her. She exulted, 'This door to be opened I command!' I intended to clean the toilet bowl but did not now dare. I opened without sufficient care of my nether regions, which felt messily moist and sticky. 'Ha!' cried the matron as I emerged, head hung low, and felt the white girls examining me. 'Ha! The vorter! The vorter you have not flushed!'

Obediently I turned, entered the cubicle, performed the required operation and returned to stand in the entrance again, unable to look at anyone. How absolutely awful it was! I who, unlike a lot of the other girls in my dormitory, had sat on flushing toilets at an early age now being humiliated in this fashion! It was so horrible I could not comprehend how it happened. I could not believe I had behaved in such a silly fashion that resulted in my being caught, as it were, *in flagrante*.

Because of this behaviour of mine the black mark was entered against my name. The horror of not making the honour roll, of not being honourable, loomed. To make it worse, we were summoned, a day later, to Sister Emmanuel.

5

In the evening of the day of the summons, I sat in prep, still feeling uncomfortable because of my terrible behaviour, but not suspecting anything more disastrous than the mark. I was memorising my geography about Bongo in the Congo and his admirable house on stilts, as Ntombi put in little addition and minus signs on a chart, symbolising the charges on the elements in the periodical table. Margot Shales, an upper sixth prefect, entered soundlessly, so we did not hear the warning whisper of the sheen of her pantihose, nor the pat on the grey tiles of her leather pumps. She whispered briefly to the other prefect, Stephanie, who supervised us that evening. The latter put on a noncommittal expression and nodded.

Margot did not look at anyone as she walked down the aisle between two columns of desks. I kept on going over the same phrase concerning the species of snakes Bongo and his parents avoided by their wiliness. A lot of effort went into that concentration, as I was working on the principle that, if I ignored Margot, I in turn would be ignored.

'Sister Emmanuel wants you,' the prefect said. 'Ask Miss Plato to be excused a quarter of an hour before recreation ends.'

She stood, as she spoke, at a point between me and Ntombi. My dorm-mate sat behind me in the row to the right. For my part, as soon as she started speaking, I became resigned. They had every right to haul me up, because you couldn't deny I'd done what I did. What I wasn't prepared for, though, was that her speech included Ntombi. It was an awful moment. We were being singled out, and I felt despicably guilty at having been the cause. Just like Netsai! I moaned in my heart. Because of people like my sister we were all suspected of being guilty of being terrorists! Now I was doing the same as my sister! I am not well, so you are not well too! That was the new philosophy.

Approaching Sister's office, regretting the last of the recreation we were missing, Ntombi and I realised in a moment we were not alone. Benhilda and Patience emerged from an archway to peer in our direction. Behind them, as though they were hiding from the sharp white lights in the foyer, you could just make out Irene and Anastasia. Margot was waiting with the rest of my roommates. As Ntombi and I arrived, she receded into the darkness. We spent a long time gathered in front of Sister's office, we members of St Ignatius' last dormitory, without saying anything.

When she spoke, I was glad it was her, my classmate and not me, who was troubled enough to express her frustration.

'People!' Ntombi turned her lips down to force the word out in a spit. 'Those who want to unforbid themselves, as though they were the ones who forbade themselves in the first place! People who want to put themselves up, up there! Now look where it's put everyone!' She glared at me.

'Can you swing them to and fro?' We heard the question faintly, the roared interrogation of some other pupils letting off steam on St Ignatius' corridor. To take my mind off what was happening, I concentrated on this cheerful rowdiness that emanated from the junior corridor bathroom.

The bathrooms were close by, down the corridor and to the left. There was an indeterminate half hour at Sacred Heart, between recreation time and prayers. The juniors took recreation in the gym, which meant *Sisi* Anastasia and our middle schoolers came too, looking too big and incongruous. The gym was equipped with a horse, mats and ropes that descended from the ceiling. After an hour's prep with Latin verbs and strange, if not dubious, geographical practices, we chased each other round, sprang cartwheels, attempted to vault, and some of the more fearless girls swung from ropes in the ceiling. They bawled as they flew, yet even as they defied gravity, getting their subjectivities all mixed up, 'You Jane, me Tarzan!' Tarzan was a man whose acquaintance I had made too recently. I wasn't about to go up on those ropes, high as a leg that leapt against the moon, a moon that arced above the dark mountain slopes. But we often began that silly song surreptitiously down in the gym, with a mad sense of being audacious and unseemly, and carried it up to the corridor. The further you proceeded away from authority, the louder you could sing. So the bathroom was a good auditorium. Before now, I had always stopped in front of the wooden swing doors and chanted in a muted way as I looked round in order to dodge Miss Plato.

'Do your boobs hang low?' the young ladies screamed, the sound coming faintly like a lullaby in the calm evening air. 'Can you swing them to and fro? Can you fling them round your neck and tie them in a bow? Can you throw them to the ceiling with a free and easy feeling? If you can,' the last triumphant line was shrieked, 'your boobs hang low!' Ntombi turned her back to me, and I turned mine, as though I didn't care, to her. Meanwhile Irene, who in fact did not care about such things as summons and absences of decorum, was humming along with the bathroom brigade. 'Imagine!' she breathed during a lull from the ablution block, 'if Emma came out and we all burst out singing it!' The first former put a hand to cover her mouth. Splutter, splutter she gurgled quietly with suffocated giggles.

Anastasia looked at the little girl pityingly. 'The trouble is,' she said gravely, 'our trouble is people who don't know *anything*, who think they know *everything*, but when you look, you see there isn't *anything*.' It was the kind of comment that made everyone uncomfortable. Irene stopped giggling and leant against the wall to Sister's office, the merriment drained from her expression, leaving a mark of upset bewilderment. Silly child! I ruminated silently. Idiotic women! The fools who couldn't use a decent sewerage system! If they'd only shown they were conversant with those contrivances, I was sure there wouldn't have been any bans – not on anyone from any bathrooms! Had these people I was forced to identify with been more able, those bathrooms would have been open to all. No one would have been standing here in this humiliation. Now, I had to be here when I had received proper training at my uncle's! Oh, I felt yet another surge of dislike for the other girls in my dormitory!

'She said after recreation!' Anastasia was growing more and more restless. She looked around helplessly. 'What shall we do? Shall we knock?'

'Man!' murmured Irene, 'Man! Come on, girls, what are you?' We all stared at her, daring her to follow up with action. To our disbelief, indeed to our dismay, she raised her hand, bunched it to a fist and banged.

No one but Irene herself breathed until the response was given.

'Enter!' Sister's voice instructed, enabling us to act, as we had now been commanded.

'I thought you'd never get round to it,' our headmistress admonished with bright amusement. 'Come right in!' she advised as we huddled timidly to a halt just inside the door. Again, Irene was the first to move, and we shuffled into a half moon before the nun, our sandals sighing over the rug in the middle of the floor, whose pile was as deep as our breathing. Our headmistress surveyed us critically. 'I see you've all made it. Good.' She clasped her hands on the great mahogany desk cut lengthwise to the grain so that, in the warm dim lamplight from an ornate stand behind Sister, it looked like a broad swirling moat.

'What I have to say to you,' Sister continued, with sufficient awkwardness to prevent her from looking at us for part of her speech. 'What I called you here to discuss is not at all pleasant.' She paused, searching. When she found the words, she leaned back in her chair, leaving one hand stretched palm down on the table. 'Neither is it Christian. However, there are many things that are not Christian going on, and we are compelled to deal with them.' Sister picked up her reading glasses that lay on top of a piece of paper. She put the spectacles on and observed us again keenly. 'As a result, girls, we receive, and have to deal with, directives such as this one.' She picked up the piece of paper on which her glasses had been sitting. 'I would not want you to read this for yourselves.' She held the sheet by the corner, waving it disdainfully. 'It is a directive from the Minister of Education.' Here Sister Emmanuel paused again, for she was once more at a loss. Nor could we help her as we were keeping our heads uncomfortably downcast, with our foreheads wrinkled and our eye sockets aching from swivelling our eyeballs up under our brows. For each one of us had learnt in infancy how to respect, but we had all, since that early teaching, discovered white people expected you to look straight at their eyes when you communicated.

Being compelled by her breeding to look at us also for a significant amount of this time, but not really wanting to do so, Sister searched for relief. She found it in her slightly sadistic humour. 'Don't you worry,' we were reassured with an enigmatic smile. 'Nobody's going to be cut in half.' Anastasia, Irene and all the other girls shifted their weight from one foot to the other in shock. I was the only one who stood still. Halves of people! I could not comprehend. I did not know what Sister was talking about.

'There are,' Sister informed us, 'quotas. Unfortunately, yes, the government puts in place quotas of students!' Her voice rose a third in indignation. 'We have been aware of it. In fact, we have known about these quotas since before any of you girls who are here today were admitted to Sacred Heart. The quotas are part of our regulations for admitting any African pupils and being multiracial. We have always interpreted the quotas generously. And we haven't had any trouble in the past. However, now, with the security situation deteriorating as is the case, the Ministry is asking multiracial institutions like our own to be particularly vigilant.' She surveyed us calmly now. I wrapped one foot around the other ankle. I was sure the headmistress was gazing at me. Oh, damn her, that young sister of mine! What would happen to me if they found out? What would the security forces do to us? How could I hope to explain away a one-legged sister in the village! Where had she sustained her injury and who had helped her? The whole family was going to pay for it. After Babamukuru had already been beaten by the freedom fighters! Back, away, over the mountains in Mozambique – that's where I hoped Netsai was.

'You mustn't worry!' Sister was reassuring us. 'We have always interpreted these quotas generously. As a result, we have always been in excess of them. We are not going to go back on that decision now. Don't worry! We are not going to send anyone away in order to comply. Everybody is perfectly safe, whatever those percentages.' Sister Emmanuel pulled one corner of her mouth down, then up while her eyes frosted with a cold humour. 'Whatever memoranda they send us, we aren't going to chop anyone in half, nor in any other portion. That is what I called you here to inform you.'

It is a joke, so we titter. Ntombi put her hand to her mouth, but Patience poked her. We all, including Irene, giggled openly.

'I'm glad your fears are now at rest,' the headmistress continued. 'I understand what you must be going through in these trying times. Just understand these are trying times for everyone.' The headmistress stared at us more keenly than before. 'That is why, even as things are changing, we feel it is realistic to continue to enforce some of our old regulations that might make it appear we are not moving with the times. In fact,' Sister divulged, 'I would not have spoken to you about this memorandum, if I hadn't heard of considerable discontent in your dormitory. I wanted to assure you we are fully behind you. All sorts of nasty circumstances could emerge from the present situation, and we want to protect you from these. We don't want a situation where Rhodesian farmers come in here and insult you for using their daughters' bathrooms!'

We muttered consent, shifting from foot to foot.

'Does anyone have anything to say?'

No one did. Sister looked pleased that the nasty business was over. 'Thank you girls,' she dismissed us. But how angry I was with Sister, talking to us like that, making jokes about our flesh and how some people thought it was divisible. Or else it was all lumped as one: your flesh fractioned or piled together! To make it worse, she did not ask for our view on the subject beyond the end of audience formality. Not that we would have spoken anyway, or perhaps Irene might. If Sister had given us sufficient space for the enormity of the matter, while we of the more senior forms hung our heads meekly, the first former might have spoken. Thinking like this, an impulse made me stubborn as the others filed out. 'You may go. All of you,' Sister repeated when I stood there. Ntombi was pushing me to move ahead. I did not budge. It had to be done. But what could be said to bring one's voice into the room, which at the same time did not annoy anyone? It was so impossible, I crumbled. I decided it was best instead to show Sister my breeding, how I would remain calm and gracious no matter what happened. 'Thank you, Sister. Good night, Sister,' I wished her politely. The nun looked at me thoughtfully, with another amused glint in her eye as I followed my dorm-mates. Ntombi trailed a hand over the black iron railings at the side of the corridor as we filed quietly to our quarters.

Around the corner we came upon the juniors taking their milk and biscuits. It was Marie biscuits this evening, and butter shortbread, both dry, while I preferred custard creams or chocolate digestives. Anastasia pretended not to like biscuits at all and pushed her woman's body past the thirteen and fourteen year olds. Benhilda, who was almost as senior as *Sisi* Ana, followed her. The rest of us stepped up for a bedtime bite.

'Stop it! Not for you!' Miss Plato came hurrying over.

'Oh-oh' gasped Patience and then her face went quiet. Ta-a! stung a slap on the third former's wrist. It takes a moment at a time like that to work out that it is Patience's wrist that is stinging. 'Do you not shame yourself!' cries Miss Plato indignantly. 'You should shame yourself!' By this she meant Patience should not be indignant, but rather ashamed. 'You are senior, but you take the food I have put for the young ones.'

'Go up to Saint Agatha's' Ntombi advised our third former.

'Yes,' concurred Miss Plato. 'It is the middle school corridor, vhere your form is! There you vill find your biscuits. But you must hurry, for I shall the lights soon out put!'

'Have mine!' Tracey stood at the table behind us. She held out a biscuit to Patience, who looked at it, and then at Tracey as though both were dirty. Tracey started flushing and the biscuit was still held out as the middle schooler turned and started swinging her hips like that, *fasha-fasha* like a stately woman, down the corridor. I felt unhappy for Tracey who was doing her best to do what was right and whose offering had been rejected. In any case, my classmate was still holding the confectionery. I reached over, relieved her of it and popped it into my mouth. My class-mate regarded me while I chewed with the too dry flakes rough like sand in my mouth and not wanting to go down. Her examination was such that she observed something about me that repulsed. As I realised this, I felt a great need to encourage her to like me, and to help her understand I had acted as I did to wish her well, so I smiled. For a long moment Tracey's expression did not change, but in the end, to my satisfaction, even though it was painful, like someone giving up a long cherished object, she shook her head and grinned, 'G'night, Tambu!'

I swaggered down the hall after that, Ntombi behind me. It was only at the door that Ntombi pushed past and exploded to everyone inside the dormitory, '*Vasikana*, girls, can you believe it! Me I can't, but yes, it was her! It was Tambudzai! She took that biscuit!'

Oh! Ntombi produced another cookie from her uniform pocket and held it out to Patience. Our dormitory mate was sitting on her bed, already changed into a long cotton nightdress, and holding her wrist. 'Oh, *Sisi* Peshi, was it so hard, is it hurting?' Ntombi turned from looking horror struck at Patience to question everyone. There were tears in her eyes. 'Is that what they are allowed to do? Are they really allowed to smack us?'

'My God, Tambu!' said Anastasia crossly. 'Why did you have to go and do that? Man, really! Go and take that biscuit!'

'She *ate* it,' cried Ntombi desperately.

'Tss!' That was Patience hissing in air between her teeth. She took a small steel-rimmed mirror from her chair and started poking at her acne. A blob of yellow ooze squirmed out.

Anastasia squeezed sadistically at a tube of toothpaste. 'Shit,' she said, 'I've got too much! Does anyone want a bit?' Benhilda retrieved a notebook from the chair beside her bed and flicked through her geometry equations.

'Didn't anyone hear?' Ntombi was incredulous. 'Are you all wanting not to hear what I said about *Sisi* Peshi's biscuit?'

'We heard,' nodded Anastasia, brushing, her mouth frothing.

'Then what are you doing?' How outraged Ntombi was! 'I told you, that cookie, the one Patience wanted, Tambudzai ate it!'

'We are,' returned Anastasia calmly, 'doing what's best. We're keeping quiet.'

'Or concentrating,' offered Irene from her bed, 'on the real issues! Come off it, Ntombi. Let's just concentrate on what we're here for. You know, pie-r-squared! And all those other squares, like the one on the hypotenuse!'

Irene giggled and looked pointedly at me. 'I don't mean pie as in crust, you know, and not square as in biscuit!'

Blood rushed to my head immediately. Who did that little girl think she was to ridicule me, when I was her senior, and soon to be on the honour roll, not just in any school, but a college for Europeans!

'Oh, look at her!' chanted Ntombi maliciously. 'She's puffing up! It must be the biscuit bloating!'

Patience was as mad with me as I was with Irene and Ntombi. 'Oh, aren't you ashamed, you Tambudzai! Eating the biscuits away from your own sister! OK, they put me down here with you guys, but I am your sister, and I am also your senior! And I was on the honour roll every time last year, except for bad luck at the very last grading! OK, they stick us in here with you guys, but we're your seniors. And you should learn to respect us!' Anastasia and Benhilda, the other two hard done by seniors, started grouping around her. Even Ntombi was edging over to the faction, while Irene sat on her bed, smiling cunningly as tempers disintegrated.

'What kind of senior do you think you are!' I fumed back. 'Making such a fuss about a biscuit! Who should be ashamed? Not me! You should be for . . . for making Tracey feel bad when she was just trying to help! Oh, you. . . you!' I was at a loss for words, so resorted to an assault from childhood. 'Oh, you! You, you with the great big spots! You. . . *mazikupundu*!'

Ntombi immediately lost another great chunk of her temper. 'No, you! Why don't you respect *Sisi* Patience here? Are you talking like that because I said the truth, and told them you ate that biscuit! Now leave us in peace! Don't say another word,' she shrieked out an ultimatum, glowing in the solidarity she had with the seniors. 'If you want to talk, just go, leave us! Just go and say something to that *murungu* of yours, that Tracey!' Her glaring eyes were red. The little group closed around Patience on her bed in a solid phalanx.

'Not just pimples!' I shot back irate. '*Mazikuzamu*!' I shouted at Anastasia. 'It's also much too big tits! Too much bullshit in your heads! And in your toilets! Too much everything!'

'What! And doesn't yours? Is yours pure, so it doesn't give off anything!' screamed Ntombi. 'Hey, you think it's pure! You think it's myrrh and frankincense!' She launched herself through the air, as though enraged beyond endurance by her own sacrilege. Anastasia half-heartedly put out a hand, without any real intention of restraining our agitated dorm-mate. When my classmate landed on me, hurling me back onto my bed, she hit me hard enough to draw tears. I retaliated by grabbing whatever soft parts I could to pummel, twist, scratch and pull.

'There's nothing wrong with Tracey!' I screamed. 'Do you know where my sister is? Do you know Netsai! She's my little sister! Do you know where she's gone to?'

'What shall we do! *Sisi* Benhilda, *Sisi* Anastasia, what, *kani,* what?' Patience sat on the side of her bed, her arms crossed now above her head, keening as though there was no consolation.

The door to the corridor opened, without anyone paying attention. Patience, who was the only one adequately detached from the fight to notice, said it was Miss Plato. In any case, Ntombi and I only stopped damaging each other as savagely as we could when all the other girls held their breath, and a voice exhaled in alarm, 'Girls! Girls! Please! My goodness, what is happening?'

This was Sister Catherine. It appeared Miss Plato had not been able to stomach the sight when she came in to investigate the source of the uproar, and had gone to call the nun on duty. We were lucky it was Sister Catherine. She made you feel ashamed instead of belligerent. My nose was bleeding. Ntombi's eye, a soft part, was swelling badly, enough to suggest injury to the tissues behind it.

'Straight after. . . well, after everything, after you've had to speak up for yourselves. This very evening.' Sister Catherine was extremely disappointed.

It was difficult. Words like that made you want to glare

at each other again. But it was Sister Catherine, her long slim frame bending all over the place with distress, her one hand under my chin to see how bad the bleeding was, her other on Ntombi's head to tip it back in order to observe the swollen eye. A white hand on hair! We gaped! We had never seen it.

'Oh, N-tombi! Oh, Tamboodzahee!' She looked from one to the other desperately. Sister was one of the few staff who did her best to get our names right, and didn't mix us up one with the other. 'Oh, Patience!' Sister addressed the third former in distress. 'Go and ask Miss Plato for the first aid box.'

Patience pulled on her dressing gown and ran out. Sister shook her head, looking from Ntombi to me, from me to Ntombi, until all three of us were close to tears.

6

'*Ekani*, yes, Tambudzai,' beamed Babamukuru. '*Manheru mwana wangu*! Good evening!'

I was home for the holidays. Or more precisely, I was at the place I called home, which was the mission. I had long ceased finding the homestead appealing and could not now contemplate going there again having seen the satiation in my mother's eye during Babamukuru's beating.

'*Manheru, shewe*! Good evening, my lord,' put in Maiguru, sweetening her voice to smother a pout, as it was not proper for Babamukuru to greet the young person I was before recognising the woman he married.

'Ah, *maswera* here, Mai? How have you spent the day? Good evening! Good evening!' my uncle now included Maiguru in his greeting. 'Yes, Nyasha!' my uncle nodded at his taciturn daughter. With this he deposited his briefcase by the mantelpiece and finally took his place at the table. Prudence, whom we called *Sisi* P, the new maid, brought in the dish for him to wash his hands. We were sitting down to supper. The meal was taken in the dining room which was the shape of half an octagon and a window with many small panes was set in each segment of the wall, giving the room an atmosphere like a captive fairy queen's tower.

Through the window behind Babamukuru, in the brief twilight, Maiguru and I could see the dusty, deserted road as it snaked towards the centre of the mission like a wide drought-stricken river bed, down which Babamukuru had recently proceeded. There was relief in knowing he had walked down it safely but at the same time there was apprehension. What else before we finished eating, or between prayers and bed and waking up, would make its way along it? The curfew had come now to the mission, the time restraints creeping out like a devastating chronic illness from the village and spreading. The Rhodesians said the curfew they imposed began at six o'clock. Tonight, as had happened every day in the two weeks since my return, my cousin Nyasha, Maiguru and I waited, peeping cautiously out of various windows, peering for long squinting moments without bothering to exhale up the road to see the precise moment the lights went off and darkness descended on Babamukuru's office. Not yet, though, dared we breathe out. My uncle had one room for his office in the mission's central building. He sat at the end of the wing that stretched down close to his home, while the clerk's room opened off at the front of it, and the administration offices, where the mission residents paid their utility bills, and the telephone exchange, and the station tuck shop extended in front of this. Nobody in the history of the mission, except its founding father, Bishop Deergood himself, had ever worked such long hours as Babamukuru. Babamukuru prided himself in, and Maiguru complained about, his ability to come home several hours after midnight, and still be in his office by seven the next morning. This my uncle continued to manage even after his beating at the hands of the Big Brothers. It took the Rhodesian government to dampen my uncle's habit of diligence. Shortly after news of the mission headmaster's beating became well known and people whispered various reasons for it, the Rhodesian army sent up the red earth mission road a green and khaki camouflaged vehicle. Out of it stepped an embarrassed and annoyed-looking officer carrying official notice of the tighter security status that the Government of Rhodesia now conferred on the mission.

Babamukuru overcame his frustration with the authorities by the expedient, somewhat unseemly, playing of *chisveru*, in English, tag. You crept awfully close, but not so close as to allow them to touch you. This was novel to me, that games could be conducted in this way, even by adults. It was most astonishing as I had ceased playing in that way many years ago, at the time, so satisfactorily remote now, that my uncle came to the village and singled out my brother rather than me for an education. I did not even like to remember that time anymore, for it was so painful having been passed over like that, and also I lost the will to play such games during it.

Besides, when finally provided with the opportunity, I vindicated myself so superlatively in obtaining a place at the Young Ladies' College of the Sacred Heart that there was no reason to return to a past that ached just as acutely as I imagined Netsai's amputation must pain her. My possibilities were infinite in my present circumstances! This I truly believed, and was ready to face the little inconveniences to be dealt with along the way. All in all, I felt I was all right now, and so was the world. I was on a direct route to a future so bright it – or I in those tomorrows – would light up more than my community; probably, I imagined, the whole universe. There I was, a student at the most prestigious private school in the country, and not only was I there, I was an exceptional pupil! Taking my cue from my uncle, I was very glad to remind myself, with a degree of superior gloating over lesser individuals who did not have the ability, how you didn't enter institutions just like that by playing – unless it was at sanctioned games. My list of lesser mortals included Baba and Mai, whose better qualities were, as far as I could see, not more than an envious sluggishness. I, in contrast, was sufficiently focused to have the honour roll within sight. Games, the sanctioned ones at which a girl was required to excel, added to your chances of honours. In my case the sanctioned sports included hockey, tennis, swimming and athletics, as prescribed by the playing fields between the iron gate and the cedars. Bearing this in mind, I assiduously played hockey for the school B team. I was, though, only reserve for the A team, having not played any hockey until I came to Sacred Heart. In any case, there was a tendency not to include you in the A team unless you excelled widely beyond mere excellence, as playing in the government schools was difficult for girls like ourselves. Miss Whitley, our games mistress, I recall now, wanted me for the under-sixteen As, but I tossed away her offers. It was the school team or nothing. I would not play for less.

Another issue was that in my form I should have been playing for the under-fourteens. My natural enthusiasm for exhibiting my prowess was diluted by the discrepancy of my age compared with the ages of most of my classmates. It was a life of discrepancies, of vociferous demands during under-sixteen house tournaments, 'why didn't you go to school when you were meant to? Couldn't you go in at the right time?' How I suffered, hearing that interrogation whittle away at me, to expose my inferior origins. As a result, my limbs moved more stiffly in the under-sixteens than when I battered the hockey ball for Sacred Heart B. I was not aware of how much this approach lacked boldness. On the contrary, I commiserated with myself, without demand. So, I passed up excelling in the under-sixteens, preferring mediocrity in the Young Ladies B eleven, and as a result of frustrated ambition ended up again mistrusting games.

Now here was the mission, placed under curfew. There were only a few Europeans at the mission. They were reigned in by the curfew too. So a lot more people were frustrated at the settlement than was the case with the girls in my dormitory at school. Before the curfew came down at Babamukuru's station, the school clerk emulated his headmaster at least once a week by keeping his office light aflame admirably far into the night. A yellow glow shone from the administration office windows for long periods after closing time regularly enough for the mission dwellers not to be surprised on the evenings the illumination was seen. Now the curfew transformed everything. Staff packed their papers and files away at half past four instead of five, pointing out you never knew with the Rhodesians. They said the curfew began officially at six pm, but wasn't there something on the piece of paper that brought this information about changes occurring without notice? Well, did you want your *body* to notice, people asked, that the curfew times had changed! So what was efficacious when a Rhodesian decided that, as a temporary austerity measure, notice was not to be given? Ah, who could think of anything else but submission? Up and down the station many people marvelled at the efficacy of servility against the military's move. That was how the mission folk went about their business. I, on the whole, agreed with this strategy, remembering the regulations we complied with at school. What could be done for or against a deed, if it was prescribed by those who could prescribe that that deed was or was not to be!

Babamukuru, however, did not like being made to feel himself less by being reduced to indolent mediocrity, and so he opted for games. On dark days when thunder clouds pressed on the tops of the ashen leafed bauhinias that lined our central mission road, Babamukuru's light was never out by six o'clock as prescribed by the authorities, not unless there was a power outage. During outages, my uncle lit a paraffin lamp, and you saw after some seconds of darkness and flickering as the first few matches went out, a dim warm light that seemed unnaturally distant. On the dot of six, if you knew my uncle, you could see him looking at his watch, the one he boasted he bought in England over a decade ago and wasn't it a testimony to all those magnificent British abilities that the watch was still accurately ticking on! Having assured himself the hour had struck, the man put away his papers, meticulously selecting the ones he proposed to work on at home in the evening, and filed these in his briefcase. If the sunset still streamed pink and gold over the mountain, you saw him at ten past the hour emerge from his office, look down towards the house, then turn to lock his door. If it was towards winter when the haze of wood-smoke suffocated the slivers of daylight, you had to wait until he emerged from the shadows a minute later. Then, Babamukuru marched homewards, walking in the middle of the way very deliberately and extremely provocatively.

'Why does he have to go so slowly!' sighed Maiguru with another eternal inhalation. She was usually in the kitchen at this time, from where she watched her husband's progress through windows that were bare – disregarding spatterings of oil and fuzzes of dust – rather than prying blind slats apart in the sitting room as we, my cousin Nyasha and I, did. There was a lot of forgetting to breathe, of sucking in air and omitting to let it out, amongst us, the wife and daughters, as Babamukuru descended home.

All three of us tried, as he disappeared in the shadows of the fir trees along the drive, to decipher how he was feeling. There were shorter loquat trees further down the way, then a canopy of grape vines. We could see him better as he passed under these, and still we tried to read from his face, in the angle and tension in his shoulders, out of the tightness with which he gripped his briefcase, whether or not he had spent his day well.

As Babamukuru approached, we scurried into the dining room to sit at our places so he would not have to wait for us when he entered, but could take his meal at once, with the minimum of irritation. Prudence brought the dishes of *sadza*, rice, vegetables and meat stew in quickly and silently. Maiguru picked up a dishing out spoon and held it in a hovering, indeterminate fashion, so that if Babamukuru appeared to want to eat immediately, she could dig rapidly into a serving dish; but if he was in an expansive mood she could ask him about the day and go into a long praising prayer to God for providing and at the same time bringing Babamukuru whole, down the mission road.

My uncle was smiling today. 'Tambudzai!' he said, as he sat down. There was an undertone of satisfaction in his voice that he could not quite hide, and he was speaking very kindly. 'Tambudzai, something has come today. It is addressed to me. But it is about you.' He reached into his inside jacket pocket and brought out a beige envelope decorated with a burgundy heart. 'It is your report card, Tambudzai. You know, Mai,' he turned to Maiguru, who was resting the dishing out spoon between her fingers on the rim of the *sadza* dish. 'You know, I always say I wish Tambudzai had lots and lots of them. Enough to put into a novel! A good, long book! Her reports make the best bedtime reading.' He waved the envelope, took hold of his dinner knife and slit it open with a flourish. As he extracted the beige sheet with its burgundy heart-shaped crest in the middle, Babamukuru spoke more about how enjoyable he found my report cards. 'It is not like Chido's,' he mentioned my cousin who was away on a canoeing trip with his friends, the Baker boys. 'Well, if they gave them marks for football, or rugby, then perhaps we would have something good to say about Chido, our son! As it is, the marks he gets are very useless, and sometimes I have to stop myself from throwing them away with the rubbish!' If this was intended as a compliment to me, it had the opposite effect of making me feel uneasy. Nyasha beside me started breathing heavily and drumming her fingers under the table; but although she was back at school at the mission, because Maiguru said boarding school would be too stressful for her, she was still made at least partially tranquil by taking plentiful doses of Largactil so that she only ever these days became somewhat and never dreadfully unstable.

'How did our sister Tambu-pie do?' trilled Maiguru, digging the spoon into the *sadza* much more forcefully than her voice would have had you believe, and eyeing her daughter distractedly. She turned to me, 'You know, sister Tambu-pie, Nyasha's report is going to be extremely good when school closes and the headmaster . . .' she giggled coyly at Babamukuru '. . . gives them out to the parents.'

'History!' Babamukuru read with the air of someone settling down for a long, often delivered and well-loved sermon. 'Eighty nine per cent – exceptional grasp of all the facts. Very good, Tambudzai, very good! Geography, ninety eight. A prodigious feat of memory,' he went on reading out the next mark upon the paper and the teacher's comment. I looked down embarrassed now that I was being praised for it, at how well my memory had served me. Geography was Babamukuru's subject, the one he taught at Deergood High School up to A-Level standard. Up until now my marks in the subject had peaked in the seventies, which Babamukuru himself pointed out to me was unacceptable, especially as he himself had never obtained less than eighty per cent in his geography tests, and as the conditions I enjoyed were better than the ones he had laboured through, I was expected to produce better results. So I had taken the textbook the teacher prescribed for us, and the notebook in which I had written the dictated notes. I had committed every single word of each to memory and regurgitated them back out onto the paper during the examination. What had I left out, I wondered; was it a comma or a semi colon that deprived me of a perfect tally?

Meanwhile Babamukuru proceeded down the list of fabulous results. I tuned back in for that delicious distress that comes from being told you are fantastic when at the same time you have to be modest.

'Sister Catherine is your class teacher, isn't she?' my uncle confirmed with me. I nodded. 'Er,' he paused considering. 'Er, Tambudzai, this Sister Catherine says she thinks you were somewhat overworked.' Babamukuru looked from the paper to me with a lack of comprehension. 'But, my daughter, if hard work brings you results like these, then it is worth it and surely that will just make you work harder! Anyone can work harder, and do better, my dear! Because no one is ever as good as they should be! I think, my dear, you must try to develop more stamina!' I gazed at my hands in my lap, thinking of my mother who sat under a tree when she grew fatigued at the fields and had a rest, instead of churning up the earth in greater, more productive portions. My head dipped and rose imperceptibly, from shame. How right Babamukuru was! Why had I allowed such a comment to be written? If I didn't work, it was evident I would end up like my mother!

Meanwhile Babamukuru was scanning the page for more information about his favourite niece's progress. 'Ah!' he exclaimed after a moment, his tenor trembling up to falsetto in indignation. 'Ah-ah! What can this be that I am now reading?' Nyasha looked up with a ghoulish smile on her face. Maiguru promptly deposited a dollop of *sadza* on Babamukuru's plate. She followed this up by raising up the rice bowl and thrusting it towards her husband. 'How about some of this, my Daddy-pie!' But that bowl pushed at the paper Babamukuru was reading. 'Mai!' he silenced her tersely. Maiguru slowly set the rice bowl back on its sisal mat. Babamukuru lifted my report paper clear of any interference and turned to face me. His countenance melted from expectation to sadness. Finally his expression grew pained as he observed me, as though he discovered only now there were several zeroes too few on one of the cheques from overseas donors towards his mission school programmes.

'Tambudzai, I am shocked,' intoned Babamukuru. Nyasha held her breath to stop herself giggling. 'I did not believe a daughter of mine – I did not believe you,' he corrected himself, 'after everything we have invested in you, would spoil your chance at this school and engage in such behaviour!'

It was one of the worst moments I had ever lived through. The last comment on the report was the headmistress' conclusion. With Babamukuru signalling as he did, I had a nasty premonition of Sister Emmanuel's observations. Why did the nun dislike me so much! I had not the least understanding; and the matter was all the worse for taking place at table. As we were at dinner, it was unrefined to speak of bodily needs, or rather the need to dispose of what came out of the corpus, and the arrangements at Sacred Heart which made fulfilling those eliminatory needs in the last dormitory on St Ignatius' corridor logistically difficult. I sighed, and Nyasha darted a glance at me. I was thinking how they were right, how those needs could not matter that much, if in order to fulfil them you ended up breaking rules! Hadn't Sister explained to us, and hadn't we all seen the sense of the situation, and appreciated the school authorities' protection! How could that behaviour of mine be justified – I disowned it! I was certainly to blame. A little more patience and control of my nether muscles would have avoided all this trouble.

'First of all, my daughter, my dear daughter,' my uncle scanned the report again. 'Well, you are at that school, which truly I did not want to pay for! Even with your scholarship, Tambudzai, I am paying more for you, for one,' he stressed, 'just for one of your terms at the Young Ladies' College of the Sacred Heart than I am submitting each year for my daughter, Nyasha, here at the mission! Then, when everyone is making such sacrifices,' Babamukuru expanded, 'first you go and say there is too much work! Then because of this laziness, you not wanting to work as you should, you become very troublesome! Listen!' his voice started to rise again. 'I am a headmaster myself and I know a head teacher does not lie. Listen to what Sister Emmanuel has written!' My uncle bent his head once more and read out in a surprised tone, 'Tambudzai has a complex. This makes it difficult for her to adapt to the spirit of the Young Ladies' College of the Sacred Heart. She believes she is above convent rules designed for the welfare of the pupils. Her inability to be a part of the college causes her considerable distress. If she is not happy here, perhaps it is best to remove her. Constantly she wears a supercilious expression.' Babamukuru concentrated deeply on the paper as he folded and unfolded it again. The spiral of steam from the *sadza* dish was dwindling. Maiguru gazed at the cooling plate despondently. Nyasha was shocked into absolute silence, as I was. What had gone wrong? After the headmistress had taken the time to reassure us so kindly, what had I done to make her so aggravated?

Babamukuru, too, was waiting for a response to this question. He ran his fingers along the report crease as though he was preparing to tear it in two and cast it into the rubbish bin along with his son's.

'It's my eyebrows!' I finally whispered idiotically, without conviction. I wanted the earth to open up and remove me from everything even as I said it. In the dismayed silence that followed, I went on, 'They're high. They make me look supercilious!'

'I told you,' said Babamukuru. 'I am a headmaster myself! Do not think you can make Sister Emmanuel into a fool with this kind of lying!'

Nyasha was staring at my forehead closely. I prayed she would not talk. She looked at her Dad, opened her mouth, but observing the thunder that had gathered on his brow, opted for silence.

'Tell me!' the command came. 'Tell me, what I have just heard is wrong, Tambudzai, that it is wrong, the thing I am hearing! Are you saying the headmistress did not know anything when she wrote those words we have just read on your report? Are you saying she had not looked at you and observed the shape of your eyebrows? Remember, she interviewed you for a long time here at the mission when you sat for the entrance examination, and after that she did not say anything was wrong with your features! Something has changed! It has changed! You are raising them, those eyebrows, at other people!'

All I could do was let the tears roll down. Then I put my head on my plate and started sobbing. Into my distress, Babamukuru issued the demand that I depart to my bedroom. There I was to write a letter of apology to Sister Emmanuel.

'You will tell her you are very sorry to have caused her to write such a report!' my uncle ordered. 'You will tell her that you will improve your behaviour, particularly the behaviour that determines whether or not the people at this convent respond happily to you. You will tell Sister Emmanuel,' he decided finally 'that you understand why she should write the words we have read, and why you deserve them. The last thing you will include in your letter to the headmistress, Tambudzai, is that you are grateful for this lesson, which is also the chance to improve. In the very last sentence, you will thank her for giving you these instructions as to how you can become a better young woman.'

'Do you think that nun really wants her to transfer?' Nyasha was anxious, knowing what would happen to me if Sister did not relent.

'No one, no daughter of mine will be asked to leave a school,' decreed Babamukuru, 'or any institution. Just the idea of it is much too shameful.'

It was so horrible. I stood the chance of losing my uncle's patronage if I did not return to grace with Sister Emmanuel. Once in my room, I fetched my pencil case and composed the letter. By the time I was finished I was full of shame for myself at having distressed Sister so extremely that she wrote the observations she had at the bottom of my report card. I was so upset I crawled into bed. When Nyasha came and sat beside me, I turned to the wall. She didn't have much to say that comforted. 'You're there now,' she stroked the blanket, somewhat absently. 'You'll have to deal with it. Maybe it's not so bad. You'd have to cope with. . . well this kind of thing, sooner or later. You know that, Tambu, don't you? I always told you a lot about England.' She broke off and sat silently, motionlessly.

'Nyasha,' I called softly, feeling the weight of her hand light above the cover, where it stopped in mid-stroke, as though the energy that moved her inexplicably dissipated. She was deep in a reverie. She had done this ever since she became ill, departing to dream of flight where none was possible. I moved cautiously, beginning to panic. If Nyasha did not wake up, kept on sleeping with her eyes staring like that, what was I going to say to everybody! Wouldn't it be clear to all I had shocked her when I shouldn't! She let me place her hand in her lap where it rested, abject and corpselike, seemingly without a pulse. She kept staring at the wall, but not seeing it, as though not a part of her body was moved. You didn't know what it was that did this, that sucked being from a person as the sweet sap from a segment of sugar cane!

'Do you want to read the letter? The one to my headmistress?' I scrambled for it and pushed it under her nose. It was a great relief when, after a few moments, she shook her head. A little later she said it was like shock treatment that I could be so foolish.

'Honestly, only you could push something straight under someone's nose, like that, hey, something that caused all this trouble in the first place.' Then she relented. 'I suppose it's like curing, you know, curing people not killing them, by using just a little bit of poison.

'Anyway,' she returned to being herself, 'I wasn't sure about your vocabulary. I knew I'd have to correct it!'

So we spent the rest of the evening making my phrases of self-deprecation yet more annihilating.

Still later, when the clatter of washing up had ceased and that day was done, we lay in bed. Maiguru came in with Nyasha's round white pill, which Nyasha took making a face. 'I wish they gave me the syrup. It sends me off, you know, well, away faster.'

'Good girl, my lovey dove!' Maiguru took back the water glass from her daughter. 'You too, sister Tambu-Wambu! Goodnight my girly-wirleys!' With this she left us.

'Where do you want to go to?' I whispered after my aunt had departed. When Nyasha did not answer, I turned to stare at the crack of light seeping in from under the door so as not to be frightened. I was afraid she would finally journey there, to the place she went earlier and, without anything to come back for, simply not find a reason that made her return.

'Don't you think about better things?' I inquired. 'There's so much we can have. Like doing well, winning things. Like growing up, really becoming a woman. Doing your own thing, finding someone to love and having a family. You know, what's going to stop us having all that?'

'I suppose,' she began. I grinned into the darkness in relief – she'd been listening after all. But she was speaking too slowly for comfort, as though an indispensable part was running down. 'I suppose, if you're going to be out there and find all that, you've just got to have the fuel. Let's say all those things do exist, right, how're you going to get to them if you haven't got anything to run on? What can you do if you've run out of fuel?' Her voice petered out. The frangipani waved against the window panes, making shivering shapes out of the light of the moon.

'It's horrible, isn't it,' she said. She was watching the window too. 'Look at all the fuel we spend on just being afraid. Aren't you afraid now, Tambu? I am! How're we going to get all those things? I don't see us getting there before we run out.'

'Afraid!' I repeated. 'You can say that again. Pup-chicken,

hey, shitless!' I mouthed the language of the convent, my mouth twisting. Nyasha snorted. I conceded, '*M, iwe*, Nyasha, you! Of course! I'm afraid.'

The pattern of frangipani leaves on the curtain shrunk and sharpened. I heard Nyasha stop breathing in the bed next to mine. I pulled the blankets up under my chin while fiends swirled up out of the room's darkness. The beam intensified for a little while, as a vehicle wound its way up the main mission road. Then the brightness faded. It was not the Rhodesian soldiers come to shine their headlights into our bedrooms all night. Strangely, they had started to do this after Babamukuru was beaten. They'd come and stationed their jeeps in the back yard the night after Netsai was discharged from hospital. Nyasha told me about that event. Now she said, 'Thank God it's not them. Imagine, doing all that, Tambu, all night. What for? To make us frightened!'

We both jumped as the floorboards creaked. Babamukuru was going down the hall to his bedroom. We didn't like noises in the dark and waited apprehensively for the next one. The door to my uncle and aunt's bedroom clicked as he entered.

Then we heard the crackle and pop of distant static. Nyasha started singing before the needle tuned into the station. '*Kure kure! Kure kure! Kure kwandinobva, vana mai na baba, tondo sangana kuZimbabwe!*' Then she was quiet and listened expectantly. Above the static the song swelled in different parts, the men, women and children who were gathered, not at all like that meeting, but like another gathering, a more triumphant kind. Then came a rough exultant voice, 'This is the Voice of Zimbabwe broadcasting from Maputo!'

'Imagine, Tambu! Just imagine it. Can you? Imagine living in Zimbabwe!'

Babamukuru lowered the volume and I pulled the blankets up around my ears.

'Imagine what it will be like!' whispered the young woman next to me fervently. 'You'll be able to go into whichever toilet you like! And any school, for that matter. And you won't all be packed in, crowded in a stuffy dorm! You'll be treated like everyone else.'

My armpits were prickling more and more with tension. What if the Rhodesian soldiers came while the 'Voice of Zimbabwe' was haranguing like that? Would Babamukuru be able to turn the words off in time? I wasn't a dreamer like Nyasha, energising myself with what could be. I wanted to manage what was attainable. What we had was that the Rhodesians were part of the country. They wanted to fight for their right to a beautiful land. Most people doubted, in any case, that you could win a conflict with them, as they were superior Europeans. In my case, I was a pupil at the Young Ladies' College of the Sacred Heart, which made me a member of a specific educational elite, but apart from that leap of intellectual upward mobility, I was a disaffected member of the *povo*. My jaws clamped at the thought of the Rhodesians forcing their way through the veranda, sitting room and hall to close in on the tuning needle that pointed at the 'Voice of Zimbabwe'.

I was so frightened and upset, 'Your Dad!' I hissed through my set teeth at Nyasha, across the little space of darkness between our beds. 'Why's he doing that? Those people beat him up, Netsai hasn't got a leg because of them!

Why does he want to forget all of it and just make it worse, open us up for anything!'

Nyasha did not answer. Her deep breathing, induced by the effects on her brainwaves of the major tranquillizer she had to take to find any kind of peace, punctuated the subdued yet haranguing voice from my aunt and uncle's bedroom. It was a puzzle to me, as I listened to the crackling short-wave broadcast, why Babamukuru, who insisted I write a letter of apology to Sister Emmanuel, should be listening to this 'freedom' radio station. Wasn't I meant to have freedom myself? Is that why I had to hand the letter to Sister Emmanuel? Was it, the lack of bondage, meant to come when I was of an age like Babamukuru's and able to appreciate it? Or were we talking about different, relative kinds of freedoms? This seemed more acceptable.

The Rhodesians did not come. I fell asleep.

I handed the letter for Sister Emmanuel to Maiguru the next morning. I did not hear anything about it even when I left the mission at the end of the holidays. By the time I left, none of the events I feared had come to be. The only thing that unnerved me was the curfew continuing. I was also most glad there had not been any visits from freedom fighters, which could have brought Babamukuru to the Rhodesians' attention. In spite of all this, I felt as usual. I was very sad when I left the mission to go back to school. My bags were on the veranda at noon on the day, ready to be stowed in Babamukuru's car by three o'clock, as this was the hour Babamukuru had decreed he would come down from the office to drive me to the Young Ladies' College of the Sacred Heart. I spent the time between lunch and the agreed upon time shuffling about in the garden.

Maiguru's garden stretched out to the side of the house, beyond the dining and sitting room windows, and it was like a lake with bed upon bed of iridescent flowers shining and glowing upon it. Phlox, nasturtiums, marigolds, pansies, African violets, roses, bunny snaps, dahlias and roses cascaded like a burst chest of treasure over the section of earth that was allocated to my aunt, or rather to my uncle as headmaster at Deergood High School. Maiguru loved that earth as though it were hers and passers by stopped to gaze on their way up the main mission road, whatever the errand, whether to visit a sick relative, or answer a case of misconduct involving a child enrolled at the school, or whether they were simply on transit to another destination. I imagined the jeeps sometimes, when everything was too much for their drivers and they came to the mission in daylight – because I could see the people in the jeeps when I thought about it – I imagined the jeeps too stopped sometimes to admire Maiguru's garden. But now I didn't want to think of that. I scuffled about in my aunt's garden, dirtying my newly polished uniform sandals. Doof! Doof! Doof! You heard the mortars going increasingly often at school. The garden was still here. I was glad it was the kind of war where the mortars didn't tear up beautiful things like Maiguru's garden.

7

What happened after that took a long time, although it seemed as if it took no time at all; as if I stayed always in the same place, trudging, trudging, exhausted, and stayed exactly where I was, treading space and time like water. Did these things mean people weren't beautiful? Or was it merely the fury of a vicious spirit at those enduring containments that define different beauties which made some people tear off other people's extremities? I was occupied with these issues as Babamukuru drove me through the tightly fenced Mubvumbi suburb. For how could I understand why anyone would want a young woman to go hopla-hopla as it was said Netsai now did. I turned it over and over again secretly, in the cave of my heart, in case I saw something that did not bear light: why a person is satisfied when my sister cannot walk. Could anyone bear a brother or sister going off and killing people because they looked like this and not like that, singing all sorts of hideous songs about smashing in their heads! Never! No human being could countenance that! All the same I thought Netsai should have her limbs so that she could move herself, I hoped forward, away from all that.

'Here,' informed Babamukuru when we stopped in the convent grounds, in a parking bay beneath the jacarandas. 'Here, Tambudzai, are some oranges.' Babamukuru opened the boot and took out a pocket. My uncle always stated obvious matters when he was being kind, as though his having the wherewithal to be generous while others were obliged to have generosities bestowed upon them was a disturbing, impractical situation. It was, 'Here are some oranges,' instead of 'Tambudzai go and get the oranges I bought you.' Sylvester, the gardener, had put my suitcase in the car. The fruit was a surprise. Uncle preferred to drive to Alpha Estate beforehand, instead of stopping on the way to college. I pulled out my suitcase and set it beside the bag of oranges.

'Thank you, Babamukuru. Bye-bye, Babamukuru!' I dipped a little curtsey as I spoke and brought my hands together in a clap, gesturing as in prayer, gently and without sound. Babamukuru was in the car before I looked up. He was already revving the engine.

'Maiguru! Tell her that she should stay well!' I called. 'And Nyasha. And Mai, my mother. Baba too, when you see them!' Babamukuru did not hear me, as the Mercedes Benzs, BMWs, Volvos and Jaguars were growling up the drive to find parking spaces. Back and forth, back and forth, back and forth I waved, reluctant to move. I watched my uncle wind the big lap round the college green. There was a swan in the middle of the pond, the pond in the middle of the lawn, the lawn whose growth was supervised by Felipe. Felipe came to the country when his own homeland was going through a difficult period. The convent employed half a dozen local gardeners, who periodically moved the sprinkler on the lawn to another location, or took the filter out and sluiced it for the swimming pool. They executed their tasks under Felipe's jurisdiction. Felipe often raked together bits of time to sit under the mimosas or the jacarandas, talking to Miss Plato. Nobody knew what they whispered about, but the girls were full of their adolescent variations. Now Babamukuru pulled round the last bend in the roundabout while I waved. His dented Rover rounded the corner beyond the cedars that demarcated the division between the sports fields and the places of learning. Out Babamukuru turned, left into Mubvumbi Suburb with its impassive, orange-overalled gardeners, ferocious dogs and sly, cavorting garden gnomes. Away the road streaked in the vehicle's rear view mirror, northwards again to the mountains at whose base stood another school like ours, Mt Sinai Preparatory College. When my uncle had been gone for some minutes, I leant down and picked up the sack of oranges and my suitcase. I slouched past the white roses and music rooms, down St Ignatius and into the dormitory, reluctant to move in this direction without being able to say exactly why because there were too many incomprehensible reasons.

That night we realised again where we had come was not a place of safety. Doof-doof! the mortars shuddered after we knelt in the corridor for prayers, and Sister Catherine went back to the cloister. Doof-doof! they murdered sleep like a damned spot because they were too near.

'Sinai!' whispered Benhilda, her voice scratchy with fear. 'They've come to Mt Sinai!'

'You have a head on your pillow, Benni, isn't it!' snapped Anastasia as quietly as she could. 'So why don't you try using it for thinking! Nothing has come that close to us! Or we'd be hearing the sirens running up and down our tar road. *Vasikana*! Come on, girls! You know that!'

'Those poor boys!' Irene was more subdued than she usually was. 'They're not even as far away as we are! Even if it isn't at their place you can hear that it's much closer!' Our first former mutinied against senior *Sisi* Anastasia's position because she was the youngest and therefore closest in age to the boys at Mt Sinai. The students at that neighbouring college ranged from six to twelve years old as it was a junior establishment. 'They're boys, but they're little,' she went on whispering, in a sort of awe that the boys should be made to cry in spite of exhibiting the latter feature. 'I bet they're crying now! I bet they just want their mamas.'

'For God's sake, get a grip!' directed Ntombi as impatiently as was possible, for, as it was after lights out, she was obliged to speak quietly. 'Tell me something, you, Irene, what's so special about those boys over there? Are they the only ones who are crying? Now, don't tell me,' she managed to snap in spite of whispering, and contradictory with reproof, 'don't tell me that's what your little first form brain is thinking? Just wait,' she went on more loudly and ominously. 'Just you wait until you've been here a bit longer. You'll have a lot of other things to worry about, like not being able to travel with the other girls on the train, or staying behind when the team plays away because they don't want people who look like us playing on those government schools playing fields! My God!' Ntombi was working herself up into a frenzy, one that strangely matched the tension in the room which came in the wake of the mortars close to Mt Sinai Preparatory College. 'They don't want us *playing*! It's OK if we walk on them with a garden fork, or what's that thing, you know the tennis court thing, a roller. But what they don't want is us *playing*!'

We were silent for a while, ruminating on this fact to find the logic. Doof-di-dhi-dhu! went the mortars, and after a couple of minutes, Irene quavered in a tight reedy voice,

'Well, even if I'm thinking about those things, it doesn't mean I shouldn't be thinking about those others.'

'What if it does? What if it does?' retorted Anastasia with a desperate misery. 'What if sometimes you just have to, hey? What if it's a must to make choices?'

I didn't like the direction the discussion was taking, at low volume out of concern for Sister Catherine and fear of Miss Plato. The debate hissed from bed to bed, so that there was no sleep to blot out the Armageddon of mortars, the explosions accompanied, I was sure, by people bearing the loss of limbs, their own or the rending of limbs from the body of a beloved person.

'I-i-ih, I'm glad I'm not them!' I whispered.

'He-he-he!' The girls wriggled under their blankets giggling, amazed into merriment that one of us was so idiotic as to express openly such an egoistic sentiment. Of course you thought so and did what you could to keep it 'them' in preference to you, but to carry such a selfish spirit into the public, as everyone knew, was inviting a curse.

'Oh, oh, who's been lying?' gasped Ntombi, 'about, you know, that honour roll,' she managed between swallowing fat gulps of mirth. 'Who's been going on about that honour roll in this school being inherited only by the biggest morons?'

'Yes, that's surely been said. Let's find out,' Anastasia joined in. Her laughter was controlled now, but you could hear her grin in the dark. 'Let's find out whose been lying to our companion here.' But she said *'mumwe wedu'*, 'our other', generously including me in the search.

'Oh!' remarked Irene. 'You mean she needed someone else for that? Couldn't do it herself, you know, lie to her?'

Including mild Patience and prayerful Benhilda, every-one in the dormitory once more spluttered. I did not need my dorm-mates reaction to censure me. I was already ashamed of myself as soon as I heard myself speaking. Now the girls' muffled gurgles made me wonder what in the world I was turning into. Was I developing into a mammoth joke? Could this be due to growing ideas too big for my sta-tion and thinking I was more important than the others, the sad little youngsters at Mt Sinai Preparatory College? The dormitories at the beseiged institution, because of the site the fathers from Ireland had chosen to build on, lay closer to the mountains than Sacred Heart, and so occu-pied a more beautiful part of the highlands. Unfortunately, as a result of this location, Mt Sinai abutted on the border with Mozambique, and was therefore more surrounded by peril than we were. Ntombi snorted, in response to Irene, in a way that indicated what little regard she had for me, and showed that the sentiment I'd just whispered corrobo-rated her poor opinion. 'Same here!' I thought as loudly as possible.

On the other hand, I was now truly ashamed. What could it be? I wondered, so as not to locate the deficit in myself. It thus became clear to me the trouble lay in the Europeans. Yes, this was always the trouble with white peo-ple, I decided. With some relief, I consequently indulged in the idea that living with them was making me as bad as they were. For if I'd been similar to the young boys, the small white students at Sinai College, my remark would not have been so heartless. It would simply have been the case of a teenager enduring the same wretched trauma as the children, who was glad to escape the war's intensity, although the younger boys were not fortunate enough to do so. But now, there was this difference of appearance between us, with neither of us looking like the other. So the logical end point was, I deliberated, as one by one the other girls in the dormitory fell asleep, that I was glad the Sinai boys suffered their fate because they possessed different skin colours! *Aiwa, kwete!* How could that be! I was appalled at the very notion of it, the idea that, like the worst of them, I was myself metamorphosing into a racist!

Of course, I had not heard then that I could not be this, but only a reverse variety. The possibility that such a transformation was occurring because I was absorbing tendencies of people I congregated with was, that night, deeply perplexing. It annihilated my very thought processes to imagine how anyone could make a better world when you reproduced the very things that in this one caused so much pain and anxiety to so many, when you recreated the forms that were so reprehensible. Now the headmistress's handwriting revealed itself in the dark within my head. It was like the writing on the wall, explaining the inexplicable. I was wrong, as Sister Emmanuel showed in my report. My reaction to the boys at Sinai proved it. No, there was nothing ungodly in the nuns' behaviour when they had given so many of us scholarships! And surely the nuns were doing God's work by keeping our sad and threatened white schoolmates within their zone of comfort! Babamukuru was right to make me write that apology. He did it to teach me, to remind me, 'Tambu, I am well if you are well too!' – the essence of *unhu*, of being a person. So I fell into adolescent sleep lightly and restlessly, with the hammering of hate raining down distantly for me, but close around the poor boys at Sinai.

I woke up feeling tired, as though I had been labouring at a never-ending job. *Unhu*, that profound knowledge of being, quietly and not flamboyantly; the grasp of life and of how to preserve and accentuate life's eternal interweavings that we southern Africans are famed for, what others now call *ubuntu*, demanded that I consoled myself, that I be well so that others could be well also. By the time I went into the bathroom to wash before the bell clanged and Miss Plato descended, I was proud of exhibiting a great deal of *unhu*. With this *unhu* I reflected, as I scrubbed my back and lathered my underarms very copiously and meticulously, I would be able to meet the challenges at the Young Ladies' College of the Sacred Heart courageously, and so advance in due course to a useful job, one that brought all the comforts of occupations that are valued by one's community. Comfort and useful, a contradiction? Not at all, if you were one with the community. Besides, useful jobs did not only bring comforts to be spread amongst yourself and your family. They were useful in a sense beyond you: for when you were good at your useful job, you inspired others to work hard so they could take up useful jobs later on too. You only had to look at Babamukuru. He had inspired me to be hardworking and useful. Perhaps one day I would inspire someone else to be hardworking and useful too. We could end up with a nation of inspiring, useful, hardworking people, like the British and the Americans, and all the other Europeans who were guiding us and helping us in our struggle. So being good at a useful job was quite different from being useful at a useless job like prostitution or politics, where no one benefited.

'Doof-doof!' It made you start, like last night's mortars,

but it was my irate classmate at the door. '*Iwe*, what can you still be doing in there? You are making yourself do this, just on purpose! So others will be late. OK, if that's how you want it, let's leave it like that!' spluttered Ntombi.

Ko-ko-ko-ko-kongolo, the bell rang behind the door and Miss Plato's shrill voice accused, 'Vhy have all of you not yet been vashing?' I quickly rinsed myself off, and proceeded out, towel around dripping body. As evidence of my newly resuscitated *unhu* I gazed apologetically at Ntombi who was waiting, washbag in one hand, the other angrily tapping the door frame. I then breathed I was sorry, as I indeed had taken too long in the tub, but it was no use. My classmate's opinion of me of the night before was confirmed, so she was no longer speaking. 'Tss!' she pushed past giving out an angry click of her tongue, as Miss Plato cried in triumph, 'Today a black mark I give all of you!'

I decided to show Miss Plato, and Ntombi too while I showed the former, just how much *unhu* I possessed. I kept my head down while we were threatened with detention and, even when Ntombi came out of the bathroom muttering about people who oppressed other people by not allowing them to remove their body odour, I quietly continued dressing.

Ruminating on this – the amount of *unhu* I possessed and how to show this to people – kept me very occupied. I often, thereafter, walked all the way from assembly to class, or from class to library without knowing how I'd come from one place to the other. I was often so sunk in myself I frequently did not notice anything or anyone. Between the library and dining hall, however, was the school notice board, where the bad conduct marks I so dreaded were entered for all to see on the way to meals. I hated to catch the smallest glimpse of that board, where the black mark pushed up by Miss Plato against my name hung, a horrible blot on the white expanse, disfiguring the paper on the board, just as I feared it might do my life. Four of those little black blobs in a single term could keep you off the honour roll. So I became very determined, every time I thrust my chin onto my chest in order to pass that dreadful board, that I would soon show Miss Plato I had so much *unhu* she would never again need to press the tip of a thick black pen beside my name.

One night, a few weeks after we spoke in the dormitory about Mt Sinai and Miss Plato came bursting in, in the morning, Anastasia could not sleep and went to have a capful of sherry in the washroom.

Her insomnia began in the second form, she revealed, when her seniors regaled her after lights out with horror stories concerning what the nuns did and their reasons for doing it, perfidious practices such as keeping her back forever, without any hope ever of proving either her seniority or worthiness for privilege, incarcerated in the last dormitory of St Ignatius' corridor. Our plump senior roommate fought the cruel inability to find rest in the third form, although she was indeed in the aforesaid dormitory. Nevertheless she managed to defeat insomnia by sheer strength of will concealed within the comfort of her flesh, so that she slept well when she was a third former. By the fourth form, however, the problem was severe. By the fifth form it was unbearable. She continually dropped off in class which gave her several black marks for laziness, until she began to treat the problem with a cheap brown sherry. Now, in the third term, with exams looming, she was taking the potion more or less regularly. She poured it down her throat by the capful, and did so in the washroom for there was enough light there to see how much she poured so that the bottle cap would not overflow and waste the precious numbness-inducing liquid, nor stain her sheets and blankets. At the same time there was in that room a legitimate reason, such as a running stomach or one that did not move, for having the light on after bedtime. That night, while the detestation of some people for other people hammered the air, Anastasia pushed open the toilet door and whispered in a voice that was strained and full of terrible wonder, '*Vasikana*, girls, come and see in here!'

We all jostled into the bathroom. Patience and Benhilda, who were tall, took up positions inside the bathtub and hung onto the window sill. Ntombi put down the lid to the toilet seat to climb upon it, while Irene and I clambered onto the tub's rim. Anastasia was short, but she stayed on the floor as she said she had already seen enough of the sight she had called us for. The sky was alight as though the blossoms from the flowering trees in the gardens had exploded.

'A storm!' I breathed, knowing dispiritedly it could not be that. What was best, I wondered, thinking about *unhu* again, the way of being that Babamukuru and more distantly the convent had taught me? What would *unhu* be at this moment? Would it be better to comment on the magnificence of the sky, or in a sisterly, roundabout way, hint that Anastasia could have foregone bringing us in to watch illuminations in the heaven that increased our already unbearable anxieties?

'*Sisi* Ana!' Ntombi began boldly, although Anastasia was

very much her senior, which meant, if you were exhibiting *unhu*, communication with *Sisi* Ana required distance and tempering. Anastasia sighed but did not answer. '*Sisi*, Ana,' continued Ntombi with a hint of severity, 'this can't be why you called us, can it? To see something in the sky we don't really want to see? It would have been better to let us sleep. Don't we all know what's happening?'

Benhilda, Irene and Patience still had their eyes glued to the little frosted window.

Ntombi turned around to face Anastasia completely. 'If we all knew, just as we were, lying down, what good does it do to stand up and walk to see it?'

The distant sky lit up once more. 'I thought it was a ssshtorm,' muttered Anastasia. We all turned round and looked at her gravely. She poured herself another capful of sherry. This she sucked up, before she corrected herself, 'At least at first.' She was defensive.

'It's the rain clouds,' I put in, prevaricating constructively. 'If it wasn't for the clouds you'd have seen immediately, Si'Ana. Anyway, we all thought it was thunder – and lightning too – right girls, when Si'Ana came in and called us to watch it.'

'I didn't think it was thunder!' insisted Ntombi. 'I never did! That's what I told you!'

'The rest of us did!' I held my ground, as by now Ntombi and I had a tacit agreement not to agree, and I wanted to comfort our tipsy *Sisi* Ana. So, 'We did! We did!' my voice without turned truculent. 'That's why we didn't want to get out when Ana called! Why on earth would anyone get out of bed just for lightning and thunder?'

'Well, some of us did,' pointed out Patience, without

specifying who did what, which turned out to be very pragmatic, as it allowed us to change the subject.

'Anyway, it's much further away than last time,' Irene remarked. 'So those little boys aren't in any danger.'

'They'll be closing the school soon,' Anastasia told us. 'They've already evacuated the boys to Umtali Boys High for nights. It's happened already. I heard Sister Emmanuel talking to Father O'Shea.'

Ntombi froze on top of the toilet lid. 'It's all right,' soothed Anastasia. 'They're taking the other boys to St Matthews, you know, that Catholic school.'

'Sakubva!' Ntombi sneered horribly. 'Oh, stick them in the townships, hey. Or let them stay and be blasted to pieces.'

'Shut up!' I snapped with a rush of choler.

'Shut up yourself!' my classmate snapped back immediately.

'No, I won't! And who's going to make me!' I found it very strange that I was shouting such undisciplined words in spite of my recent acceptance of *unhu*, but even stranger was how I enjoyed it.

'Just think about those little boys! Oh, God, I just hope their parents let them go out to Sakubva. You know how some of these people with money can be!'

'Are you telling me I don't care about people?' I squared up to my classmate.

'No, you don't!' Ntombi's nose and lips wrinkled up as she snarled. 'You just make me sick! You don't unless it's them! The honkies! You don't care about anything, Tambudzai, unless it's yourself! And that's why you just love those Europeans!'

130

They tell me I dealt the first blow. Now there was no satisfaction in it. It was just blind, numb flailing, and I believe Ntombi retaliated in much the same way. Once more we punched and pummelled at each other. I sustained another bloody nose, and Ntombi a great tract of red meaty flesh where my fingernails raked down the shoulder exposed by her nightdress, before the other girls managed to stop us. I felt her skin bunching under my fingernails when we went to bed. I went back into the bathroom, sat on the bath tub and spent a lot of time scraping the blackness out from where it was lodged, with the tip of a hair grip.

So I was brawling again and I could not believe it. Once more I was ashamed of myself. I cannot say I thought much about Ntombi and the rawness of places without skin; but I was distressed and could not see how the fight had happened when I was so taken up with making sure I had enough *unhu* to behave in the right manner. Why on earth did I keep on doing these meaningless things that made me like myself less! The mere thought of why this might be so, having to do with a fundamental and inalienable state of not being worthy, gave me a handful of fingers that flicked up and down in my stomach with a fluttering so sickening it prevented conclusion. When I walked past the notice board, the fingers clenched into a fist.

One Saturday afternoon I was on my way back from the library where I had retreated to revise instead of swimming. Ntombi was swimming with Irene and Benhilda. Patience was on an *exeat* as an uncle had come down from Harare, and she had taken Anastasia with her in order to help keep the senior's chin up. This uncle was an alcoholic. On his way to secondary school at Goromonzi in the 1950s he had disappeared, only to turn up a couple of years later blowing a saxophone in Johannesburg. The cross-border brass had not lasted, and he was back, with blackened teeth and jobs as a session musician that kept him in brandy, and memories which he sought out Patience for, in order to tell her. The library closed on a Saturday at four o'clock, which did not please me. I would rather have kept on revising the vegetation of the low *veld* until supper. For how else was I to get on? I was pondering this question, with head bowed so as not to observe the notice board, while thoughts of Patience's uncle brought the smell of tobacco to my nostrils. I dipped my head further, so as not to be fascinated by what the man and the two girls were doing. But up ahead were footsteps. St Sophie's corridor, the penultimate most senior corridor, opened on the upper floor from a staircase off the main foyer. Several sets of footsteps approached. Of these, one pace was unmistakable. Miss Plato was coming down.

'The smoking!' the matron's implacable accent remonstrated from the stairs which led to the penultimate senior dormitories. 'The smoking may only in the common room place take! That for the seniors! In other places not. No! Not also in each other common room! There vas never in this whole school a dormitory vhere the girls can smoke!' The edge of the irate woman's uniform descended around the corner of the staircase while the matron continued in utter disbelief. 'How you come upon it, I do not know, that in a dormitory the girls may smoke! No, I do not know and therefore I must immediately tell Sister Emmanuel!' I ducked off into the alcove at the back of the foyer so as not to meet Miss Plato in her fulminating mood.

Standing in the alcove was a cabinet and inside this were shiny shapes. Each was made of silver and glittered in a superior, yet enticing way. Here, at the top of the main entrance, the large, magnificent and luminous school trophies were displayed. Being presented with one of these meant you had performed a feat worthy not only of recognition, but also of record for posterity, by the school. There was not, on the shelves of dark wood, one of the copper shields for the roll of honour, which I was endeavouring to obtain. That prize, even for an achievement of such proportions that not a girl in my dormitory had yet managed it, was not sufficiently distinguished to be displayed. Had I not set my sights high enough? Was I like my mother, making do with a few buckets of maize? So even if I earned one of those copper shields that were not in the cupboard, what was the meaning of it? What difference would that make? I began to feel tired, with the exhaustion that comes from being constantly discouraged. It was a frightening matter, that sucking out of me. I didn't want to feel it. I continued to gaze at the trophies, which excluded the one sort I had thought I might contrive to win, and cast anxious sidelong glances at the group that was now mid-way across the foyer. If only they would walk faster, I itched, so a girl could move.

Miss Plato rolled like a storm across the entrance hall. The group of seniors shuffled behind, the straps of their sundresses cutting into their shoulders so that the flesh swelled up on either side, looking as belligerent as they did. The matron knocked at the headmistress' door. I continued staring at and around the trophies. 'Come on, relax! Relax, man!' I pleaded with my reflection to make me appear believable. My hope was in Ntombi, Patience or Benhilda – the white people might assume I was one of the other girls, if I did not move in a way that persuaded them differently. These were my thoughts as I gazed at the shiny metal. For even when we behaved as though it was not known, it was known. A person was a nanny, a cook, a boy gardener, boy messenger, boy driver, a member of the African dormitory until this nanny, cook or boy became a terrorist. Then the person achieved a name. With the name came a photograph printed in the *Umtali Post*, or even the *Rhodesia Herald*, or, if the person were particularly notorious, the *Sunday Mail*. The new found name was printed under a blurred but recognisable registration card photograph. A little later, there was often a second photograph in the same paper (even if it was simply a reprint of the first) accompanied by a satisfied epitaph: another terrorist brought to justice was executed this week. One day someone close was a cook, gardener or student, another day a terrorist ripe for decapitation. That is how it was for people whose husband, son, father, aunt, or sister, made the transition from sustainer of life to one who trampled it out. But also, in this lack of identity, one could hide.

In any case, it was sensible not to face a group of senior white girls receiving a talking to by the matron en route to goodness knows what punishment, presented so deflatingly by Sister Emmanuel. 'If you want to contract cancer at this school, at least have the courtesy to wait until you can do it in the right place!' That was the headmistress' talk. No, their conversation would not be about cutting in half, but Sister would find something appropriately demoralising with which to scalp them. It was like that. 'This is the only

African girl in the school to. . .' 'In spite of the size of her calves, Bougainvillea Edwards has managed to become the runner up in the Manicaland junior championships!' Sister Emmanuel was one of those people who even in praise erased you. Under these circumstances, it was bad planning to end up close to a group of disgruntled white students, especially ones who resorted to the unstable pleasures of drugs. Girls like that might resent you seeing their humiliation. Or they might simply let out on you their frustration caused by being barred from their chemicals. They'd find a horrible name to call you that would be taken up by the entire school. Or they'd mimic you to make you look foolish so that everybody laughed whenever they reproduced your particular personal gesture, whatever it was, or worse, whenever you passed.

Most dreaded was that they wouldn't bother with the effort of it. 'Hey, man, there's that *kaffir*!' one could simply call out. Wherever you were, whatever you were doing, if you belonged to the last dormitory on the junior corridor you froze. Then you started whistling or singing under your breath. Or you resumed whatever you were doing nonchalantly, but with much more energy than the task required. The items you were using to perform the job – that pen, toothbrush, comb or tennis racquet – would, quite often at this point, and inexplicably as far as you could tell, mutiny against you and break. Non-believer. We in the dormitory did not bother to go to the dictionary, as we had been taught in history and religious knowledge, even before we came to the Young Ladies' College of the Sacred Heart, what *kaffir* meant. Nevertheless, when the white girls used it, it was like a pronouncement of impenetrable magic. By the audacity of seeking it and applying the term – as one might pound the private parts of one's daughter into a potion at a *nganga's* discretion – the desired outcome was won. But that was the problem with the white people. You never knew when they would smile, yet underneath think like that, like a person with a potion of potent parts, derived from terrible places, to smear wherever they walked.

As I stared, drowned by these anxieties, at the shelves, features bulged back at me, looking hideous and bloated from the sides of the cups. Naturally I had known of the trophies before this moment. You saw them towards prize-giving time whenever you passed through the foyer from the classrooms or library to the dormitories or dining hall. Besides they were always displayed when the talented girl strode up to the stage during the ceremony, and returned to her seat, her arms proudly cradling, as later they would a child, a gleaming goblet. I was aware of them, but had never looked into the trophies sufficiently to see any reflection I could recognise, because you thought, yes, that is what it is like – like a girl with her sister, these trophies are happy with other people. This afternoon, though, I was captive. I shuffled from foot to foot. The white girls shuffled too and bit the ends of their hair. I gazed at the silver while Miss Plato knocked on the headmistress' door and waited. To fill the moments, I resorted to reading the inscriptions on the prizes.

Stephanie Rivers, Frances Millar, Barbara Blacking, Karen Browne. There were individual prizes for Mathematics, French, Latin, Geography, History, Physics, Chemistry, Biology and English – all the individual subjects.

There were trophies for houses that had won at sports, and other trophies for houses winning in 'citizenship' which encompassed performance at social, sporting and academic endeavours – all the aspects of a young woman's breeding attended to at the convent. I was not interested in any of these as they did not mean much to me. The individual prizes were given to students who were completing upper sixth. That was too many years away to think of. But on the right were two tall cups engraved impressively with leafy decorations. One was slightly smaller than the other, apart from which they were more or less identical. 'Best A-Level results' was inscribed in a firm though curly script on the larger. 'Best O-Level results' was engraved in the same style around the lip of the smaller. Miss Plato entered the head-mistress' office after glaring at the girls. They remained, still shuffling, still gnawing the ends of their hair, but now gazing out over the stairs down to the assembly patio, then further, over the lawns with the swan upon the goldfish pond and trees with blossoms, beyond the tall conifers at the bottom, and in the distance, hazy purple, the mountains with the blasted green of the wattle plantations, as if at this moment they were of the same opinion as the guerrillas: in that direction you would find freedom.

I was not thinking of those people anymore. Best O-Level. Best O-Level! I read what the cup said again and again. Me! I could be that person with the best O-Level results. I'd show them I had what it took – grey matter that was grey enough, white matter that was white enough, in fact greyer and whiter than theirs. They'd see I had more brains not only than them, but also than Ntombi! Number one! I'd be number one in class, and then at the end of my fourth form year,

I'd walk down the aisle in the hall, cross to the steps on the left and receive my gleaming trophy. But who would be the guest of honour? The headmistress from the government girls' secondary, who didn't shake hands? For a minute I felt cold and the image of myself in that exalted position began to crack from the frostiness. But I shook myself until a tide of determination rose in me. Why not? I would and I could. Nor did I have long to wait. I was in form two, coming to the end of the year. Alot of subjects started the O-Level syllabus in form three. I'd already proved how well I could memorise. The Geography teacher and Babamukuru himself were impressed by my ability. I'd memorise everything for O-Level, there was no problem. That cup, the one for the best O-Level results, I promised myself I would have it, and my name would be inscribed on it for everyone for ever to see: Tambudzai Sigauke. Then people would know who I was, a person to be reckoned with and respected, not a receptacle of contempt like the gardeners, maids, cook boys and terrorists. My life, I promised myself again, was going to change in two years time, at prize giving. As for the head-mistress from the government school, what would I do? I would smile! I would be sure not to cause embarrassment to anyone by proffering a hand.

'Sister Emmanuel says you must come in!' Miss Plato confronted the group of distressed seniors. They shuffled more slowly than ever to the entrance of the headmistress's office. The girls in front made way in a courteous fashion for the girls behind, but the girls behind seized the arms of the front girls and pushed them back in to the head of the queue. Miss Plato looked on with her nose raised in disdain. 'Vhat vith you is the matter!' she began, as though she already knew the answer and so realised the girls' position was hopeless. 'You have already enough done, but you start again already vith the senseless behaviour!' Then something was said sharply from inside, so that the girls shook themselves, pulled their shoulders back a trifle and entered.

I continued at last to the dormitories, a smile curling my lips. You came to a school where you frequently had to pinch yourself to see if you really existed. Then, after that was confirmed, you quite often wished you didn't. So you ducked away to avoid meeting a group of people. That's when you found out how you were going to manage after all, when you'd almost given up hope, to bring people to admire and respect you. Life could be like that, in the end, with all the pieces dovetailing in together and becoming beautiful! I had an aim in life. Now life was good! In the days and weeks which followed, I did not pick fights with Ntombi so much any more. I rose from bed at four thirty to bath quickly and quietly so that the water would heat up by the time the other girls started. In the meantime I sat on the rim of the tub, reading over subjects like Chemistry, Latin and French whose syllabuses began in the first form. Sometimes I merely enjoyed a novel, as that also improved my English for the composition I would write at O-Level, as well as the essays on literature in the English language.

8

An aim could move you further. I cherished mine and nurtured it throughout that third term of my second year. I also anticipated my third year and the year of the O-Levels. To facilitate everything taking place according to strategy, I repeatedly pictured myself sitting in the library until it closed. Thereafter these motivational visions were of myself in the bathtub in our bathroom, lying there wrapped up in the blankets Babamukuru had bought for me to take to school, my head between the taps so that I would not loll to sleep, and plastic bags fastened to the spouts with rubber bands, since the outlets had a habit, although it was irregular and depended on the water pressure, of dripping. At the same time, while my imagination reinforced me like this, I continued my assiduous reading. Ah, I told myself when I grew tired, but all this hard work is going to add so well to my *unhu*. Babamukuru thought so too when I went home for the holidays, saying with a contented smile he could see how hard I was studying.

At the mission, Nyasha, with the aid of unpalatable medicine coated in sugar, was coming out of her depression. She was more involved with her work at school although, being the headmaster's daughter, she still did not have many friends at the mission. So my cousin was lonely and was now glad that I returned, so she could challenge my own development with discussion. Nyasha had missed a year of school, because of her bulimia, so she was only in form three. As a result of her being held back, combined with my new aim that pushed me forwards, I felt equal to engage her. As she was at the mission school, where Maiguru could keep an eye on her in case she relapsed, Nyasha's books were of the inferior African syllabus. However, that her texts were beneath the standard of those we possessed at Sacred Heart did not matter in my cousin's case as she was herself so superior. With me, that situation would have been disastrous. With Nyasha it was a kind of evening out, far different from what would have occurred if I, an inferior sort of girl to begin with, had then gone on with inferior syllabuses taught through inferior text-books. The best thing about the whole situation was that as Nyasha was now only one year in front of me because of her illness, she paid attention when I questioned her about issues. She deigned to discuss seriously the matters of contention that I found in her school books.

'Were,' I murmured one afternoon in the first week of the Christmas vacation. I sat on the purple and brown bedspread which striped my bed, my pillow propped up behind me next to the window. My finger pointed patronisingly at a line completed with a pleased red tick in one of Nyasha's English language exercises. 'If I were taller, I would reach the top.' I was proud of having spotted this mistake that so many would overlook. 'It's were, Nyasha, not was! How come the teacher didn't see it?'

'I know,' she said tiredly. 'I used to try and tell the teacher all the time. And it used to drive me silly looking at them all wallowing in all that mediocrity! But just think about it, Tambu, how could that woman know what's right? And if she doesn't know, of course she marks me wrong when I do it properly! After all, she's the teacher. So I've taken to doing it the way they do, for the marks, because they're the ones that give them.' She shrugged a shoulder at the exercise from her own bed, where she was reading a book she had not bothered to share with me, which rather than being revolutionary seemed to be about agriculture for it was called *A Grain of Wheat*, written as far as I could see, by someone like poor Bongo in the Congo, a starving Kenyan author. I sighed in regretful surprise at the changes in my cousin's character as a result of either the illness itself or the life she lived or the drugs she was taking.

My exhalation vexed her, for she sniffed, although more gently than had been her manner before she became depressed. 'It's just like syllabi and syllabuses! I honestly, no matter what you tell them, they keep on doing it! It's not just Mrs Zvimba, it's all of them,' she exonerated her English teacher. 'And Mum teaches Latin! They all sit in that staff room together and drink their tea! Just think of it, Tambu, they drink tea! You'd think it pickled their brain cells! Because,' she waxed crossly, 'I can't think why else they don't talk about their subject matter. And if they wanted to know about all that grammar they could easily ask my mother!' She closed her paperback energetically, so she could answer me by continuing, 'They could ask Mum about any of that English and Latin stuff! She's got a degreee, from London! But, Tambu, she's a woman, isn't she? Just like you and me, and that's the trouble! Imagine that, having to go back to the class and say yes, this is correct, a woman told me. Because, whether they said it or not, everyone would know. You know, everyone knows everything at this mission. And you know this place!' her voice was withering, on the brink of drying up completely and catching flame. 'It's a mission, right, but that's the way they're still thinking of . . . I mean not really thinking at all, not many of them do that. I meant that's the way they're conceiving of women!' Nyasha was about to become impassioned, but, 'It doesn't matter though,' she stopped herself with more resignation than she'd ever shown. 'It's not about was and were, is it, all that syllabi and -buses! It's about what you're meant to know and what you're meant not to know!' She picked up her book again with not another word concerning the status of women. I turned to watch the waving frangipani outside the window. The new calm Nyasha was frightening. When she was ill my cousin used to fume and rage. I found the young woman's fury frightening, too – you could say I was frightened of everything. I feared the rage because it consumed everything, including a person. For how rage consumed my cousin then, in those recent months! But at the same time, Nyasha's rage reassured me, confirming I remained whole and was not burning. Today the absence of that bumptious and at the same time blazing belligerence of my cousin's was unexpectedly more disturbing than had been its presence. What I piece together now is that it was comfortable for me to have someone else being angry for me, so that I did not need to become crazy myself from outrage. I cannot really blame myself for this position, since I did not have the wherewithal to do differently, for *unhu* did not accommodate furious emotions of any sort. *Unhu*, as we knew it, required containing, and even negotiating and renegotiating passion. So, little could be done

143

in a situation where negotiation was not practicable. Then you came up against a pane, as of glass, through which you saw *unhu* was dysfunctional. There was a reason for this dysfunctionality, obscure to me then, which was the key to the philosophy itself. In a phrase, this was the principle of reciprocity. *Unhu* did not function, unless the other person was practising *unhu* also. Without reciprocation, *unhu* could not be *unhu*. The practice of it assumed that *unhu* was given. We believed, as had been the case over the months, years, ages, of the concept's development, that we were all together in extolling its excellence, and in wanting nothing but the practice of *unhu*. How confident all our ancestors and we ourselves were that this practice led to the preservation of the world, and added further to the world's benefit! It was hard now for me to see Nyasha exhibiting less anger than she had done, speaking with increasing enervation, the tamed flatness, even in strong emotion, of women whose genitals have been carved into and mutilated. However, my concerns were not for the young woman, I must confess. My thoughts then were, 'Could she be turning into a person with more *unhu* than I?' If she was, I ruminated, still following the waving frangipani leaves, was it because she was once so bellicose but had relinquished that behaviour? Or was her greater *unhu* a direct result of her new containment? Would I then have to be more contained than I already was if, in spite of everything, in addition to all I did at Sacred Heart and learnt from my textbooks, I had nevertheless to increase my *unhu*?

'All the same, you know, about the "were"s and "was"s...' Nyasha began again with a small, suppressed smile, her voice small too, as she lay her book upon her knees.

'How she suppresses!' flashed through my mind, with admiration. It was surely this suppression that had caused her to relinquish her anger, I reasoned. Yes, this suppression was the basis of her *unhu*.

She patted the book's cover, stroking it gently and could not look at me. 'There's this one teacher. He takes the A-Levels for Chemistry,' she murmured, retaining the new, slight smile on her lips. 'Even though he's a science teacher, his English is still very good.' Her smile broadened somewhat, but still did not extend very wide, and remained distantly focused, meant for someone who was not in the room. 'In fact, it's excellent! There aren't many English people, you know, who'd know that, whether it's "was" or "were", better than Mr Samukange does!' With that she dived back into her book, but I could see she was not reading, which made me more disturbed. A world in which Babamukuru caught his daughter with a teacher was a world not worth imagining. Not even for the sake of superior *unhu* to my cousin did I wish this to happen and so saw it was good she was suppressed. I returned to flipping through the mission texts, and focused on how our discussion exercised my faculties and so added to my chances of winning the coveted cup. This intellectual exercise, I reminded myself, and the moral manoeuvring that resulted, were a part of building up of the character I needed to make my way in the world. I decided it was best to monitor my cousin's suppression keenly and see how she progressed, so that I obtained the mental activity I required, but when the danger of Mr Samukange was over, ensured that she did not end up outdoing me with her new measured approach in the *unhu* stakes.

Just how important *unhu* was could easily be seen by what happened to the smokers Miss Plato caught and brought down to the headmistress' office while I examined the trophies in the foyer cabinet and made my resolve to forge further and further ahead in the world. The unfortunate smokers were all in their O-Levels year, writing these exams in the fifth form like Anastasia. During the investigations, initiated by Miss Plato's discovery and conducted at first by the nuns, they slunk through the school halls, all the time trying to appear defiant but they only succeeded in looking sullenly depressed. Their complexions were blotchy with anxiety, so that I imagined them anxious about what their parents would do to them when the Christmas holidays came. I trembled many times, picturing what would have happened if I had been the girl, and the parent had been Babamukuru! 'Oh my God, I am heart ily sorry!' I immediately resorted to the Catholic penance whenever I thought of the possibility. I was never going to defile my body by smoking cigarettes. Nor was I going to join Anastasia for her bouts of sherry drinking in the washroom. But just in case I did something grievous that would distress God and Babamukuru enough to induce a rage, I wanted to build up on my capital of contrition.

Our poor smokers were expelled. Caroline Nicolls, Susan Winterfield, Janice Fraser, Alice Walters and Paulette Hudson, the school was astonished to hear one morning at assembly, had been inhaling smoke more hallucinatory than tobacco. I imagined Sister Emmanuel going down on her hands and knees, finding a roach behind the foot of the bed, emerging with it pinched between her fingers and seething 'Expel them!' Or plump Sister Henry, who took us for Biology, searching the room with forceps and a plastic bag into which she deposited specimens for examination under the microscope in the laboratory. Did Sister Henry know what *dagga* looked like, I wondered, or did she take her samples to the police station? Or did the smokers have so little *unhu* that they forgot you had to hide if you were bent on transgressing, and that if your transgressions were discovered, your remedy was contrition?

The price for the smokers not knowing these facts was to be chased out of the school. In spite of the defiance they finally affected, the injudicious young ladies could not defy Sister's directive to pack their suitcases in the middle of term.

'It's not fair!' breathed Bougainvillea at lunch a few days after the expulsion was effected. 'They've all gone! Every one of them! Caroline Nicolls was the last. I bet he didn't know he was doing it, but you should have seen how slowly her poor dad was driving!'

We were eating this meal of fish baked in white sauce. There was broccoli, in the same glutinous floury substance that smothered the fish. The maids came and slammed the plates down in front of Ntombi and I at the table as usual. When they had something – a platter of bread, a jug of milk – to set down in front of the white girls, they did it smiling gently. I wasn't very concerned with Bougainvillea's opinion. I eyed the dishes, knowing the other girls at the table wouldn't take much, for, to promote my new aim, this menu had evolved into one of my favourite meals.

'My mum,' said Bougainvillea venomously, 'wouldn't put up with that! No ways, man, not for a minute! They've paid their fees, haven't they! They've been paying those fees for years! They're entitled to write their O-Levels at this place. My mum would do something about it,' our classmate vowed. 'She'd jolly well talk to someone, and get someone to do something!' I gazed at this girl who sat opposite, one eye still on the food that was going to fill my stomach, considering this new surprising notion that mothers came in active kinds. I'd always believed people relied on their aunts, but even an aunt's ability was a passive, clinging variety. As for Mai, the picture I had was of her writhing forward, like a snake, on the ground. Bougainvillea's could! My mother, she wouldn't be able to tackle someone like Sister Emmanuel about anything, not in a thousand years.

'Come on, Bo!' Tracey passed on the fish and forked a dab of broccoli to the side of her plate, accommodating a pile of mashed potato. 'You know what they were up to, don't you! It wasn't just ordinary smoking. They were into dope! And they even did it in the bedroom! I mean, how stupid can you get! I mean, Bo, really, I ask you!' Tracey rolled her eyes and relayed on the broccoli. I put a lot of this on my plate, beside the fish, as I was now informed both were excellent brain food. The empty carbohydrates, on the other hand, whose emptiness had been confirmed by the same magazine article that extolled the fish, occupied a small heap the size of a teaspoon. As far as Bougainvillea and Tracey were concerned, though, I could not make up my mind as I agreed with both of them. The smokers were foolish to indulge in such behaviour in the first place, and even more wanting in wisdom to be caught doing it. They must have been too full of themselves, and didn't drugs contribute to wild delusions – girls thinking they could do anything anywhere, no matter what anyone else stipulated, and get away with it without any consequences! How odd! I could not understand this kind of perspective denoting an awful lack of *unhu*. How could you just go ahead like that with what you felt like, no matter what other people agreed on? *Unhu* only allowed that when your strong-headedness benefited other people, as was the case with Babamukuru. 'How are you?' 'I am well if you are well too!' That is how people with *unhu* greeted each other. It was, of course, as is always the case with such salutations, a normal greeting, having been used for centuries, so that people without *unhu* knew the form and also employed it. Nevertheless, I reflected, chewing on the broccoli, the position of *unhu* with respect to what other people desired was clear, regardless of who used its verbal expressions. In spite of having this position, nevertheless, I sympathised also with Bougainvillea, and agreed girls in such a trying situation needed strong parents who were not afraid to speak up for them. How awful it must be not to write your examinations! Not be able to get on with your life after you'd spent so many years preparing! I could not conceive of anything more terrible.

'Come off it!' Tracey's face settled into a little sneer. 'You can't tell me Caroline Nicolls actually wanted to do all that. You know, sit in the hall and fill in those papers, and write for hours so Cathy could send it all off to the examination board! More like the censorship board!' she snorted. Deidre and Angela, and Ntombi giggled.

'It's the principle!' Bougainvillea held her knife upright on the table and insisted. 'For your information,' she divulged witheringly, 'some people who smoke dope do want to do their exams. They can be,' she paused dramatically, 'exceptionally intelligent. That's why they have to smoke it. Just look at the French existentialists! And any-way,' she inquired from a lofty height, 'dope! What's dope? It grows all over the place! Don't you think God put it there for a purpose! Why wreck someone's life just 'cos of *ganga*!'

I wanted to sort it out in terms of *unhu*, for I felt this way I would gain knowledge. The notion that kept recurring to me concerned the loss of *unhu* – that characteristic that was so essential for becoming a person – which the girls faced because they were expelled. Looking at the matter that way showed something was wrong. *Unhu* meant other people shouldn't lose it; it was like being well – everyone should be. The unfortunate smokers had made a mistake, which meant they'd already lost a good bit of *unhu*. Now people were making sure they lost more, instead of helping them to retrieve it. If it was blood, would people do that? You might as well leave the blood vessels to empty, if you weren't going to staunch people's *unhu*. I kept feeling sorry for the girls. After the main course, the nannies came in to clear the plates to make place for the dessert, but before it was brought in, Sister Emmanuel picked up her small silver mallet.

It was bad news. 'Girls, you are soon going to be busy with exams, so I thought I would have this over and done with now,' the student body was informed. 'There will be some strange men walking around in the corridors and in the grounds.' Bougainvillea and Tracey exchanged looks, and Bougainvillea quivered an eyebrow. Under their table, as they too sat together, to rationalise distribution although the principle was for students to be seated according to year, Benhilda and Patience slapped palms; or rather they merely brought their fingers together, in order not to draw attention to their natural practice for fear of looking ridiculous. At the same time, a titter spluttered up and down the hall. But Sister impatiently cut off our adolescent innuendo. 'These men are the special police unit concerned with detecting drugs,' the nun revealed, and paused after the revelation so that we should understand it. We did understand, and silence settled over every inch of the dining hall. The nannies also stopped, pudding trays in hand, to stare at Sister Emmanuel.

'Girls, I want you to realise the drug squad will be here because of the behaviour of some of our students.' We waited breathlessly, wondering how our lives would be disrupted next. Sister went on, 'You also need to realise the young ladies involved were supplied by individuals here on our campus, members of our domestic staff. Yes,' Sister pointed out, looking over the maids who held trays upon which were dishes of tinned peaches and custard. Sister looked down, past the bearers of food and threw out amongst us like cannon balls, her angry countenance. 'Yes, some of our domestic staff who were approached by these young women are now to lose their jobs, because of the behaviour of some spoiled rich girls.' The said domestic staff serving me threw the dish of custard and sliced peaches down. Luckily I knew she was going to do it and grabbed it before it could spill.

'If anyone knows of anyone at all who is indulging in drug use on the premises, please, inform a person in authority. It would be much simpler for us to know of the fact now, than wait until the drug squad completes its investigations.' Ti-ti-ting! Sister touched the shining hammer to the sides of the triangle suspended from a small frame before her. All the girls grabbed their spoons and began a somewhat subdued clattering of enjoyable eating. I glanced sidelong at Ntombi. I couldn't ask her because we were not on those terms where you simply asked things, and anyway it couldn't be done in front of the white girls, nor would I dare to speak Shona and risk getting another mark. But I was thinking about alcohol as I ate my pudding. Alcohol, I speculated, was a drug! What did that say about Anastasia? She was using an intoxicant and so had to be reported to the drug squad. But what if she was not breaking the law? Sister mentioned the drug squad, but she did not talk about people who were merely breaking school rules. If only I had not thought about it, our fifth former and her sherry! Ntombi was eating her peaches and custard peacefully because she had not identified the link I saw so clearly between Anastasia and drugs, and law-breaking. Oh, the law! Now it had to be observed to see how far Anastasia could bend it, without it actually breaking! I finally took my spoon and dipped it into syrup, but not before the young woman serving our table pulled my dish away so that I ended scooping up air from my place mat.

'Ah,' she said in Shona, causing me to feel hot and uncomfortable, 'as you were just sitting I thought you were already finished, not wanting pudding!' She allowed me to pull the bowl back.

'*Sisi* Ana, when's your birthday?' I queried when we returned to the dormitory, having finished eating.

'Eh-eh-eh! Stop! Right now!' Ntombi breathed quietly in Shona. 'Don't think I didn't see you cooking it, cooking it there in the dining room!' Poison thickened in her voice. 'And next time someone talks to you, maybe you could answer! I was embarrassed! I was embarrassed right up to the point of not knowing, to be next to you when you treated that young woman so badly! In the dining room, girls, *vasikana*, can you imagine what she did. Imagine,' she turned to the room indignantly, '*Sisi* Jeleska was talking to her! And what did she do? All she could do was pull the plate, right out of *Sisi* Jeleska's hands! Pulling it, without saying anything.'

I was exasperated with Ntombi and irritated with the maid, but did not think about any of it further. I continued to feel sorry for the smokers who were the subject of Sister's special announcement. I tell myself today it was this sympathy for the seniors, along with the new submission in my cousin, to whom I still looked for direction, that caused me to behave the way I did when I returned to school the following year.

The term began distressingly.

'They've closed Sinai!' whispered Benhilda the very first night we were assembled again in the room.

'No!' breathed Irene, who was now in the second form. 'Why did they do that?'

'Who d'you mean, they?' asked Benni. 'It wasn't them, the comrades, our elder siblings, if that's what you mean.'

'Well, *vana mukoma*, the elder brothers and sisters, they have been closing schools. They have! Everywhere!' Irene insisted.

'Not quite everywhere,' pointed out Patience, who had this year progressed to form four, moving up behind Benhilda. 'Have you heard of those elder brothers and sisters, as they call themselves, have you ever heard of them going in and closing a school where there's a European?'

There was silence, broken only by the sound of our breathing as we pondered Mt Sinai Prep's closure, which was uncomfortable to think of, because whoever had performed the act could also come and close the Young Ladies' College.

'What's Sinai?' piped up Cynthia, our new little first former who was a bit lost. 'What did they do that for? Was it a bar? Or was it,' she hesitated before she used the word, 'a brothel?'

As we older ones were too busy with our worries, we did not bother to answer. 'Well, then,' demanded Irene as quietly as she could. 'Who closed it? Was it the government?'

'Just imagine!' continued Benhilda, worried. 'My sister's married to the Jereras. The ones who own that Kumhanya Kusvika bus service! Well, her Maiguru, the one who's married to the second eldest son had a little boy there in grade two, at Sinai. He was a boarder, you know, one of the ones who had to go to Sakubva. Of course, the parents were mad about that! Paying the same fees,' Benhilda recounted with wonder, 'but legally not being able to have the same treatment! So they tried to bring the other parents on to their side, but those Euros wanted their sons to be segregated! Just think of that! Wanting your son to be segregated! Why don't those people want something better! I think,' Benhilda related, more and more anxiously, 'my sisters-in-law threatened to complain to our elder brothers and sisters. I think,' she reflected further with some shame, as though she were confessing a sin for which there was soon to be penance, 'I think, because they have all those buses going to all those way out places, you know, down in the rural areas, my sisters-in-law, they have to... well... get on with them, you know, the elder brothers and sisters! So,' she went on sadly, 'either they did go to the boys, or they just talked about *vana mukoma* at a school meeting, saying *vana mukoma* wouldn't like it. And all the white parents at the meeting said nothing. But afterwards, they just started writing letters, asking for their children to be transferred because they were saying their children couldn't be safe in a place that also allowed the children of terrorists.'

A chill slouched through the room. Those Jereras were fools. Was it better to be the child or the sister of a terrorist?

'Hi-i, hi-i!' Benhilda was crying quietly. 'Now he's been taken! My brother-in-law's been taken. We don't even know who did it! One day he just wasn't there and no one can find him. We don't even know if it was the security force or if it was the Elder Siblings! Oh, oh, me, *ini zvangu*! What shall I do? He's the one, when things were difficult, who always came forward to buy me things and pay my fees!'

We were quiet, considering all these matters. What if our school was closed? Who would pay our fees, or make sure that we moved to another place of learning? Even Cynthia forbore to ask, until the next morning, 'But *Sisi* Tambu, please tell me properly, what is Sinai?'

A few days later Ntombi came back from lunch and inquired of the dormitory, 'Girls, have you seen those Swanepoel twins? Have you seen them when they look at that classmate of mine and me?' She glanced towards me, indicating I was the classmate, as we made strong efforts to speak each other's names as seldom as possible. 'Whenever they look, it's as if something's devouring them. Shame, hey, something's got inside them and it's eating them! Completely! It's even digesting them!'

The picture in the paper the next day disclosed what this was. There was a quarter page sized photograph of a man sprawled out on the soil of his farm as though worshipping some old earth goddess. He had an axe in his head, carving the cranium into two equal half moons, so that it looked as though his head, perhaps because of his thoughts, had curiously turned into buttocks. The man was Mr Swanepoel.

Sister Emmanuel grasped a dozen copies of the *Rhodesia Herald*, enough to pass one down each line that morning at assembly, and have another to wave indignantly. 'We are not a political institution,' said Sister, speaking with magenta lips out of a face that was as white as a furnace. 'What we are is a Christian institution. As such an institution, we cannot condone murder. Acts of murder cannot be justified under any circumstances, and certainly not these acts of butchery!' I nodded. I twisted my head round to observe, surreptitiously, so people would not think I was not affected by the gravity of the occasion. Down at the back of the Three A line stood Ntombi. She was even less interested now in a place up at the front, close to the headmistress, as she wished to ensure that she did not provide my back with protection. The assembly bell rang each morning while she was deep in discussion with one of the girls in the dormitory about whether or not to squeeze a particular spot or whether Michael Jackson sang better than Donny Osmond. Meanwhile I was turning my aim into a goal. At those times, when the bell sounded, I held a diagram of photosynthesis in hand, quotes from 'Wuthering Heights' or pointers to the rise to power of Oliver Cromwell. I easily put these away without causing any offence, or losing out in any argument, as soon as the bell went 'kongolo', and I was out of the room before Miss Plato progressed past the bathrooms.

So now Ntombi was at the back, but she was also nodding. The seniors, Benhilda and Patience, also gravely lifted and lowered their chins. The two juniors could not raise their eyes and kept their heads permanently lowered. Pictures in the paper of the awful things the elder siblings did had that effect. They made you nod. They made you agree. They shamed you.

'I have thought about it for a long time,' our headmistress continued. 'I have made the decision that we shall accept an offer that has been made to us by the city council.'

The paper reached me. I examined it perfunctorily and passed it on, using the moment to check my form line again, head still low, to catch a glimpse of the Swanepoels. They were not at assembly. They had already left, it turned out, to discover they had lost not only their father, but also their mother.

'I regret to tell you Mrs Swanepoel passed away a few hours after her husband. Kim and Katherine, two very fine young women, members of our first under-sixteen doubles pair, are orphans. This is after they were subjected to unspeakably obscene horrors during the holidays.' Sister spoke in a drilling voice, without inflection, as though she was past understanding how humans could behave in the way *vana mukoma*, the elder siblings, had towards others. It sounded, though, as if there was something in her soul which she did not like, that was more dreadful than her decision. I did not look at her anymore, and all the other girls from the dormitory were also now looking down.

'There is a matter I would like you young ladies to consider carefully,' Sister informed the school. 'There is an effort to counter these dreadful events in all the communities in the country. We have a similar initiative in this municipality. Those young ladies who would like to join the women knitting comforters and gloves for the troops, please put up your hands. A bus will take you to the town hall on Fridays.'

The sun became too hot, the crazy paving sparkled too brightly, the sky undulated up above us and shone too potently. It was too quiet as if everyone had suddenly stopped breathing. The girls who lived on their parents' farms and ranches with the threat of violence looked wide-eyed ahead, as though harm had inexplicably tracked them into the place they prayed was safe. Bougainvillea stared at the headmistress, her mouth cracked and gaping wide. Traccy and other town girls shifted their eyes uneasily from here to there. Now, apart from the security checks of handbags when you went into department stores, the war had come to them. We of that dormitory kept on darting glances to see what was going on. But for the most part, because we were distressed and embarrassed, we looked down.

Sister saw we were all demoralised. 'Now, let's not react as though alarm and despondency have been spread on this campus!' A little colour came into her face as she groped for a lighter touch. 'I wouldn't want to alarm you or make you despondent,' she toyed with the terminology of the crime we heard of practically every day on the news, of spreading alarm and despondency. If you did that in Rhodesia, you could be punished with many years in prison.

'Girls, there's no need to be alarmed,' our headmistress told us. 'I hope you've been sleeping well!' Sister regained her manner of saying 'go' and expecting it to be gone, borne of her absolute authority over marks, awards and examinations and which, her confidence made many of us think, also extended to the affairs of war and nation. 'I,' the headmistress went on with a personal element that was encouraging, 'am a very light sleeper. But I'm glad to say since the drug squad examined the premises, I am enjoying a decent night's sleep once more. They discovered in our area some lapses in security, which have now been rectified. In fact,' Sister looked encouraged herself, 'there has not been a single incident within our radius since the beginning of this term.' Having raised morale in this fashion, Sister now surveyed us in the way she did when instructing us to start preparing for examinations. 'The troops are mounting a great exercise,' she stressed, 'to enable us to continue with our mission to educate you in a Christian way. I think it would be appropriate to show our appreciation. Volunteers, please raise your hands.'

Put up your hand.

Don't put up your hand.

Do the right thing.

If you do, the terrorists might find you.

The impossibility of it, of the putting up of four fingers, of the stretching up of a hand on an arm, and then the impossibility of everything else after that moment of raising up, impossible because legs and other limbs you knew of tangled in heaps as they fell, tramped through my thoughts like a too heavily armed force. Meanwhile ahead, on each side, and behind, along the form lines, beige sleeves fell back from young white arms, fingers waved and more and more arms ascended. Sister said lists should be made, which task was given to the class teacher, as so many of us came forward for the war effort. Mine was amongst the arms that were raised.

On the Friday, I collected from a table in the back corner of the town hall several skeins of dark green wool and a photocopied booklet of patterns that produced garments to warm various limbs and other parts of the body. 'You do what you want, dear! That way you don't end up bored, and you can carry on much more quickly,' a woman I did not know beamed at me, her back very straight behind her desk. There was coffee, tea, cake and sandwiches for sale on a table at the top end of the space. I had enough pocket money from my uncle and went over to treat myself to something tasty, so that I could speak about it significantly to all the other girls who stayed behind in the dormitory. I selected a bag of home made caramel, and sat popping one into my mouth then muttering as the sweetness ran over my tongue, knit one, purl one for the throat band of the Balaclava helmet I began.

9

On Saturdays Miss Plato prowled, to peer in and out of all the cupboards on St Ignatius' floor in order to predict our eventual success as graduands of the Young Ladies' College. Her predictions were based on orderliness and neatness, criteria that, on those Saturdays in particular, caused pandemonium in the last dormitory on St Ignatius' corridor.

Order and neatness were attributes naturally in short supply in the junior dormitories. Bougainvillea was now housed in St Agatha's, the middle school wing that looked over the swimming pool. But while she lived on the junior floor, she spoke for us all when she defined the character of tidiness. 'Order,' declared Bougainvillea, 'belongs to a lower class of mind. In fact, a lack of randomness denotes an abysmal spirit.' There was great admiration along the corridor for the girl's turn of phrase, the jut of her chin when she made the comment. In spite of the admiration though, no one, besides Bougainvillea herself, ever demonstrated that theory to Miss Plato. Indeed, apart from Bougainvillea, not a soul on the junior corridor was foolish enough to neglect a jersey, a towel or a book upon her bed when she went off to the classrooms. And at the weekends we were doubly diligent, intensely more painstaking. For during her weekly inspections Miss Plato did not merely pounce on obvious offenders. She spent several minutes in the room, her head half hidden in the cupboards, examining every recess. At these times the matron proceeded to scour every nook and cranny of the dormitory. One after another, wardrobe doors were pulled open, her eyelids pressed together like callipers over her small grey eyes. Shelf by shelf, she conducted her scrutiny, to see whether a blouse protruded over the item of clothing upon which it was folded; and if the blouse was the first item placed on the shelf, Miss Plato inspected to see if the cloth did not lap over the woodwork.

Now, as the rooms in the junior corridor were meant for four but because the nuns' great favour towards us resulted in us being six, there was even more tension than usual on Saturdays in our dormitory. This came about as, with four cupboards and six people, four girls must of necessity share two cupboards. The seniors were allocated their own storage space, while sharing was left to middle schoolers and juniors. So Cynthia shared a cupboard with Irene. As the two next youngest, I was required to share a space with Ntombi.

Miss Plato patrolled without notice on Saturdays. Carrying her large brass bell into the fourteen rooms she inspected each week would inhibit the matron's execution of her duties. Which hand would then run down shelves of gym culottes and blouses, arranged as inconsistently as foreign participles? Besides, the bell was too vital to the smooth-running of the school to relinquish, once she was inside a dormitory and conducting an examination, within the reach of pupils. If Bougainvillea got her fingers round that bell, there would not be any saving of any people's faces, as Miss Plato herself was acutely aware of.

The matron compensated for the time she spent without her alarm by calling us to receive our pocket money at the top of the hall with a tumultuous clanging of the bell. This occurred a quarter of an hour after breakfast on Saturday, after which we returned briefly to our rooms to brush our teeth and wait in trepidation for the weekly checking of cupboards.

Kongolo-kongolo-kongolo, the stationary chime rang, Miss Plato standing imperiously at the confluence of Saint Ignatius with the route from the dining room so she could keep watch over two corridors simultaneously. In this position, she also presided over a small wooden table on which squatted a grey metal box. This box contained small manila envelopes, fatter or thinner, depending on the amount of pocket money each parent had given a daughter. Because of Babamukuru's generosity towards me, my envelope was comfortably full. It was embarrassing, though, to look at some of the envelopes that belonged to the girls in our dormitory, especially the envelopes belonging to the older girls. Benhilda's and Patience's were as thin as cows in a drought. We filed up form by form. Seniors proceeded first, so at least Benhilda and Patience were in the front, although they had very little cash to receive when they advanced. Counting coins, or, if there was only one to take, patting the half crown from palm to palm, we walked back down the corridor to tidy up our dormitories. When this was done, as I was now so engaged in my objective, I did not take time these days to saunter down to the gate to visit the ice-cream man who came by on his tricycle, and was required by the college regulations to remain outside the portal, as a strange male was not allowed onto the grounds in spite of many pleas to the school authorities to reconsider by the manufacturing company. I spent my free time at weekends curled up in a spot behind the hall where nothing but *chongololos*, which were silent, came. I carried a blanket with me and a pile of books.

Plotting and planning how to achieve my goal of obtaining the best O-Level results in the school and being rewarded with a big silver cup that bore my name also influenced the orderliness in my cupboard. Taking time to be precise each time a pair of socks or shirt was pulled out would reduce the time spent overhauling on Saturday and give me as much as a whole half hour more for my books.

'So you're dashing off again? Where to?' asked Patience this Saturday. 'It makes us wonder what we are like now. Ehe, it began last year, Tambu, and it's getting worse. You're making us wonder what we are like since now we aren't the people with whom you can sit down and do anything!'

I pulled a pile of gym knickers a fraction of an inch forward, examined them to see they were now properly aligned with the edge of the cupboard. Having completed this motion, I stepped aside, trying not to listen.

'Ehe, that's it!' Ntombi spoke pointedly across me to Patience. 'Aren't there other people she sits with now? Those ones we know of! They are the people who go there also, these new people of hers, the ones where she goes knitting!'

There was silence in the dormitory, as we did not comprehend how to talk about these things. Even the white girls who climbed into the bus on Friday chose mostly not to talk about their knitting.

'Never!' Patience decided to brush things aside. 'Ntombi, do you think anyone can do anything like that! No, no one can be that stupid! Knitting everywhere in the school! Even on your own, how can you do it! When *vana sisi* up at the compound, or *vana bhuti* down in the garden can any

164

day be *vanachimbwido,* or *mujiba*, and any day go and tell! Mm! Not even the white girls, they're just as scared! No one would do it, sit knitting! No, it's just that she's reading,' Patience guessed shrewdly. 'As if there isn't enough time for prep! I'm always done an hour before the time is finished!'

In fact it was true that there was plenty of time for studying for those who did not have an objective that demanded more input. The bell for us to file to the classrooms rang at eleven o'clock each Saturday morning. Our desks were occupied until one o'clock, which was enough preparation time if a girl's mission was merely completing her homework; but my aim was set much higher than that! Naturally I could not tell anyone in the room, in case I did not manage to achieve my ambition, so that someone else, Seema Patel or Tracey Stevenson, or perhaps even Ntombi, curtseyed in front of the trophies on the stage instead. If I failed, how delighted my dorm-mates would be, delirious that I had pulled myself down so they did not have to do it for me. How they would thrust down their lips and mock and laugh, especially Ntombi! My classmate was already dreadfully exasperated by Patience's talk of classrooms and prep, combined with my industry, for the words reminded her how far behind me she was falling in the intelligence stakes, whereas in the first two years she had constantly out-studied me.

'Of course they would! Be that stupid, of course they would!' Ntombi snarled. *Unhu's* decorum required she keep quiet, but she was so exasperated she simply could not do it. 'Haven't we seen how stupid they are, going there in the first place, for that knitting! Getting into the bus, there under the jacarandas, haven't we seen them! And haven't we heard them singing that song, there with all the Europeans!' With this Ntombizethu turned to face Patience, her arms full of clothes. 'This land is my land! This land is your land! From the Vumba Highlands to the Sabi Valley!' That was the song bawled in the burgundy school bus as we drove through the suburbs to the town hall. Tight and high, Ntombi's voice strangled her words. 'Now, girls, what do you think? The driver's in there at the steering, right! What if that driver is a *mujiba*, or knows someone who is? When he's finished the driving and he goes back to say what he saw, what is he going to tell people?' The girl's nostrils flared. Her breath was loud as though she could not draw enough air through them. Her exasperation was bringing her very far past *unhu*, to a place where the dangers of speaking vanish. Next the girl flung her armful of clothes onto the floor to lunge with outrage into my part of the cupboard. 'See! See what I mean about this one! What if *vana sisi* who clean this room see this kind of thing in this room in this cupboard?' She waved my ball of wool and knitting needles at me as though they were monstrous weapons direct from a brutal dictator's arsenal. 'Then who will remain! Tell me, who will stay here and remain behind! Will your mouths be able to say anything about anything that helps us? Which one of us will still be speaking if the elder siblings decide some people here must stop being sell-outs! Oh, do you think any one of us will be excluded from it! By saying "it isn't me"! Tell me, *mhani*, do you think just saying that to someone is going to exclude you!' Everyone was quiet, knowing how the pain that pushed Ntombi beyond what it was appropriate to voice ached in a more deadly way than the mere smart of school-girl rivalry.

Now I nearly stopped breathing. I found it impossible to know myself why I had done this thing. Looking at Ntombi – or even not looking at her – now it was so surprising I had not thought of it: the agony in the thin, thin air, the silence and the breathing, the slow, slow grace of the leg arcing in the air; and then Babamukuru in a strange way, like a dancer, finally moving. All of it was gone at the time of the decision. Not a bit of it was considered. For of course these things cannot remain, lest they claim, by the act of being remembered, to have had existence. That is why one does not think of these things, because a girl is not as wide as the sky, which is wide enough for the conjuring into being that is the act of thinking. As it was like this, and I was not the sky but was a girl, standing in the dormitory, I said, 'When the Swanepoel sisters come back.' I addressed the room quietly and was surprised to hear my voice breaking, as I did not feel the force that shook it, but when I heard it the sound revealed to me how I was caught up in terrible self-defence against my accusing classmate. 'When the Swanepoels come back, I thought if. . . maybe if someone said, I knitted a helmet and some gloves, I thought maybe it would help them,' I finished quietly.

Patience sat on her bed without speaking, while Ntombi opened her mouth wide and wrinkled her nose. She grabbed my arm. I shrugged to free myself. She circled her fingers more tightly around the flesh of the upper arm and shook it. Benhilda, Irene and Cynthia crowded around Patience's bed, the closest, and gazed at us with anticipation. But because of the last fist fight we had, and the sense of what wasn't remembered, I no longer had the will to fight. So I covered my head in case my classmate struck.

Ntombi could not shake so well with my arms in the new position. She became enraged. 'You're saying I'm going to beat you! That's what you're saying, aren't you, doing that. Putting your arms up like that! Even when I haven't done anything! No, I haven't done anything to you! You poke me, and when I touch you, you say I'm going to hit you. Ho-o, you want me to beat you, don't you! Keep on! Just keep on like that, I'll do it!' Her free arm swung back. I tightened my elbows about my face to protect my eyes. The blow did not come. There was commotion in the room as I continued cowering.

'Hey!' Patience came to grapple with Ntombi. Now that the motion had been made, Cynthia, Irene and Benhilda also sprang forward in the little room.

'*Sisi* Ntombi! *Sisi* Ntombi! No, don't do that!' the juniors remonstrated, reaching out to hold Ntombi's limbs.

'No, Ntombi, not like that! No, that's not what we do!' Benhilda resorted to Shona and spoke with so much passion anyone would have thought she was the first instead of the last to move.

'*Vasikana*!' panted Patience. With one hand she was holding onto Ntombi's arm and was trying to get a grip round her waist with the other. '*Vasikana*, hold her, hold her! Don't let them say that's always what happens here with us in this dormitory.' Patience now turned to Shona also, as she held onto the lunging Ntombi. 'Is that what we want, he, *vasikana*? For them to say, ah, those, that's what they do, so just leave them like that!'

There was no need to tell us who she was talking about,

who spoke like that. An ominous, undefined 'they' in the dormitory always meant Europeans.

'Why are they saying it? Why? Isn't it because of people like her!' panted Ntombi, still flailing. 'Benni!' she turned to the middle schooler, who had now prised Ntombi's grip from my shoulder. '*Sisi* Benni, what if your relatives hear you! What if those relatives who know *vana mukoma* hear you talking about that one!' Ntombi jutted her chin at me venomously. 'What if they hear you talking, you know, about some of the things that some of the girls put in some of the cupboards in this room!'

Benhilda looked down, unable to speak, being so anxious that she was confounded. Patience, pulling Ntombi onto the bed and keeping a firm arm around the third former, gave Benhilda time to recover. 'Oh no, we don't get on with them! No one from our family talks to them, apart from, you know, *vanasekuru*, the grandfathers,' our fifth former disclaimed. 'All that I know, about the boys from Sinai, it's just from what the elders said.'

'Iiih!' wailed Ntombi. 'That's making it worse!' Her eyes were large. She looked very stricken. 'Those relatives of yours don't like you, *Sisi* Benni! Isn't that why they didn't talk to you when all those things about your brother-in-law happened! If people don't like you these days, if they hear something, if they hear you saying something about some people like the ones in this room, they will immediately know who to tell! It all just makes it worse! Oh, because that's when people tell the elder siblings!' Ntombi jerked this way and that, so that it was not clear whether she wished to throw herself at me, or merely to dash herself to the floor. So Benhilda and Patience pushed her down onto Patience's bed. There they sat one on each side of the impassioned and disconsolate third former, one arm each stopping Ntombi's hands from lashing out, the other arm gentle but alert for quick motion around her waist.

'Oh! I know them!' Ntombi moaned. She had a look in her eyes that made me stand still for a moment and wonder what, in her own holidays, she had been brought to witness. 'These days, when people don't get on, that's when they do it! They – those relatives of yours – they'll just say there are people who need to be taught a lesson, together with your niece at that school of hers. That's all! That's what people do, *Sisi* Benhilda! Then, once those words are spoken to *vana mukoma*, it's the end! I know it, it's nothing but the end!' Ntombi sobbed and twisted up with a new spurt of desperation. Before she could take a grip on me again, our roommates jumped up and surged towards her. They caught her arms, then tried to bring her back to the bed once more. They made little impression on Ntombi, who was shouting about the limbs we would miss, the nature and temperature of rods that would be inserted into our various orifices. 'Oh, you, Tambu! What's making you do this! As if you don't know some things are cursed! Oh, just jump into a pot of hot oil! Or just water, go on, water will do it too if it's boiling! Just jump in, *usvuukue*! *Usvuuke*! Then you will be what you want. It will make you look like them, all pink like a European!' It was very horrible, what she was saying, and as she did so, Miss Plato burst in.

With all the noise that was going on in the dormitory, it took a while for us to realise the time for judging the neatness of our cupboards had come, therefore the matron was in the room before any of us noticed. By the time we looked at her, she was standing a step from the doorway, completely rigid. The door-handle was still in her hand. This she slowly relinquished. Just as slowly the terror of the junior corridor brought her hands back to her sides. She stood very straight and tall, and very still. But as we were, in our surprise and consternation, looking at her closely, we could see the prow of her cap tipping up and down and from side to side, and sometimes describing little circles. Her chin was doing the same, with the difference that, at this part of her body, the circles trembled.

Although Ntombi's warnings were still in our ears, it was difficult for us to see this other party, who was more immediate to us than the elder siblings, so angry with us that she trembled. This being so, we could not look at Miss Plato's face for long. We were at least half ashamed at having caused such anger. For if you had *unhu* and you lived with people, you were meant to know what angered them; you were meant to know what precipitated uncontrolled, unsociable feelings and what caused good humour, so that you ordered your behaviour in such a way as to inhibit the first while reinforcing the latter. At the same time, what if *vana mukoma* were here, or had recruited their *chimbwidos* and *mujibas* upon the premises? What might become of this shaking woman? It was difficult to look at her with these questions and issues in mind and so we stopped returning in a mild way Miss Plato's gaze and did what we knew the Europeans did not like, or at least did not respect as a reasonable action when people talked to people: each of us turned her eyes from the chin and cap and furious forehead, to stare instead at the floor or out of the window where doves in the pines behind the cloister cooed and pushed out their breast feathers. Irene dared to become interested in the ceiling.

'I have come,' spluttered Miss Plato, 'your cupboards to be checking!'

A splutter now came from Irene too, who immediately pressed her lips together and gave the ceiling another, more serious examination.

Miss Plato opened and closed her fingers by her sides, as though she was girding up her authority. 'To whom are belonging these?' she demanded, her voice as penetrating as any bullet, her finger pointing at the heap of Ntombi's clothing strewn over the floor as though it were a gun barrel. No one wanted to own those clothes that lay upon the linoleum. We kept gazing into distances. However, Ntombi was the most uncomfortable of us by now. She stepped off the cardigan she had trod on.

'So! These clothes are yours!' The matron pounced. Ntombi, who was already excited before the matron came in, lost her wits sufficiently to bend down and pick up the jersey. She stood there dangling it in her arms, while silence reigned in the dormitory apart from everybody's increasingly heavy breathing. What was going to happen? Was Miss Plato going to confiscate the jersey? Ntombi, of the thin pocket money packet, and her parents would take that badly. Confiscated belongings did not often find their way back to the original owner, but into the thrift shop or else, in the form of donations, to a charity or school for the underprivileged in Sakubva township.

'Why? This I do not understand! Vhy are lying your clothes on the floor all over around! They should inside your cupboard neatly be, but into your cupboard you have not packed anything!'

As Ntombi could not answer, the third former merely kept picking fluff from her jersey. The silence went on for long enough to make some of the bolder of us peep at the matron.

'Ach, so!' the woman exclaimed next. 'Ach, it is always so! You must now your clothes pick up, all, Ntombi!'

Even I dared take a glance at this calmer rejoinder. Miss Plato was standing tall. Her hands hung by her sides easily. There was a detached tolerance about her, on her face a faint, yet definite and satisfied look of recognition, as though a matter of small significance was concluded finally, in accordance with expectation. But we did not understand it then. That was the trouble with Europeans in those days: it took a lot of effort to know what they were thinking.

'You will have two black marks,' decreed the matron with the new, calm, practically contented expression we found so inscrutable. 'Now, quickly your clothes pick up, Ntombi!'

Ko-ko-kongolo! That was the prep bell after we finished half an hour of silent tidying. Then the next one sounded for us to end our prep and proceed to the dining room. We verified the two small fat blobs against Ntombi's name as we filed off to eat, past the library. Contentedly I contemplated how, if my classmate obtained two more, she would not be received onto the honour roll. I must confess yet again, I was not concerned with my roommate's suffering.

'What did she have to go and do that for! *Vasikana*, what kind of thing is that for a woman to do!' Ntombi was morose after the meal that followed the pilgrimage past the notice board. She grumbled without stop, wanting us to tell her she'd been badly treated, but nobody really answered.

'Mm! People like that!' sighed Irene. 'Mm! Like that woman!' She paused to stretch on her bed and wiggle her toes before she rolled over to take from the chair beside her bed a Cadbury's bar she had bought at the tuckshop that morning. Rip! went the wrapping. 'Mm, those ones!' Irene chewed on the crunchy bits thoughtfully. 'If they start talking gently like that! Mm! I think it's better maybe if they just remain behaving the other way to us, being angry!'

No one had anything to say to that. Ntombi spent the rest of the afternoon sobbing.

'Remember Anastasia and her sherry!' recalled Patience. 'I wonder if that's what she's still doing!'

Cynthia had a radio. She snapped it on. The Mahotela Queens from South Africa were singing, and Mahlatini, the lion of Soweto, roared. Pa-pa! Benhilda struck her palms together, sitting on the edge of her bed. In a minute she stood up, moving. One by one Patience, Irene and Cynthia joined her. Pa-pa! clapped hands. Step-step, skipped feet. Clap-step, clap-shake, step-clap, clap-twist! It was first the right foot, then the other one. Soon the head was shaking. There was an atmosphere, almost like joy, in the room; still it was too grim for that, yet the girls were laughing. I wondered what it must be like to have so much money you could afford a radio for a first form girl. Not even Babamukuru could do that. There was, in his house, only the wireless on which he listened to the news and the 'Voice of Zimbabwe', beaming in from Maputo.

Ntombi went on crying, although you couldn't hear it so much because of the music and laughing and dancing.

I slipped out with my blanket and books. No one noticed me leaving.

Miss Plato's serenity had other consequences. My roommate communicated with me even less after that day our cupboards were checked and Ntombi waved my green yarn and grey knitting needles. I was concerned, not so much because I missed communion with the other girls, but because their avoidance resulted in a decrease in my quota of *unhu*. You said, I am well if you are too. *Unhu* required a minimum amount of interaction in order to establish the mandatory reciprocation. Apparently, now the first former's radio exhibited more *unhu* than I did. It went 'click', girls leapt up joyfully and started dancing. I became concerned with the existential question, and felt very superior to be so preoccupied, as the French existentialists had pondered similar matters, according to the information Bougainvillea gave us. So my question demanded: what about radios and other things that returned people's happiness, the things purchased with money, which you obtained after getting a good job as a result of your studying? Did they constitute *unhu*? Undeniably, for example, Babamukuru, who had a good home and many fine possessions, possessed a great deal more *unhu* than my father. Did that mean Cynthia, who had a fatter envelope of pocket money and a radio that made sad young women stand up and move to the roaring measure of music, possessed more *unhu* than I did? Was it the *unhu* you possessed that earned you your possessions, or did you acquire *unhu* once you possessed them? If you did not have *unhu* in the first place, then were you doomed, for how could you reciprocate with people? At this point I approached clarity. The white girls had fatter manila envelopes than we did residing in Miss Plato's cash box. The whole world wanted to reciprocate with them, so surely they possessed more *unhu*! Thus I wondered until it became apparent one path to *unhu* was the way of material preponderance. I spent more and more time memorising every word of every text, every strange scientific sign and symbol, the succession of British monarchs.

The third year examinations arrived. I began to near my objective. I was top, overcoming Seema, Ntombi and Tracey. My prowess continued in my fourth form year. I worked harder, being convinced now my goal was attainable. By the third term of our O-Level year, even Bougainvillea was wandering around looking hounded and muttering quotations from our prescribed prose: 'I have no pity! I have no pity! The more the worms writhe, the more I yearn to grind out their entrails. It is a moral teething. . . '. I too had memorised chapters of *Wuthering Heights* for the English Literature examination, although I was concerned I had forgotten several sentences and therefore could no longer be perfect, but would be obliged to resort to mere paraphrasing.

Three or four days before we sat, I turned my attention to the necessary quotations from our prescribed drama, *Romeo and Juliet*. Absently my fingers fumbled in my desk in the O-Level classroom, while I looked out, above and beyond the mountains, mentally reciting the first lines of Romeo's soliloquy. 'Oh, she doth teach the torches to burn bright! / It seems she hangs upon the cheek of night / Like a rich jewel in an Ethiop's ear. . . '. That kind of beauty was good to imagine! My fingers touched first my Chemistry text, then the History, Geography and Biology book. Enthralled by the picture conjured up by the words, dreaming of being part of that opulent beauty, it was minutes before I understood the book sought for was no longer in its place. I turned instead to the features of Mediterranean climates vowing to search at the end of preparation, since having trained my memory as I had, it was now very easy quickly to memorise everything. By the day before the examination I had not revised, however, for the Shakespeare was still missing.

'Who's taken my book?' I cried out in despair. The form room was full, as it was just before the study hour, but nobody paid much attention. My blood boiled and powered me like a steam engine over to the girl who also slept in my dormitory.

'Where is it?'

'What?' Ntombi was somewhat feverishly jotting down Geography notes amidst that noise of the class, looking at a page of text, covering it up and jotting key words on a piece of paper.

'My book! Where did you put it? I want it!'

Tracey and a few white girls stared at me. I drew in breath to demand once more. Ntombi's eyes in her midnight face sparkled like starlight.

'Quiet please!' Sandra, the prefect, stood in the doorway. 'Please proceed with your work,' she instructed, as desks opened and closed for the last time, pages rustled and fountain pens scribbled.

I kept my awful desperation under my tongue until the study period was over. Then I proceeded to make sure I would pass English Literature and walk up to collect my trophy. It was an act fraught with the risk of a black mark, for Miss Plato leapt on anyone who arrived late at the hall where we took a period of recreation after our nightly study. However, my ambitions weighted the silver trophy more heavily than the copper plates, of which I now had two, so that, in spite of Miss Plato, I remained determined in my decision.

After the study hour was over I stayed behind, ostensibly to close the windows, an offer made to the prefect with a smile shining out in the way in which, at that time, most Europeans liked to be smiled at. I closed two or three windows with the long metal pole that had a hook at its end. Eventually Sandra's footsteps died away and the dark corridor outside was deserted. Immediately I darted forward to the desk ahead, to fling up its lid and turn books feverishly this way and that to establish its contents. When nothing was revealed I threw the lid back and progressed to the next one.

When I came to Ntombi's place my heart beat hollowly. Up the lid went, in my hand plunged, pulling out her pencil case and rulers. Many times I searched through and through, to find only one copy of the play, with her name Ntombizethu Mhlanga, then Form 4A, Young Ladies' College of the Sacred Heart written neatly on the inside cover and underlined firmly. There was nothing to find in three more desks. The fourth desk was Bougainvillea's. There, nestled between the pages of the A4 exercise book she used for Latin was my Shakespeare, complete with the annotations! Holding it in palms that sweated, I sat down shaking. I did not challenge Bougainvillea. It was hard to understand why anyone would do that, especially a European doing something like that to someone like me, when I was knitting Balaclava helmets and scarves for our common security! I did not discover what happened until many years later.

The examinations progressed. I too now passed up fish in white sauce with broccoli, for I was nauseous with tension. If I did not pass the O-Level tests, Babamukuru might decide not to support me. Then my life would be finished only four years after the miraculous transfiguration when I was accepted by the nuns at the convent. For comfort, I imagined myself, as I sat in the great hall at flat desks which did not open in order to prevent cheating, upon the stage at the front with everyone down below cheering and clapping. There were Babamukuru and Maiguru, two proud relatives, beaming. Baba and Mai were shining and oiled, brought in especially from the village. Swaying between these two extremes pressurised me terribly. I was always exhausted.

'You have ten minutes,' Sister Catherine's soft, encouraging voice called out towards the end of each paper, although it always seemed as though only ten minutes had passed. I was not able to finish a single paper to my satisfaction, and knew I could not face Babamukuru again in my life. Miserably, as I lay in bed, I saw myself return ignominiously to the village and listened to Mai's spiteful consolation: 'Did you think you could, Tambudzai! Do you think others who didn't couldn't! So, it's coming back, is it not! Ehe, now, with all that not succeeding of yours, that's when you know who your father is!' I was more petrified of failure than of anything else, so that imagining Mai's sarcastic sympathy sanded my tongue with panic.

A month into the first term of our lower sixth – I remember it was a day after a thunderstorm, with dust and smoke

179

washed away by the downpour so that the leaves on the rose bushes around the edge of the crazy paving gleamed and the air around them sparkled – Sister Emmanuel addressed the lower sixth at assembly, with an instruction to congregate outside the dining room. Up on the first floor, we clumped together in a nervous group, while other pupils began the day's first lesson.

'She's coming! She's coming!' That was Tracey, who was watching breathlessly. Po-po, po-po went Sister Emmanuel's rectangular heels on the grey linoleum as she advanced towards us. Gravely she held in her hands a large brown envelope.

'Girls, your examination results are here,' the headmistress greeted us, as though it were an ordinary day, and this were an everyday occurrence. Saying this, she dipped her hand into the envelope. It reappeared grasping thin strips of paper. Seema, Angela, Bougainvillea, Tracey, Ntombi: the narrow slips were accepted into clammy palms. My hand closed over the paper the nun proffered, of so little weight in order to keep down the cost of informing millions of teenagers all over the world whether or not they had passed their O-Level examinations, but of such heavy import. Tracey was by now jumping up and down and hugging Bougainvillea.

'I got six! Six ones!' my classmate yelled.

'Congratulations, Tracey,' nodded Sister Emmanuel, and finally conceded this was a special occasion by practically smiling.

'Shame on you!' retorted Bougainvillea. 'Six! What happened! For one reason or another, my girl, I thought you wrote eight subjects.' Then Bougainvillea, shining in a pleased way, held under Tracey's nose her own slip of paper.

'English Language, English Lit. . .' they proceeded down the list, comparing.

'Attention girls!' the headmistress called. 'You may stay up here for fifteen minutes. Then Miss Plato will ring the bell. After that, I am afraid it will be back to your usual routine.' The headmistress glanced at my fist in which my sliver of paper was disintegrating in sweat. Sister gazed at me intensely. 'By then I hope all of you will have summoned up the courage to take a look at your results. I think only in very few cases are they as unpleasant as anyone expects!' With this she strode away to her office, head precise and high, pleased with what was a good year's result in one of the most intelligent classes the convent had enrolled since its founding.

'Look!' This was Ntombi, for on an occasion as important as this, grudges were less important than they had been over the years. 'See!' Ntombi held out her piece of paper. 'Maybe I beat Tracey! Hey!' There was a pleased challenge in her tone. I gazed at the list of ones broken only by one two and one three. 'Just imagine, hey! Maybe Seema too!' There was satisfaction in her face at such grand thoughts. Next, however, she turned to the topic of real interest. 'And you, Tambu? How did you manage?'

My stomach lurched and I felt very sick so that I could not answer. What I knew was that Sister looked at me when she made her remark about small numbers of cases and unpleasantness. The nun's long scrutiny and impassive expression meant I was one of our year's few unfortunate girls whose results were worse than expected.

'Tss!' Ntombi sucked her teeth loudly and sulkily. 'Didn't I show you mine? Go on, ka! It's only fair! Show me!'

'Hey, how did you do?' Tracey bounded up. She did not walk on the ground for the time being, but on the air several inches above it, where she bounced forward in uncontrolled leaps, as though upon a trampoline.

Ntombi forgot me and turned towards our classmate, her face tight and expectant. 'And what?' she demanded immediately. 'You said six ones. And what?'

'Well, I got five, so I don't count,' drawled Bougainvillea. 'I always knew I should have read that soppy love story, *Romeo and Juliet*. So, you six ones women, I'm the umpire! You draw, on the count of three. Right? You show each other what you've got! One-two-three!' Tracey's streaky hair fell over Ntombi's plaits as the two lower sixth formers peered over each other's hands to see what the other was holding. I walked off down Saint Ignatius until I reached the dormitory. But Ntombi and Tracey could follow easily, and so I swerved back into the hall to clatter down the fire-escape. It was not a good route to use because the steps were narrow and metal, which gouged at your heel tendons. But it meant they wouldn't come after me to investigate, or if they did, they would follow slowly.

Where to? I loosened my hold on the piece of paper to ensure it did not fall apart on the way to perusal in a safe destination. Such a place needed to be safe but not too far, as the first lesson of the day was religious knowledge, at which all the lower sixth had mandatory attendance. In no time I reached the classroom, where none of the other girls would come until the very last minute. I sat at my desk and smoothed out the crumpled information. Several readings were necessary to make sure. When I was certain of what I had done, I could not believe it, and my strength drained away, and I rocked at my desk almost fainting.

'Typical,' Tracey complained sourly, I did not know how many minutes later. She, Bougainvillea and Ntombi were grouped round me as the lower sixth waited for Father O'Shea. 'Just look at her! Put it in her mouth, butter, she'd never melt a bit of it!'

'And a good morning to you too!' a light male voice intoned from the door. 'Although I hear you have just received news that makes it a better morning for some than for others!'

Girls stopped prophesying their futures on the basis of the small strips of paper they had a little while ago received, and made their way to their seats. I was glad Father came then. I was still numb. Only my mind was alive and teeming as a swept storeroom infested with cockroaches. Tracey was angry at not having the best results. She was jealous as well of my seven ones and one two, and that made her angrier in addition. What would Mai do when she heard of my astonishing success? Would she be envious and therefore crudely sarcastic? What about Babamukuru, would he become surly and insufferable because of the one subject in which I did not excel? Was that what getting what you wanted did, permeate you with uncompromising, unanswerable questions?

How wonderful those succeeding months were, nevertheless. What progress it was clear our nation was making! Here were Ntombi and I! In spite of our differences we were alike in proudly being top of the O-Level class at Sacred Heart, the most intelligent gathering of young women since the college's founding. As our school was one of the best, we were also top of our nation. We were living proof of the benefits that would accrue to the land if only we were made equal. So almost shyly Ntombi and I took time to smile at each other. In class, in chapel, in the swimming pool, we nodded approval to ourselves of what we had done. It was a powerfully wholesome development. You marvelled, as you might at the moment of conversion, how essential it was to have a core that was happy.

Aggravations surfaced at times. However, they were the result of events that took place beyond the conifers and outside the college gates. Whatever its failings previously, it was clear the convent could not be held responsible for all that took place, especially not the deeds of an offensive government that conceived of people as divisible portions.

The largest of these problems, that resulted from the government, concerned my continued education. Ntombi did not face this new set of difficulties. She often, following her fourth form achievement, looked out over the mountains fearlessly to Mozambique, where people spoke Portuguese. She was studying languages in order to enable communication later between Africans who could not understand each other as they spoke French or English or Spanish or Arabic or Portuguese. I, on the other hand, in order to equip myself for a good degree in Pharmacy, Medicine or Engineering, chose to write science subjects for my A-Level certificate. Being the intelligent young women that we were, the cleverest class of lower sixth in the history of the convent, a dozen of us had chosen this programme. A Chemistry teacher expected to arrive from Europe became so alarmed at newspaper reports of aeroplanes shot down, and oil reserves exploding like carnivals, that he did not sign his contract. Moreover, as a result of unabated mortar attacks, permanent grinding of truckloads of grim, grimy troops through town, the shortage of fuel and the austerity quality of writing paper, many teachers were leaving. The girls in my class reading science subjects were driven each day in the school bus to Umtali Boys High School for their lessons. This secondary school was a government institution, built upon government land, so that my presence there was forbidden. I was instructed by Sister Emmanuel to identify one girl whose notes I was to copy after lessons. Quiet Angela Reid agreed to this unsatisfactory arrangement. Frustrated, as I sat in the library trying to make sense of textbooks without an instructor, and waiting for my classmate's notes, I wondered, was I a Rhodesian, if I could not sit on Rhodesian seats, read formulae from a Rhodesian blackboard and press down upon Rhodesian desks? I went so far, when I stumbled at solving logarithmic equations to plan a boycott of the school bus, an end to Friday excursions through Mubvumbi suburb, to the town hall. The notion of such a salient step, though, caused me such wretchedness and anxiety that I continued my contribution to the war effort. I decided, in a way that I felt was very mature and progressive, to bring Angela a sign of gratitude from the knitting evening instead whenever I had sufficient pocket money to do so.

There was during these evenings still a choice of brownies, mulberry pie, koek sisters and doughnuts, but the coffee was thinned with chicory, and the organisers from the suburbs apologised for the absence of cream. Green and white posters, however, reminded us that walls had ears and encouraged us to spend freely in spite of our deprivations, so as to cheer up the boys in the sticks. 'Rhodesians never die' a long banner above the cake table reassured. The phrase was not punctuated by an exclamation mark: it was a statement of fact. Nobody spoke to me, therefore I had ample time, as I twisted wool about needle points, to examine the message. To me it was a potent proclamation, one that added to my recently replenished sense of *unhu*. Those large green words proved if Rhodesians didn't die, the real content of this war was not about decimating people. So the purpose of warming the troops was not to enable their limbs accurately and swiftly to bring death to other people, but to prevent commendably these others from executing unnameable acts upon the soldiers.

Events at the college contributed to my sense of balance returning. Sister Emmanuel sent a message, one Saturday morning, after our cupboards had been inspected, that we were to come from the dormitory when the bell rang not to study hour but to her office.

'Some of you,' the headmistress nodded when we, from the last dormitory on the junior corridor, stood before her, 'will remember the last time I spoke to you about this matter.' We were, of course, tight with tension. That was the trouble with white people: you never knew truly what they were doing. So we stood motionless until Sister continued by way of explanation, 'We want to offer more places to African girls. I have asked Miss Plato to give each of you above form two a room on the appropriate corridor shortly. You will, by the way, use the bathrooms on the respective corridors.'

How elated we were! Yes, marvellously elated with our industrious efforts. I cannot say how thrilled we were with our progress, combined with the absence of marks against our names on the notice board, that had changed Sister's heart in this way so that we were now rewarded! Finally, Ntombi and I were to occupy St Sophie's, the penultimate most senior corridor in the convent, which since the time of Caroline Nicolls, had not harboured further smokers. Patience was moving to St Joan's, the senior corridor, while Irene, Cynthia and Petronilla, who was now in second form, progressed to St Agatha's, the middle school dormitory. The next morning, up early, I fixed on a veil and padded down to St Ignatius for the last time, even though I was Protestant, over the short distance to give my thanks in the chapel.

The second term came, bringing the event I had laboured for: our annual prize giving. Because of the circumstances of my education, I was not on the honour roll, although Ntombi was. At assembly a fortnight before the end of term, Sister read the list of girls who should go to the Great Hall for practice. 'Young ladies who have worked will soon be rewarded for their application and discipline,' said Sister. I cannot tell you what joy I felt. Pu-pu-rwi a wood pigeon cooed from the jacarandas, and I felt like exploding into joy with it. All the girls looked up at the headmistress expectantly. Sportswomen shuffled nervously, waiting to see if they had won colours. Ntombi nudged me from behind. I put my head down modestly, so that no one would see the furnace of triumph that burned over me.

'As you know,' the headmistress explained the circumstances of the large trophies patterned with leaves that stood in the cabinet in the foyer, 'Michaela Hammon is now at university in Cape Town. We expect her to return to collect the A-Level trophy.' Next the headmistress announced individual subject awards, for girls currently in upper sixth based on their overall sixth-form performance. At last Sister Emmanuel approached the matter for which I was waiting with uncontainable excitement. 'The award for the best O-Level results,' she looked over us and I felt it was time for me to burst with happiness. I did not even know what to do with so much jubilation. 'The award for the best O-Level results is awarded this year to a very deserving and hard-working young lady,' continued Sister. 'This young lady,' she concluded, 'is also a champion swimmer. As the Young Ladies' College of the Sacred Heart undertakes to nurture well-rounded human beings, the O-Level trophy goes to Tracey Stevenson.' There was a commotion up at the front where Tracey stood, as girls patted her shoulder. Sister called for order and read the rest of the list, including sixty girls on the honour roll. I did not look up any more. There was no need as my name was not recorded.

I read Angela's notes that day and comprehended even less than usual.

Tap-tap. It was after prep that evening. As seniors, living on the senior corridor, we no longer went down to recreation in the hall. Instead, we had a common room, but I opted, this evening, to lie on my bed in the dark. Tap-tap. The knock came again. I said nothing and did not move. Motion was fantasy in the state I was in. Certainly, I would not talk to anyone.

'Come on! Open up! You're in there, isn't it?' It was Ntombi.

Reluctantly I got up to undo the latch. She came in but didn't put the light on. The rooms were small. Checked curtains fell over small windows secured with burglar bars that threw shadows of crosses onto the material. A desk, straight chair and wash basin were crammed in besides the iron bedstead. 'Let us sit together,' Ntombizethu said. I moved over to give her space. She sat, leaving some distance between us. We both started pulling fluff off the bedspread in the dim light that came in from the corridor.

'Why don't you ask?' she suggested finally. 'Even if, well, if there was something wrong with the results, you ought to know, shouldn't you, if something was wrong, and they didn't tell you?'

I felt I was strewn over the patio still with the shock of it, this unknowable, eternal thing about too many Europeans. 'It's all right for you!' I hissed, savouring the bitterness and letting it out at last to spit at her. 'You've won something. You're on the honour roll. You'll be walking up that aisle! Nothing's been taken away from you, so you haven't lost anything!'

The breath she succeeded in drawing was short and annoyed. My stomach tightened half in anticipation, half in shock, at the memory of my angry limbs upon her flesh, the blackness of skin scraped out from under my fingernails. I could not cry, although it was time to. I could not because it was too late. Ntombi, who had wept with fear and grief while all of us watched her, Ntombi commented, 'Tambu, you have to stop. Now. You have to stop it.' She made the point quietly.

Half-hearted, desperate with one half for peace, with the other part for fury, I spat, 'Stop what? Don't talk to me! Don't talk to me about the knitting! They're for their hands! And for their feet! People's hands and feet! Can you hear that! Do you hear me, Ntombi!'

'Don't you want to find out what happened about the O-Levels?' my classmate returned to the reason for her visit. 'I know I do. We can go together if you want to.'

'Ha!' I snorted with great disgust. 'Now, who are you? Bishop Muzorewa, Ndabaningi Sithole? Robert Mugabe, hey, or Herbert Chitepo?'

'Let's do it!' urged Ntombi. 'You can't let all this just happen like that! Come on! Tomorrow, hey? Let's do it.'

I could not tell her, this girl who had not earned something and had it taken away, who was going to walk up to the stage for achieving the honour roll, how fearful I was that I deserved it, that I had not committed sufficiently to heart enough pages from *Romeo and Juliet*. There *must* have been a mistake in the results, otherwise, as my uncle had pointed out concerning the report Sister Emmanuel once wrote, the headmistress would not have done it. Worse, I whipped myself more, I had enjoyed six months of good results and the *unhu* that accompanied it as an impostor. How afraid I was that in fact I was worth nothing. If I did not know, I could at least dream I should have been the rightful owner of the silver O-Level trophy. When I looked at it in the cabinet I could superimpose upon it my name instead of Tracey's. I didn't want to take away the dream. I turned to the wall and stretched out. Ntombi watched. She did not insist. After a little while, spilling fluff balls on the floor, she left in disappointment.

10

It was hard to look at Tracey. But she was herself, as always. She blushed at Bougainvillea's inconsiderate brashness in the lower sixth common room, and passed on, in the dining hall, the broccoli and fish in white sauce that did not appeal to her taste so that I could pile generous helpings onto my plate; for the diet at the convent had not changed in the intervening period. Ntombi, having given up chocolate powder soon after she pulled out the troops' green knit-wear from my cupboard, clenched her teeth and breathed deeply when I stretched out my arm to receive the dishes. Nevertheless, as I accepted what Babamukuru was able to give me, it was clear to me how it was also appropriate to accept this generosity. Graciously, with a smile that appeared more naturally from occasion to occasion, I did so. Intermittently, without doubt, I became morose. At such times I prodded myself to consider all that was done in my favour. I took solace in the fact that while my class-mate, Tracey, was also studying science subjects, as these lessons were conducted at Umtali Boys High School, I was fortunately spared any outraged feelings that might result from sitting close to her in class.

On the day of prize-giving, the hall was magnificently transformed with awe-inspiring decorations that hung and stretched and stood triumphantly in the burgundy and gold school colours. Bowls of deep red dahlias together with roses sprayed in gold glowed upon gleaming gilt flower stands. The heavy calico stage curtains were replaced with ones of a velvet so deep it looked like a pool of beckoning, endless waters. Streamers swung from the gym ropes to the walls, and the gardeners had been up on ladders the past week dusting the window sills and blinds, and tying on bunting. Half an hour before the ceremony began parents were pouring in through the side doors. The back doors opened out onto the patio after a short walk past the classrooms. In the assembly ground a sumptuous reception, with small animals on spits and foods from across distant waters which Ntombi and I only saw during prize giving, were in preparation, so it was necessary to cordon off this area.

Inside the hall, the atmosphere was so excited people did not need to be told to be quiet. Proud parents sat holding their breath. Mothers pointed out one gorgeous flower arrangement after another to each other in whispers. Fathers folded their arms to pretend it was a women's affair, but beamed complacently. People whose daughters had not done quite so well caught the spirit of expectation that swirled everywhere in and out of the wonderful decorations. The prize winners sat at the very front. The little first formers there had places directly under Sister Emmanuel's eye. Solemn lower sixth formers who would receive copper shields were seated further back. In the first chair in this section sat Tracey. Last amongst the girls who excelled were the most senior, the upper sixth girls, in spite of their contentment, already drooping in their seats, sad and nostalgic for this was their final prize-giving, and who knew if they would fare so well out in the larger world. Girls who had not excelled were tucked behind the sixth form winners, far away from the proceedings, so that mediocrity was well hidden in an unremarkable situation. Here, at the end of the sixth form section, I shrunk into my seat. Behind the school were the teachers, and Miss Plato, although dressed in white, had pressed into her earlobes for the occasion a pair of small cross-shaped silver earrings.

The guitar club was arranged on one side of the stage. D-ra-mmm! Sister Catherine thrummed the strings of her instrument, filling the hall with welcoming music. Tapping heartily with one foot, the nun darted glances from side to side at the group of head-nodding, finger-snapping students.

'This land is your land! This land is my land!' the guitar club started singing. Backs straightened. Faces glowed. Eyes gleamed, or looked beyond the hall walls, far away, and backs were purposefully turned to the Mozambican mountains. Here and there in the audience, some lips curled into small, half-distressed, half-determined smiles. But we, the girls! Ah, we! Jubilant with youth and good fortune, when the chorus came, 'This world was made for you and me!' bellowed the school.

'As I was walking, that ribbon of highway,' came Bougainvillea's lead. Our classmate had a voice like an opera singer when she could be bothered to use it. 'I saw above me an endless skyway! And down below me. . .' she couldn't keep a slightly cynical and bored look from her face, '. . . a golden va-a-lleee!'

'This land was made for you and me!' By now the parents too were singing, and the notes rioted up to the ceiling.

When this number was finished, Bougainvillea stepped forward. All of the school stood up. A hush descended over everyone as Bougainvillea took a breath that went on and on, and swelled her chest until you feared there would be an explosion. But the melody that came out was full of grace and control. Behind, in the last row of school, you could hear the sound of fumbling in pockets, followed by that of tissues unfurling. There were sniffs. Surely among the meritorious young women, Paula, this year's head-girl's eyes were reddening too, for here, at the back, a dozen undistinguished sixth formers were weeping.

'Beside Cross Kopje's gentle slopes! 'Neath fair Rhodesian skies!' declared Bougainvillea, her eyes looking inward now, as though towards a truth hidden in the notes she rendered. 'There I first saw my Sacred Heart, in stately beauty rise!'

'Sacred Heart! Sacred Heart!' we all joined in. Our voices trembled and resonated, brimming with all that our years at the convent had instilled in us. 'We give our hearts to you! And pray that we will loyal be! And to your teachings true!'

Wa-a-a! The audience broke into spontaneous applause, and the ceiling itself seemed to answer, as though the hall were a gigantic loudspeaker that sent the message of our song out beyond the city and over the nation. We were so awestruck we forgot to sit down. We only did so when Sister Catherine thrummed again and the guitar club started up, this time with one of the tuneful nun's favourite pop hymns.

During the last verse of this next song, Sister Emmanuel ascended to the stage. She held her back and head so regally it was impossible not to admire her. Peremptory yet poised in her dark blue tailored suit, with her hair gleaming glossily, she emanated power and accomplishment from every pore. Ah, I could not help thinking as I watched the headmistress position herself squarely behind the lectern, if I kept on, if I put my head down and simply continued, I too would turn into such an authoritative and potent woman. Me, Tambudzai Sigauke from the village, ending up as compelling as Sister Emmanuel! It was such a wonderful thought, I resolved once more to do nothing else but what I should.

Soon Sister had the entire hall feeling as calm and satisfied as the well-being she exuded. She stood for a while, observing everybody and smiling a welcoming, well-satisfied smile. After a short greeting, she approached the sensitive matters that affected us all in a marvellously encouraging and reassuring way. These were difficult times, the headmistress pointed out, as a result of which she was glad the school had done so well, when many institutions had been overwhelmed. Praise was particularly due, Sister said, to the girls who had remained sufficiently focused in our disturbed times, to excel in their respective fields. With that she called upon the guest of honour, who wore gloves and a large white hat, whom I believed I recognised as the lady who stood behind the money tin at the tea table in the town hall, but I was uncertain, because with white people at such a distance you could never tell properly.

The first polished copper shield was picked up. As I sat, my stomach turned and my hands sweated. When more prizes were distributed and we came nearer to the O-Level trophy, I tried to build up a numbing vibration by clapping longer and harder than anyone else. In the intervals, though, while trophies were passed over and hands were shaken, I imagined rushing up to the stage myself when the best O-Level result was called out. But of course it was Tracey who walked there and curtsied before she clutched the trophy on which I had dreamed so often of seeing my name inscribed. Emptiness opened up a hole in my stomach. I continued clapping and smiling, doing both as hard as possible. But I felt my classmate contained me in that goblet as a magician contains a genie in a bottle. It was as though with each step she took to her seat, her hand on the lid to prevent any spillage, she transported me far away from where I intended.

As Tracey returned to her place, Ntombizethu twisted around, as though to have her gaze touch me. She was doing that a lot these days. She had taken to staring at me mournfully, and with some reproach, as though she had some claim on my actions in spite of which I had failed her in some significant attribute. Nevertheless, at the same time as she looked at me with that reproving expression, she attempted to push in beside me in files, in front of the dining room, at assembly, or on the way to mass. I detested this behaviour. Worse, when Ntombizethu was close, the reproach gradually transformed itself into pity, as if she wished to protect me. But I smelt something terrible and destroyed in her too, that she was trying to discard in this fashion. Inevitably I flinched and shrunk away. This afternoon in the hall, I drew my uniform in tightly as though to reduce contact, although my classmate was at a distance. The other issue was that you were bigger when you gathered close together like that, and all those things that made events take place in the manner as they did, grew as a result of this visibility, more remarkable. I turned to look miserably out to the patio, driven to risk going to the toilet and not coming back. But what a vain notion that was! I did not have the will power to thread my way through these other people. Besides, once you'd filed in and were seated, you were not meant to move, and I had resolved I would move ahead by behaving as I was instructed.

Ntombi raised her eyebrows distinctly, pointed to her chest and then to the door before she mouthed 'Me too!' I pretended not to see, instead pressed my lips together without answering. Ntombi sighed. She folded her arms and looked down, while I stared grimly at the back of her plaits.

At last the torture was over. Sister Catherine's voice chimed out, 'Oh Lord we thank you!' Ntombi and I filled our chests, opened our throats and let out large sounds. That way you heard, but you did not feel. You just concentrated on the vibration of the music, and goodness music always spread throughout a body.

When there was no music to ward off despair – in the dead of night when the ghosts of angry, dissatisfied nuns slid up to our beds, or when I looked up in the library from the grip of an insoluble equation, dreading Angela padding forward with more of the same – I scarcely knew anymore who or where I was. I saw I would never find the route back to the place I had aimed at, yet I could not see where I had taken a wrong turning. For surely Sacred Heart could not be wrong. This was the place where every ambitious young woman wanted to be educated, the college to which all good and caring parents wished to send their daughters. Down the rough concrete stairs beside the hall, which you could see through the library window when you sat reading, was the secret spot where I used to memorise for my O-Levels, accompanied by the silent and therefore essentially truthful *chongololos*. It made me feel cold to look in that direction. It gave me a churning in my stomach. For that spot, and all the recitation that had gone on there, said either Sacred Heart or I did not possess the attributes that confer upon a party virtue and deserving. It was me against Sacred Heart, a scale of struggle similar to David and Goliath. But I believed in the college with a practically ferocious tenacity. I may have thought differently, but I didn't believe it. Belief prevailed. This school that formed us was an early and important post on the road to better living. You believed the signs to this superior destination were placed along the way by those who knew and wished you a safe journey, so that all you had to do was follow. Oh, how diligently I had followed, had obeyed the imperatives put out for me without question – save for that episode, of course, of the toilets on St Ignatius' corridor, and for the occurrence of the pulling of sheets; but those incidents embarrassed me so much that I disowned my actions and treated them as aberrations. Could I conceive of standing up and looking around me in a different manner? I could not. Truly, I could not imagine that I should have looked around me in another way, and analysed what was taking place from my own perspective. For to do that, one requires a point of view, but it is hard to stand upon the foundations you are born with in order to look forward, when that support is bombarded by all that is around until what remains firm and upright is hidden beneath rubble and ruins.

In this state, it did not help very much when I tried to learn how to progress further by applying the general, hitherto useful, concepts of *unhu*. The thing about *unhu* was that you couldn't go against the grain on your own. You weren't a clan, a people with a poem of praise, or a boast of war that petrified enemies. *Unhu* required an elder aunt, or a *sahwira* – someone you were related to not by blood but by absolute respect, liking and understanding – to go forward to the authorities in order to present your case, showing that what disturbed you was not the flighty whim of one badly brought-up individual. What *unhu* prescribed for one who was moving against the larger current was to come to one's senses, realise the sovereignty of the group and work to make up for the disappointment. Then you would become somebody, as more *unhu* would accrue.

This, then, in the weeks and months that followed the prize-giving ceremony of my lower sixth year, is what I tried to do. I turned towards my A-Level examinations and applied myself to succeeding there, but I could not concentrate on the lessons Angela returned with from Umtali Boys' High School. My classmate did her best with explanations and diagrams, but it made no difference how often, nor how patiently she went over the lessons. Nor could I relate this to having been demoralised, to having exhausted myself in my quest for recognition and a trophy so that I was now depressed and discouraged, empty as an old husk. Nor did any of this matter! In spite of my good intentions and exertion, everything was disintegrating.

How unfortunate it all was! To make matters worse, in the euphoria I soared into when the fourth form results were announced and I discovered I was the most intelligent girl in my class, I had signed up for more subjects than usual: Mathematics, Biology, Chemistry, and, in addition to these sciences, a fourth paper, English. This was the subject I had obtained a two in, and I was determined, when the lists were taken, to obtain an A in that in the A-Level round, as well as in the other three subjects. Wearily I applied myself. I worked longer hours in the library with my back to the window and never went down to the sunwashed spot, with a blanket to make the pebbled ground more comfortable, where warmth radiated back up from the concrete and the *chongololos* crawled quietly; the place where I had devoured my O-Level texts like a cow eating grass to be regurgitated as cud upon the examination paper.

I grew red-eyed and irritable, reading through the night in the little room on St Sophie's corridor, until the letters trooped off the page like small black ants, and I stooped to pick them up, only to find I was in a doze without hope of any real sleep, and I forced myself back to learning. So it went on each night until the mortar attacks on some tea or tobacco farm or wattle plantation beyond the mountains ceased their muffled attempts at murder, and the peaceful grey coo of the doves, soft as dawn, suggested tentatively 'Ask! Ask father!'

The days dissolved into these anxious stretches between dusk and dawn, for bed was where I frequently ended up after breakfast, as there were no classes to keep me active and all I had to do was wait for Angela to return with the day's quota of knowledge. Exhausted from hunting after rest, I frequently sat at the desk in my room and pulled out my knitting needles. But nor did this occupational therapy have any advantage. The dark green wool was the colour of glossy leaves in shadow, and when I bent so that my own shadow from the light through the high little window fell upon the glove, it looked like the fingers were severed and, in the darkest patches, that blood was upon it. The energy with which I slipped the stitches waned. Soon I could not whip myself over to the parking bay beneath the jacarandas to climb into the burgundy school bus to the hall. Several times I arrived to see the bus pulling out from under the trees. Not once did I wave or call, but watched it leave indifferently. I did not care now what the girls in the bus thought or suffered anymore and after several occasions of missing the bus, I stuffed the unfinished gloves, the wool and everything in the rubbish bin in the classroom. I felt guilty and worried that now that I did not care I was giving in to evil. For wasn't that a general rule known to all human beings everywhere! Love your neighbour as yourself! I am well if you are well also! But I could not anymore find a good reason to do the knitting.

Now on Friday evenings, times were solitary. You had to find things to do to take your attention from the thudding that flung the lives of people to the sky, like the thunderbolts of a mad god. Down St Sophie's filtered other sounds of the butcher's carnival that raged in pursuit of Rhodesia's diverse antagonistic freedoms. 'Daddy's gone to fight for the green and white!' trilled Gwyneth Ashley Robbin. After prep on the last school day of the week, with time on their hands and despair straining at the heart like an unknown, untameable animal at a leash, the lower sixth girls filled the common room with familiar homely sounds: the clink-clink of metal tapping on china, the singing of a kettle rising to the boil, the hiss of simmering milk splashing onto the little two-plate stove the college provided. Then coffee granules were beaten with sugar to a cream. The delicious foam which frothed up when the scalded milk was added calmed as the sixth formers enjoyed the new national pop on Radio 1, the European station.

For the first time you saw differences deep enough to cause partition amongst your classmates. There was, amongst the girls who lounged on the sofas and thumbed through copies of *Fair Lady* on Fridays, a tightening against the girls who every week knitted spells to dissolve bullets and ward off shrouds with the city's women. All the same, I felt strange in the common room, so that I did not go there often. 'What sings and flies into mountains?' Bougainvillea began it. One set of girls repeated the joke with giggles that bordered harshly on loss of control when the young wartime singer's jet crashed into a cliff, while the remainder looked on in frigid disapproval. But there was something indefinable yet absolute about our classmates' togetherness, and in the sharpness of their scorn, unexpressed, that was repulsive and exclusive.

'Come on!' Ntombi was unlocking the latch to her room on St Sophie's with her key. This was a few weeks after I slid into not boarding the bus to the city hall, and no longer contributed to the troops' comfort. Patience lolled beside her, one hip resting on the door frame. These days, you saw the youngsters from the last dormitory on St Ignatius moving in a hunched, shoving group along the junior corridor, like small antelopes. These two seniors, too, felt the need to congregate and form a constellation.

'Ehe!' Patience agreed. 'Come on, Tambu, *kani!* Join us.'

Tracey, walking up the corridor, coffee mug in hand, stopped to slap palms with Ntombi. 'Yes, Nnntombi!' She only prolonged the first sound and didn't, like the rest of them, put a vowel in front of it. 'Nnn-tombi' was what Tracey said. 'Patience, yes, hey Patience!' grinned our classmate. This I dreaded, this shutting out by coming over, for it was their will and did not allow you to move over and join them. Ntombi observed Tracey open the common room door to a bombardment of music. She raised her eyebrows while Patience looked sideways at me. I waited and waited until the common room door was closed, before I accepted that Tracey had not slapped palms with me.

'Sit with us for a minute?' Ntombi asked. But now I was angry. Tracey turned her back on me when I had forborne to make the slightest trouble about the trophy and the O-Level results; meanwhile Ntombi, who desired our classmate's exposure, was the one whom Tracey now slapped palms with! So I was distressed with both my classmates for their betrayal and duplicity. In addition, I was outraged with Ntombi and Patience who wished to claim me, now that I had stopped knitting, for their uselessness, gregariousness and constant fecklessness. Moreover, I could not abide the way they thought if I wasn't for knitting, I was for pointless sitting around and achieving nothing. These girls, defining the ground on which I stood! Yet they didn't have the slightest sense of my direction. If I wasn't for the town hall, it didn't mean anything: could they not understand a person came to a point where a person was against everything? Besides, once Ntombi banged the door to her room and closed it after her, the two girls' voices climbed to that sort of raucous chatter reminiscent with forests. The hall cracked with the slapping of palms. Then there were shrieks of laughter, as though St Sophie's was besieged by an army of inebriated banshees. All this with only two young women! What would happen if we were three was something that did not bear thinking of! 'I'm doing quotations,' I informed the two seniors after they issued their invitation. They were now waiting to enter the room, smiling pleasantly to make me join them. '*Julius Caesar.*' I gestured down the corridor to my door, delivering the wave so it was at the same time both self-deprecating and superior.

You had to efface yourself so that people did not think you thought you were designed in wiser detail, and with greater abilities, than they were. At the same time, you needed to know how to rise above their worthless ebullience. It would not be ignorable lapses – a prefix or suffix injected excitedly here or there. These seniors were planning to spend the entire evening trying futilely to turn back time by speaking Shona. Just imagine! Inviting a mark for refusing to accept which language was allowed and which was not when you were as far as the sixth form! We had, by this level, escaped Miss Plato's patrols, but even in the sanctuary of St Sophie's corridor roamed prefects. The upper sixth office bearers particularly did not practise solidarity due to our common form ranking, preferring instead to emphasise the difference between upper and lower. Those girls who were to leave had little against inserting crosses beside lower sixth names on the notice board. I was not going to identify with a group that spoke in the only language, out of all the ones that were known at the school, which was forbidden.

'Next time!' Ntombi promised as I went off. She was taking English as well, alongside French and Afrikaans. 'Tambu!' Her voice started rising in a way that pushed me forward faster, in proportion to its pitch and intensity. 'I'll be there next time! I'll come and help you with those quotations!'

'He-he-de!' Twa! Laughter bounced down the corridor, followed by the crack of palms slapped together. 'Hu-uri!' Even after thirty minutes, the two girls' hilarity split the drone of the common room music. There was no concentrating on *Julius Caesar*, for I was puzzled. What did Ntombi and Patience have, that I did not, that they laughed over? What made Ntombi and Patience descend for sessions in the last dormitory on Saint Ignatius' corridor, which we had so longed to escape? I was vindicated when, one morning at assembly, Sister Emmanuel asked the girls to damp the number of decibels that emanated from that dormitory.

A week later, Ntombi kept her word. She began to come to study in my room, even if she reserved Fridays and Saturdays for the strident gaiety that glazed the eyes with light and left the girls strangely satiated.

Sunday was the day she preferred to spend time with me. Within a couple of weeks I looked forward to her visits, which continued into our upper sixth year, and we both moved over to St Joan's corridor. Eventually, I told my classmate it was my turn now to carry my books across to her bedroom. It was a big move for someone locked in the misery that I was tied in, to take this step. So I was horribly deflated, one particular evening, when each knock, every rattle of the handle, as I stood before her door, a pile of books in the crook of my arm, was answered with silence. Some of her neighbours were the sort of girls one could talk to. Angela was opposite and Bougainvillea two doors down. Neither of them knew where Ntombi had disappeared to after supper. I decided it was worse to go down to St Ignatius to see if she preferred to spend time speaking an illegal language over studying, so I braved anxiety and put my head into the senior common room. Tracey volunteered she had seen Ntombi make her way to the telephone booth at the back of the classrooms. 'I bet,' our classmate grinned, 'it's her boyfriend!'

Boyfriend! Here I was struggling to find a life for myself and already had to contend, in addition to stolen trophies and relatives who would never again be whole, with the rather smelly, completely pointless competition of male adolescents. Having pulled on my nightgown I tied my scarf too tightly, felt a cutting headache come on and quickly undid it.

Go-go-go! came a knock as I squirted paste onto my toothbrush. The handle descended impatiently before there was time to answer. The girls debated again and again: was it better to have a strange object come in through the door or through the window? I now did not lock my door to enable flight when necessary. Ntombi stepped in. She stood in the doorway, inhaling deeply, which made her eyes glisten red in the light that filtered in through the chinks between the curtains.

'Hence! Home you idle creatures,' I began, exchanging the toothbrush for the small leather-bound Shakespeare, which Maiguru had lifted from the shrine for her academic books in her bedroom, and bequeathed to me in her excitement that I, as she had done, was studying this old English literature. Holding the drama out to my visitor, '. . . get you home. Is this a holiday?' I demanded, reciting.

Ntombi swished past.

'I've decided,' I said grandly, 'to simply begin at the beginning. I might as well just memorise it all.' To demonstrate, I went on, '. . . you ought not walk / Upon a labouring day without the sign. . .'

The words tasted good upon my tongue, seasoned with the memory of my O-Level triumph. And while it was unlikely that I would out-memorise Tracey at science subjects, I was sufficiently revitalised now by the weekly sessions with Ntombi to believe I might manage to capture, this time round, the English trophy.

Not responding, Ntombizethzu sat at the desk with an arm propped on the back of the chair. She rested her cheek on a limp fist at first. Some moments later, she put her forehead down on the desk edge.

'Speak, what trade art thou!' I proceeded, waiting for my classmate's smile of awe at the prodigiousness of my memory to provide me with the approbation that I required so ravenously.

'Hm!' Her breath came out harshly but she was still, and otherwise quiet, her eyes trained on the ground. 'Hm!' she grunted again, and now when the sound forced its way out, her chest heaved as though she were wrenched by convulsions. Finally Ntombi looked up, crossing her arms upon her chest like a vice. 'Tss! Ha!' Her lips curled back and she smiled revoltingly, shaking her head. Naturally, I supposed she was laughing at me, so that I stopped reciting in mid-sentence. For it was incomprehensible and astonishing treachery, where months of friendship were simply a ploy to humiliate me with this new, malevolent laughter!

'Asi, ya! He-he! Ya!' The chuckling went on. Ntombi looked up with hate glaring from her eyes like a demon. 'Have you ever seen it, Tambu! He-e! Have you ever even thought of such evil?' The sound that tore from her now was a sob. 'Iih! Hi-hi! Could you even think of it, holding its feet, upside down! Putting its head in water! A baby!

'She was only nine months old!' Her voice was as broken as the little body. 'She was already full of water, so they had already drowned her. But they still hit her on the rock, as if they were threshing *rukweza*!'

The elder siblings! The terrorists! I slumped onto the bed, appalled and hardly breathing.

'Hi-hi! They said my aunt is feeding terrorists! My aunt! Oh, my poor aunt!' cried my classmate. 'Yes, she talked, because of what they did to the baby. But it was too late. My little cousin was broken, just broken! Hi-hi-hi. Then they caught *vana mukoma*. Nobody is talking about what they did to them! Oh, Tambu *kani*!' Ntombi's anguish clawed out, making me draw back towards the wall. 'Then my aunt killed herself, because when it's like that, you'll never live. But they came back and now, at the homestead my *sekuru, mbuya, babamunini*, cousins! No one is alive! Baba was going there, with Mai. But there was a road block. The only reason Mai and Baba are alive is because those army men said they had to go back!'

We needed to grasp each other's hand and let the tears fall without knowing whose fingers were wetted by whose grief. I believe we were too young and not sufficiently pained for this; there is a curve, you come to the summit and then climb down it. Ntombi and I were still climbing. She shuddered in a deep, halting breath. 'Masters of life!' she cackled. 'Doctors of life! That's what those people think they are!' She grinned like a skull. 'Tss! What they are is doctors of death!'

'Daddy's gone to fight for the green and white!' The pop music strained down the corridor. I lay back on the pillow, feeling desperately tired. Ntombi sat motionless. When the song was over she shook her head.

Then she looked up again with her red eyes. 'Blood. . .' she began her lips working up and down, with passion, but her voice soft. 'Blood,' repeated Ntombi inaudibly quietly, under the music, 'and destruction shall be so in use, / And dreadful objects so familiar, / That mothers shall but smile when they behold / their infants quarter'd with the hands of war.' Coming to the end of her quotation she asked, 'Shall I go on? Do you still want to do it? And maybe it's better that we do this Shakespeare now, Tambu. Otherwise, what it says there, otherwise would we have known! But Tambu, now we know that we must stop smiling!'

I nodded, clutching at the words and what they would do for me at my A-Level examination, and not the sense she spoke of. In a moment, faintly, tra-la-la-la la-la-la-la, the news march started up in the common room.

In order to hold onto self control, I reminded myself it was only the radio. On television you saw what the radio anchor talked about: flies buzzing around pus-drenched holes that previously saw, while the nostrils beneath flared futilely and the lips moved, so that you thought they were praying because you could not hear them speaking. In any case, no one held the microphone to the mangled mouths.

Only the anchor turned round and told you in the last sentence. There were people on the television in cattle trucks, with their hands tied to the rail high above their heads in the gesture of the praying hands on copper plaques that were sold at Meikles and OKs and Kingstons, then their heads drooping at an improbable angle between shoulders whose blades flared like wings, all of it making you remember paintings in library books of Christ at his flogging. Preferring not to see, still you searched the images called reporting, because if it wasn't Mr Swanepoel, it was your sister, and if not her, it was Ntombi's *mainini*.

Ntombi and I did not talk to each other much after that evening, not even when we sat together in the dining room, or within whispering distance in the English classroom. Our study sessions all but stopped, as though she had released some fetid load in my room so that it was not any longer a place of comfort for her to visit. She spent more of her free hours on the junior corridor, and when she came back from there she drooped with exhaustion. I did not care particularly. I frequently exhibited strange behaviour, yet I could not make sense of the unfamiliar seizures. It took me an hour to master a soliloquy. If I so much as looked out over the pine and wattle plantations, two minutes later every word was forgotten. When I began again from the top, I succumbed to fits of weeping.

11

You craved relief when it was like that; a way out of the world Europeans wove in a pattern that was so exhausting, escape to a destination far from here, where people were benevolent and gracious, and by consensus everyone, women and teenagers too, were included. But a girl's fantasies are ineffective. Days proceeded without many options.

There were a lot of students who could not go home in the year of our A-Levels, because their homes had been taken over. Occupied the girls said. The 'Voice of Zimbabwe' on Babamukuru's radio, broadcasting from Maputo said liberated. So there was more whispering and there were more tears than usual in the common room that end of term, when we left Sacred Heart not to return to it. Angela, who was head girl that year, and Tracey were returning to bungalows in Hatfield and Mabelreign, far away from the smells they grew up with and knew, and their girlhood memories.

'Tambudzai,' Babamukuru said when he came to pick me up. In a sort of subdued celebratory mood, my uncle had allowed my aunt to come with him. 'Tambudzai, you have finished your A-Levels,' he nodded contentedly to the back in the rear view mirror as we drove through Umtali, past the post office where the queues were no longer segregated. 'You have done well. You have made us proud, my daughter! Yes, parents become very proud when they have such a daughter as you are!'

'And Nyasha,' ventured Maiguru, seeking to have the child she bore acknowledged.

But my uncle was sufficiently engrossed in praising me so that he did not hear her. 'Yes, you are a wonderful daughter, Tambudzai!' he added, delighted. 'I am sure that since your O-Levels were so excellent, your A-Level results, when they arrive, will not disappoint us.'

A few metres before the Inyanga junction, a roadblock was set on the tarmac like a clot in a vital vessel. People spilled all over the place, around battered buses which had been cautioned to the roadside with rifle butts, and around ancient Peugeots that still ran border routes to Watsomba and Nyanga, roads infested with *mbambaira*; thus we laughed at war as though it were plenty by calling land-mines sweet potatoes.

'Good afternoon! Good afternoon, officer, sir!' Baba-mukuru remained cheerful because he had not been paying the army trucks much attention as he spoke of my achievements.

A man in camouflage, with a ruddy face looked in. 'Chitupa?' he demanded. Babamukuru fumbled in his pocket, taking a few well-calculated seconds longer than necessary before he handed over the bit of thick paper. The soldier looked at it and turned it over, remarking as though to himself, 'Oh, so you're the one. You're the headmaster, Sigauke.' Maiguru clenched her hands in her lap.

'Yes,' Babamukuru nodded. He added, 'Yes, sir!' and continued smiling.

'I'll have a look at your boot,' the patroller decided.

Babamukuru drew a breath to speak. Another soldier, a weapon like a third arm folded across his chest, walked up behind the first. Babamukuru regarded the newcomer for a second, then opened his door and walked to the back.

'What's in there?' the patroller demanded, eyeing my suitcase and metal tuck box.

'It's hers.' Babamukuru nodded at me. He swallowed and continued reluctantly, 'Sir, we are just bringing her back home from school. It is the end of term there. They don't have a timetable like we do over there at the mission. For them it is already the holidays.'

The officer walked round to investigate who was in the car. 'Oh, yes, Sacred Heart!' His gaze rested on the badge on my blazer pocket. His eyes narrowed as he pondered. 'That's a good school to go to,' he made up his mind. I felt myself exhaling. 'You're giving your daughter a fine education!' The pass was handed back to Babamukuru. The soldiers stepped back while Babamukuru negotiated the car once more onto the highway. Two young men, being frisked with their hands against a bus, twisted their heads to see who came away so easily from this roadblock that had caught them.

Maiguru regarded the youths as they dwindled to dark specks in the distance. 'M-m!' she breathed with foreboding. She observed the scene for a little longer before she turned to her husband. 'From what I could see, I didn't recognise them. I don't think they are anyone who knows us.'

'No!' Babamukuru agreed by dint of the negative which he so frequently employed when speaking to Maiguru. 'No, they are not familiar to me either, Mai. There is no need to worry.' My aunt relaxed slowly. Babamukuru went on before she could finish unclenching. 'Even if those young men are people who are watching what is going on, what have they seen that can be told to anyone? The soldiers also made me get out of the car. I opened the boot. What does it matter if then they did not want to search me. No, Mai!' My uncle spoke with great and deliberate conviction, which simultaneously was sad and wistful so that it made Maiguru once more tight and nervous. 'No, Mai!' my uncle emphasised. 'It is not what they see. It is something else that makes people say these others are sell outs!'

'That is it! There are people,' shivered Maiguru, 'who feel they must make these things matter! They make things like that important. Some people, as we know Baba, some people do that. Those are the people who talk a lot, too freely everywhere, going pwe-pwe even about what is not, so they can fill the ears and close the eyes of other people.'

'Nobody's eyes are closed, Mai!' At his wife's persistence with the matter, something sensitive in Babamukuru grew offended. 'So if the eyes are not closed,' he answered my aunt curtly, 'and people can see, what can people be looking for to keep bringing up things that do not help? We do not want, Mai, also to start talking too freely! Not everybody can manage the things which go on today when these things are told to them!'

'Anyway,' Maiguru vacillated between conciliation and retreating to a milder offensive, 'it is true, that bus was going to Salisbury. Those two cannot have much to do in these parts. All the same, Baba,' she finally insisted, 'my feeling is, sometimes one has to talk about these things. Now is a good time to do it, when no one who should not be is listening.'

214

'I do not see the point of it, Mai!' objected Babamukuru. 'I do not see why you just want to bring about bad feelings! Mai, that is not what a good woman does, nurturing those kinds of spirits that pull down families.'

'Asi, Baba!' Maiguru's voice fluttered towards exasperation. 'Who hasn't got one of these families you are talking about? Are you saying it is only one family that has worth? Even if you are talking of totems, that one of yours, that wild cat, haven't I borne it? So what I am saying is, my family also matters!'

Maiguru clenched her hands in her lap again and looked down at the interlaced fingers. It was clear, because of this talk of totems, that the argument involved me in some connection. I looked out at the bare, blackened hills where leaves no longer grew after the army destroyed the elder siblings' cover. It was hardly better than listening to my relatives speaking in their undecipherable code and knowing something dreadful and bare as bones was the cause of their simmering antagonism.

'Anyway,' went on my aunt, after we had travelled another kilometre, speaking increasingly indignantly, 'aren't you bonga yourself! If something happens to that bonga, who will anyone call? Where will they look? And don't we know things are happening these days? Just look at what happened just next door, at Samhungu's!' In a belligerent, disillusioned rush, Maiguru flung out the name of our village neighbours.

I pressed my nose up against the window, willing myself not to take in and remember anything. Oh no! Not Samhungu! Samhungu's place was closer than the guerrilla's clearing. How many lost their blood, drained over the floors they slept on? How many limbs filled with maggots lay in the earth the rest of the family tilled, and were these parts as large as Netsai's, larger, or as minute as Ntombi's cousin's? Trying to shut it out made it worse, caused too much thinking. I tried to look for familiar sights. But the kiosk at Alpha Estate where Babamukuru bought oranges for me was not there any more, so I ended up wondering whether the farmer still existed, or whether the remains of him had been dragged away for a ritual of retribution. It was a terrible thing to have in mind: that people did what they did, just as I had gone knitting, and the troops frisked people who boarded buses, because of fundamental convictions. So it was much better to attend to Maiguru's bitterness and distress. At least I could ask her, later, for clarification.

'So I think she must be told! She isn't a child!' Maiguru was continuing, quietly but determinedly closing in on her position. 'In case anything happens, or tries to happen! Isn't it better to know what will come about than just to wake up and find it is already there to face you?'

'Mai,' said Babamukuru, deftly turning the tables against his wife's demands. 'If you're saying you know something, something that is going to take place, then it is better if you tell me in a little while, when the time is right. This girl is tired, Mai! She has just finished her A-Levels examinations! And she has written many subjects. You know how hard Tambudzai always reads for exams! What we should be talking to her about now is the course she wants to take and which applications she has made for her further education.

'Yes, Tambudzai!' my uncle tipped his head back a fraction, keeping both hands on the steering wheel. He was the kind of driver who focused on nothing but the road in front of him. 'Mathematics, Biology, Chemistry! With that combination of subjects you will do much. You are not like us, your aunt here and even myself! We were not advised about which subjects a person should take to ensure a good living. Now you know better than we, and so you have everything in front of you! You can go ahead to become an engineer or pharmacist, or a doctor. Have you thought what you would like to do? All of these are good careers, with good salaries,' my uncle guided me enthusiastically, with a hearty nonchalance to make me believe I had not been there while he and my aunt were arguing.

I slouched into the back seat. 'Yes, Babamukuru. I've thought of all that for a long time,' I lied. 'I've made my applications. I am hoping to qualify for a scholarship to study engineering.' There was a smudge on the window where my nose had pressed. I rubbed at it with the sleeve of my blazer.

'Don't dirty that blazer, Tambudzai! Dry-cleaning's expensive,' warned Maiguru sharply.

Babamukuru beamed into the rear-view mirror. 'You see, Mai. Soon Tambudzai will be off on her career. She will be in the city. If she is lucky she will be accepted overseas. The British Council will give her a scholarship. She will leave all this behind her, and when she qualifies, it will all be forgotten. Jeremiah and Mainini there will live comfortably when Tambudzai comes back. What is upsetting their hearts will disappear, because of the good work of their daughter.'

Not even in her somewhat mutinous state could Maiguru resist so much talk about education and academic performance. She asked me about the exams, and I had to lie about how everything had been perfectly clear because of the high quality of Angela's note-taking.

'Yes, yes, Tambudzai,' remarked Babamukuru with great satisfaction as we turned into the mission. 'This is good! It is very good! I know we did not spend all this money on you for nothing.'

Some relief came when Babamukuru told me at supper that evening that I should not proceed that holiday to the homestead. For a lot of rifts were being rent between people by the different beliefs that abounded concerning the Rhodesians and the guerrillas, and in the infinite divisions between points of view things no one ever spoke of were happening. I was petrified of finding out what had befallen the Samhungus. Besides, with my A-Levels and the prospects they provided, how could I sit and talk, as to an equal, to a sister who did not possess a certificate, whose name was not printed on any paper of merit, and who also now was deprived of a leg?

The war only came to the mission in the evenings with the curfew, and on some occasions the army patrolled. During the day I had some respite, although I often needed to run away from Nyasha and her new-found equanimity. It rained more than usual that year. In fact, it rained more and more as the war worsened. People said the good rains came because the ancestors were rewarding our gallantry. After the downpours you felt even the earth clogged with the clots of people's lives was freed. Leaves glittered clear sharp green, washed of dust that raged through the air in the wake of army trucks or following the whirlwinds whipped up by explosions. With a reed mat to lie on, a thumb in one of Nyasha's many books, I took refuge under the loquat trees that grew on the edge of Maiguru's garden.

This piece of earth in which Maiguru set seeds was a mystery to me and many people. Sylvester, my relative's gardener, was diligent, but he received what was handed over by Maiguru. And it seemed my aunt only had to hold a seed in her palm and stroke it, to have it jumping into the earth, where it shot out green and in a short while was profusely blooming. Nor did the seeds seem to care about their fate. Whether the blossoms and fruit were to be admired or eaten, they produced prodigiously for Maiguru. Sturdy mango trees towering above her dropped fragrant fruit into my aunt's hand. Papaws plopped ripe at her feet, while leafy covo, rape and kale waved leaves as big as small umbrellas, as thick as a jungle. In the front were flower beds, in a timidly decorous arrangement, shielded from the house by jacarandas and more loquat trees, as if my aunt's productivity should not be observed by those who sat on the sofas. So from inside you gained only fleeting glimpses of flame coloured cannas skipping, brilliant roses dancing on their stems, deep purple dahlias holding their heads as though in meditation, elegant white arums looking down their noses at everything – the whole array of Maiguru's intensities that no one, not even she, could think of.

'Good afternoon!'

'Good afternoon!'

'Good afternoon!'

People with business at the mission, and those simply passing through, stopped walking to take in the magnificence of Maiguru's plot. At weekends when she worked side by side with Sylvester, she laughed in her self-deprecating way at compliments. During the week, I basked in the praise.

'If something is good, it is good, jealous down!'

'What kind of woman stays in that house? And those vegetables too!'

'Yes, it's my aunt! She's my Maiguru.'

'All that, are you eating? Do you sell it?'

'Come down and talk to *Mukoma* Sylvester.'

'Soon every woman will have a patch like that! For her to work with the strength of her hands! After the war. Everyone will have something. That's what the elder siblings are promising.'

'Ho, is that what is said?'

'After the war! Don't you know! Everyone! It is true, the elder siblings said it!'

It was good to talk to people, to pass the time of day in this way, to end the conversation by smiling, knowing they were to receive a fine surprise. 'For now, go and see *Mukoma* Sylvester!' I instructed my questioners happily. The inquirer could not believe it when *Mukoma* Sylvester told them the vegetables cost a tickey a bundle.

I lay on the *bonde*, wondering about Maiguru, the lushness she cajoled out of the earth, the eggs and vegetables she sold at prices so low it was as if she was running a charity, controlled by a law of giving. That talk about my family's totem wasn't charitable, though. What did that talk about wild cats mean? I wanted to know while at the same time I also wanted to ignore it. My biggest worry was that, being *bonga* too, Maiguru was as outraged with me as she was with the rest of the family. This aspect of matters made thinking about my aunt demanding and difficult. Meanwhile sleep stayed away at night because of fear of army vehicles. I was afraid they would hear a midnight *morari* broadcast from Maputo on Babamukuru's radio, or, with the way my aunt and uncle were behaving, they might find something else at the mission that would make the soldiers violent. I was already worn out from Sacred Heart and examinations. A soporific hum vibrated out of snapdragons' bells where bees probed. It seemed best to drift away on the burr of it, or simply gaze at the blue sky vacantly. So, in the safety of day, I made up rest under the trees, calmed by the scent of Maiguru's flowers. My mind slowed down. With Babamukuru commenting on how proud I had made everyone with my endurance and hard work, I began to smile again at my disappointments. Looking forward, turning my back on all that had happened, after a couple of weeks I had enough strength to start thinking about being useful. I began to help around the house again and went into an orgy of cleaning. When nothing was left to be made cleaner than it was, I went outside to help Sylvester in the garden that perfumed the atmosphere ever more fragrantly with the scent of healing.

'*Sisi* Tambu! *Sisi* Tambu!'

I wanted to be practical now that I was better, so this afternoon I was at the back, holding a hoe close to its neck, then with a short swing ramming the blade in and ripping a clump of broad bladed grass from the humps of Maiguru's sweet potatoes. Sylvester was loping down under the loquat trees and waving a manila envelope.

'*Sisi* Tambu, it's here, the letter you asked me to look out for!'

It was two months into my holiday, the time when, if we had been at school, we would have been watching

Sister Emmanuel intently. Sylvester disappeared under the grapevine. Was he going to come over with the mail? My heart was reverberating in my chest, doof-doof-doof, like those nightly mortar explosions. The gardener had a handful of other letters to take in and went to deposit everything in the place the daily mail went, the mantelpiece in the dining room. Running in after him, forgetting to wash my hands in the excitement and having to go back to do it in the cement tubs in the laundry, I sorted through the pile and found without trouble the one I wanted. Fumbling inside the envelope took too long. I turned it upside down and shook it. A narrow little slip fell out onto the honey-coloured floorboards. I squatted down but could hardly read it, I was so full of anticipation. This was the moment I was waiting for when the road to the rest of my life would finally open. Now, with this slip of paper I was to undo all the cords that bound me in the realm of non-being. That length of paper was a Gordian sword to destroy the knots with which I was fettered. All the energy, discipline and forbearance I had exhibited between home and school was finally to be rewarded. Oh, what was I going to be! I could not wait to discover it. The letters of the print were smudged. I held it up and squinted close. I was numb, just as I had been when the news was good, by the time I real-ised I had finished reading. I did not feel them; in fact, it is only now that I recall tears falling. On the result slip were two Ds and one E, as well as nothing more than an O-Level pass in Mathematics, as though there had been prodigious waste and nothing added to my ability in the two further years I had spent at the convent. What could I do now? I had no idea, apart from panic. I dared to think it was a mistake, but the same result was repeated on the certificate delivered later.

Babamukuru was furious when he came down from the office to supper. 'Can you tell me what good these results are? Tambudzai, what good are these Ds and Es, these low marks, and this . . .' he could hardly bring himself to say it after spending money for two more years to educate me at Sacred Heart '. . . this O-Level grading! What are you going to do in life,' he finally demanded, 'when you should have your A-Level in Mathematics, one of the most important subjects of all, but you only have this O-Level?'

'But she does have the three A-Levels, Baba!' Maiguru tried to soothe him by placing several large joints of chicken on her husband's plate. 'Have some, Daddy-dear!' she lilted on the brink of baby talk in her effort to keep peace at the table. 'I thought since *Sisi* Tambu has passed, we should celebrate with something delicious.' She turned to me and offered the plate. 'Most people only take three subjects, you know! Of course, *Sisi* Tambu, you're just as good!'

'Good for what?' Babamukuru inquired ominously. 'Good enough to do only what we did and become teachers, Mai! Are you saying she should become a nurse or a teacher, Mai? Didn't we become educated where our parents were not? Shouldn't a child, one who is intelligent, want to become more than her parents?'

'Tell us, Tambudzai,' cajoled Maiguru anxiously. 'It must have been something. What happened?'

'Life!' volunteered Nyasha levelly. 'If you're interested, Mum, life happened. It's been happening to Tambu a lot, you know. Just like it happened to me.' I gave in to a surge of viciousness and kicked my cousin under the table. This talk of life would result in my standing with both legs, not only one, in stormy waters. My cousin went on evenly, picking the skin off her chicken to avoid the fat that lurked beneath it, 'But since a lot of people live in missions and not the real world, they probably wouldn't understand that, or,' she delivered the *coup de grâce* with wry detachment that made you think of Mercutio slaying the Capulet, 'be able to advise anyone about it.'

'Be quiet, child,' snapped Maiguru.

Babamukuru's face went pale as his daughter talked to her mother, looking complacently past him. Now Babamukuru looked past Nyasha too, to impale me upon his gaze directly. There were dots of sweat beneath my uncle's nose. His chest was heaving quietly. He stretched out his arm and rolled up his sleeve. Quiet settled on the table so that we heard the material rustle as he folded the cuff over and over again, upwards. Maiguru picked up the vegetable spoon half-heartedly to heap up crisp, green, garden beans. 'I don't think it will help us now, Baba,' she breathed. 'Were you not talking of times, and right times, yourself? It will be better after we have eaten.

'But,' she continued quickly, shaking the beans back into the bowl and replacing the empty spoon, 'but if you think telling her now will help her, do it, Baba. I only did not want others to hear. Others, who might not know how to react sensibly to it.'

'I suppose,' observed Nyasha, responding to her mother's somewhat sulky reference, 'I suppose you mean like react sensibly, like to the news bulletins about the *munts* they kill, right! Like that one where that man looked like he was eating a mouthful of maggots! Not for the nervous, right, Mum? Because nervous people don't react *sensibly*!'

'What is wrong with you, child!' Maiguru looked at her daughter with a strong dose of disgust.

'I wonder,' the daughter replied nastily, 'where it came from! I do wonder where I got so much wrong from!'

'What is wrong,' Babamukuru interrupted, 'is Tambudzai here.' My uncle turned to me once more, speaking with heavy emphasis. 'Yes, Tambudzai, today you are a great disappointment! I have seen Nyasha's results. I have not yet sent these results to the other parents, but as the headmaster I have seen them. She has done very well. But I must tell you, you are a disappointment, my child, especially when I kept you in spite of everything.' He stretched out his arm. 'My daughter, perhaps I should have told you before so that you knew and worked properly. Yes, it is especially disappointing, because I have been hoping all the time after this.'

Babamukuru thrust the loose sleeve up to his shoulder, with a movement that turned time into a loop beaded with endless unbearable moments. For Babamukuru, who could not countenance his hurt, now needed to hurt something badly, so he thrust his arm closer towards me.

'Look at what I am showing you!' Babamukuru commanded, twisting his arm to reveal the lighter flesh underneath where the scars glistened more visibly. Maiguru looked at me with anticipation to see what I would feel. 'Do you know, do you even dare think of what caused this?' her husband demanded.

I could not face the scar, the old wound which I knew, without wanting to know, was there beneath my uncle's long-sleeved white shirts. And Babamukuru had hoped for me, like some kind of holy child, to wash away the hostile blood that had caused his wounds. I resorted to the usual way out of not feeling anything, of concentrating on every inch of skin, on the opening of every pore until I could feel nothing else and the sensation of me filled the entire universe. But as I was not, I could feel nothing, and when I had come to this point of not being, I took the precaution of appropriately looking down.

'Do you know?' demanded Babamukuru once more, 'or do I have to tell you my child?'

I nodded, indescribably miserable. *Bhunu! Rova musoro rigomhanya*! Hit the white on the head to make it run. It was the song one didn't want to hear that sang all the same in one's head. But it was Babamukuru who was beaten, and did not run, only walked slowly, and like a dancer.

'Speak!' Babamukuru ordered. 'If you know speak!'

'It was the *morari*.' My voice trembled, but I did not dare to disobey him. Besides, I had seen it. 'The one in the holiday. . . the holiday in second form.'

'You might as well know,' said Nyasha, 'someone at the village, we don't know who, said he was selling out.'

'It was as you say, Tambu,' Maiguru came in, disguising satisfaction as help, 'it was when you were in form two, when you were settled in that place and were doing well. That's when people suddenly saw it! That some people were being *vatengesi*!'

'Selling out,' translated Babamukuru unnecessarily. He continued in English as though he wished to keep the matter more distant and clinical. 'Yes, you were in form two, my daughter,' he echoed his wife sadly. 'That is when people there at home started saying, look at Sigauke, he is selling out! Could it be my own brother, Tambudzai? These things were being suggested, as they were happening, so I had to consider them. But no,' he went on. 'I could not believe it.'

Nyasha's hand slipped across under the table. I clenched my fist, so she circled her fingers about my wrist. They were repulsive to feel, cold and clammy with sweating.

'You have seen the road blocks. You have seen what happens here at the mission. The war is everywhere. . .' Letting her speech peter out, Maiguru stood up to close the door to the kitchen so that Prudence, the maid, would not come in. 'So why was it only then?' Maiguru returned to her seat and clasped her hands together above the table so that her mouth pressed into her thumbs.

Her eyes glimmered with a light like triumph, but it died away as Babamukuru answered the question she put. 'The comrades were told at that particular time. They were called and given the story of *tshombes*. I know you were only reading your books at that time, my daughter. You were not doing anything at that school, Tambudzai. That is why I sent you there. But *vana mukoma* were told I put you there to teach you how to be like myself, a *tshombe*!'

So, in addition to everything, it seemed I was now involved in this attempt at my uncle's murder. Now I did not know anything anymore, whether to be relieved or not, when my aunt breathed, 'Can you imagine anyone doing that? Behaving like that in a family! What kind of woman does that to the man who bears the same totem as her husband?'

Nyasha's mouth fell open. My heart slid into my bowels.

'Now I am just as disappointed by you, Tambudzai,' Babamukuru continued, his sense of proportion obliterated by a horrible distress. 'I am just as disappointed with you, my daughter, as I was by your mother's actions. You are a bright girl, Tambudzai. You could have done better than you have if you had worked properly. But by the time you wrote those exams, you were doing something else! You were playing! Enjoying yourself at that place, and making your headmistress angry. If your mother had been angry about this, that I sent you somewhere to play, and mess around, Tambudzai, that would have been something we could understand. Then it would have been endurable!'

'She wanted him to be finished off,' my aunt devastated me further with the plainness of her language. 'But your father, Babamunini Jeremiah, is a good man, Tambudzai. I tell you your father is a good man! He went and found the commander. Even though anything could have happened to him, your father, too! Remember that one. He could not allow it. He knew what your uncle has done. That is why he did not want them to murder my husband.'

Nyasha unwound her grip from my arm and arranged her cutlery neatly in the middle of her plate. 'Excuse me,' she said gently before standing up. Nobody answered.

'Look here,' my uncle requested. Now there was neither sadness nor weariness in his voice, nor in the way he held forth his arm where the hand dangled limply at the end. There was only incomprehension. 'Tambudzai, it is time for you to see this properly!' I was compelled to look again at the ragged valley rifted in my uncle's flesh, where the dagger had gouged to slit the artery, the path long and wide, so that it was better not to think of the depth of it.

'I hope you will remember!' said Babamukuru. 'This scar came because of you! I put it out of my mind until today. When you received your wonderful O-Level results, even if you did not manage to obtain the trophy, still you were doing very well, and I knew that even if I had suffered this, I was still whole. Now there is pain! I feel I am again being pulled into pieces!'

I looked at Maiguru for help, but her thumbs had crept to her nose, as though now, having seen her husband relive his pain, she would stop herself breathing. Her eyes were dry, stonily red right into the pupils which were in any case completely closed; she had removed herself for the moment, could neither see nor hear anything.

Babamukuru shook his head and rolled down his sleeve. After it was buttoned down, he picked up a chicken portion. At this sign, Maiguru hesitantly and lethargically came to life by offering the dish of vegetables to her husband, and when Babamukuru declined more beans, giving him the option of gravy. This he declined also, and I did likewise when Maiguru pressed me to understand and not be sad and work up an appetite. I looked at my plate for a long time, growing more and more numb, feeling less than on the occasion of night and moon and bone and song and jumping away from everything.

So I had not jumped far enough, I saw, around the woman who was on the ground then, after Babamukuru lay like a sacrifice to the deity of want and need so sharp it was like desire, and in the end did not arouse the pity of this god for he was not sacrificed: I had not jumped far enough around my mother. It seemed I would never move again unless I managed to go round her. Round, round, round. Round such a woman. To return to my uncle and his family, how could I progress past my mother!

Babamukuru did not go up to his office after dark any more as not even he could brave the curfew. We watched the news together, and I kept staring with my uncle although Gail Bright informed us that the footage that followed was not for the nervous. There was a rope, this I remember, and bodies attached to an end of it. You did not notice the other end until a jeep some distance away revved and the bodies bumped after it. The rope was long. It allowed the driver to manoeuvre round a pit and drop the bodies in. The flies swarmed up in a buzz of rage as a caterpillar deposited dirt. Gone, we were told approvingly. The terrorists were buried!

Later that evening, after prayers, Babamukuru asked me to remain behind in the sitting room. Both Maiguru and my cousin remembered tasks to do. Therefore I sat alone while Babamukuru described – once more, and in greater depth, going back to how bright my smile was when I was eight years old and he arrived at the village from England – how disappointed he was with my development. He showed me more scars on his shins to impress upon me how he had suffered on my behalf and had gladly borne my mother's treason. For wasn't it the normal course of events that a father should go before his children and since we were not rich in the way Europeans are, and as it was not in any case the custom, he had nothing material to leave me, therefore wished to leave me an education. This he said was better than a business, which could be lost. 'Your education,' he rebuked me sadly, 'is your greatest commodity! It is as if I have taught you nothing, because you have simply wasted it!' Babamukuru had not minded all his sacrifice and suffering as long as I behaved myself. His suffering had simply made him tenacious. Now, however, given the new tendencies to disobedience and silliness I showed, he was no longer prepared to do it. 'I thought,' he began to conclude after he had spoken for about an hour, and touched on many topics, including the wages of sin being if not death, then an existence very like being moribund, as evidenced by the way my mother and father lived at the homestead, 'I thought that after you wrote your letter to Sister Emmanuel, Tambudzai, and apologised for your bad behaviour that the trouble was over. It seems it was not! You have been doing as you wish and not listening. In that case, you may now do as you wish, since you have shown that what others want of you is of no interest to you! I just want you to remember when you do these things, I shall not provide anything else to help you!'

I went to the bedroom I shared with Nyasha, undressed, still feeling numb and heaved into bed. I believe that I went numb permanently after that. It was a moonless night, so the soldiers came and stopped their jeeps with the head-lights shining through the frangipani into the bedroom, casting undulating horrors on the wall that chilled me completely.

At least I would have been chilled if I had been feeling anything. I reflected on what Babamukuru had said and sworn to do and found, in a comforting way, how much sense it made. Of course, if your mother had plotted a man's death on one side and then he was subjected to terror by light on the other side, it stood to good reason he would disown you. I was comforted somewhat by this logic, as it was always easier to believe I deserved whatever happened. However, I made a vow.

'Nyasha!' I whispered. 'Nyasha!'

'Shh!' she turned towards me. Her eyes were large and shining. In the light that cut through the curtains you could see the blankets shivering over her thin body that was trembling with terror.

'Nyasha, do you like Maiguru?' I asked. She did not answer. She turned over, away from the headlamps. Her huge shadow heaved and rolled.

'I am never going to talk to Mai again. I'll never go back to the homestead.'

'Tambu, please,' she urged softly, 'just be quiet!'

'Ask father! Ask father!' the doves in the bottle brushes beyond the frangipani advised as the sun crept over the mountain. With no more darkness to break with unwanted light, the jeeps revved and rumbled away. Maiguru always went out in the morning to sweep away their tracks. 'Whoever comes here in the night,' she said between sweeps, 'whoever! I don't want to see it!'

'You will have to take what comes and not choose too much!' Babamukuru warned me on several occasions in the days that followed. 'You cannot expect to earn much, as you do not have a degree, only these, er, only these three A-Levels.' When Babamukuru showed Nyasha her result slip, we discovered she had obtained distinctions in all three of her subjects. As a result of the discrepancies between us two young women, Babamukuru now attempted to smile at his daughter sometimes when he admonished me. But Nyasha did not allow this and discouraged her father by scowling. Poor Babamukuru was very distressed now not to have a good relationship with either of his daughters. Nyasha maintained it was good for her father as she was soon to leave altogether, having received the scholarship for refugees to study in England that Babamukuru had hoped I would be awarded by the British Council. I was so depressed that I could not be more disturbed by my failure to secure a scholarship. I was, in fact, relieved, although I did not want anyone to know. I did not want anyone to see I had lost my fighting spirit. But I was glad I would not have to adapt to a new way of life and new kinds of Europeans.

When he was feeling particularly morose upon contemplating my future, my uncle continued, 'You will have to not want too much, Tambudzai. Even if you qualify for university with what you have, you will not qualify for a decent profession.' It was very strange to me to hear Babamukuru beginning to talk in a way that was so similar to my mother. Had I disappointed Mai so badly? How? When all I had wanted was a good education so that I could help, just as Babamukuru did! Disappoint my mother? No, it was not possible!

12

I slunk away from the mission in miserable ignominy a few weeks after obtaining my disastrous results and revelation of my family's murderous behaviour. I departed to take up a series of jobs, secured from Babamukuru's contacts in education as a clerk in one establishment, a temporary teacher of the dullest, most junior grade in another. How dispirited I was! How traumatised and discouraged! How gleefully, I assured myself – now that I mistrusted the woman completely – yet also how wretchedly my mother would mock me over my predicament, if I was sufficiently foolish to allow myself to meet her. So I reinforced my vow, and found good grounds to avoid her. If I received calls from Babamukuru, or from Baba at the telephone at the council houses in the village, to do with *Sekuru* Dombo, my maternal uncle, coming down from Mount Darwin for consultations, I promised to return to the village and then promptly forgot it. But while I was teaching domestic science at a trade school down in Gaza, near to the place Ntombi came from, there were matters to do with *Mbuya* Hanna, my paternal grandmother, to be settled, where both my mother and I were required to be present. Nor did I dare be absent, for a paternal grandmother's is a powerful spirit.

Mai made a point of hugging me eagerly, when I arrived at Odzi, where my grandmother's family came from. I stiffened at the touch, willing myself to put my arms about her shoulders. Then Mai sighed and laughed at the same time, and did what she always did, saying what she wanted in that raucous, unmodulated way of hers, in front of everyone. 'A-he, Tambudzai! Spending all that time with all those Europeans only to rot in a school that doesn't have form four! And not even youngsters who have an intellect, just any old idiot! *Vasikana*, Tambu, is this a truth of yours, that now you are at a craft school, where people work just with their hands, without any thinking! Ha but never mind!' she consoled, like a thorn pulled from a bush to dig out the first embedded in the heel. 'No, there's no point in worrying! Which of your ancestors learnt those books? The blood that's in you is mine and your father's, not Babamukuru's!' This is how I learnt a mother can speak in this way to her daughter.

I found it all so terribly revolting. 'Get on with it, my daughter! Pull yourself together! Do something for yourself,' was what I wanted to hear, in private, doors closed, strength flowing from mother to daughter. I was sickened by my mother's lack of faith and expectation. How her words demoralised, confirming there was so little to me. I wore myself down with wondering – was it something to do with my person individually, was it a recent genetic strain, or, more sinisterly, was it generic?

Nobody – not even I – expected me to pull myself together sufficiently to succeed in my new situation. Nor did I, if the truth is to be told, manage to do so. I was so depressed that mustering the energy required for smugness at having higher qualifications than my students was beyond my capacities. Being so lethargic, I did not beat the children to prove superior mental status as the other teachers did. I merely wrote lists of ingredients, or grammar rules, or insects on the board, depending on what I was teaching, and followed this up with a few interactive exercises to lessen the strain on my personal resources. Marking I turned to diligently, if with an endemic lack of enthusiasm. However, it did not seem to me logical to be other than diligent, as teaching was what I had entered into a contract to do with the administration. As to whether the children liked me or not, this issue was my least concern. Teachers taught to transfer knowledge and discipline, not to arouse friendly feelings in children. I had neither heard nor experienced anything achieved by dint of affection or liking, for in the end not even Sister Catherine had been a remedy: achievement meant application. The form two English I was from time to time required to teach was a language even my mother spoke in my dreams, in a quaint old form from Shakespeare. 'Fie, Tambudzai!' Mai scolded at night, 'Prithee, Babamukuru!' in the long flat tones of Sister Emmanuel. With my abilities at a comparatively high level and without the stamina required to lash knowledge into my pupils, I acquired a reputation for competence. The hopeful youngsters interpreted my disciplined inertness as a kind of stern compassion. Their work improved and several started passing. I began to enjoy again the knowledge of executing a task effectively. I began to feel I taught the children well. Just as they now had hope of passing, my own hope in life's potential returned, like one of Maiguru's perennials during the rainy season.

I cannot say what happened to the classes I taught, since I was not interested. My own hopes, however, I remember very well, began to be realised at Independence. Ah, that Independence! It is not a time you forget. People thronged the streets rejoicing so thoroughly that there was no place for remembering the acts their hands and their feet, and their teeth, and the fingers, boots, and mouths of their children committed. So we never remembered and grieved together as women sorrow in groups many years after a birth, 'Is there a pain like that! And so much blood! It is like the blood of slaughter, my sister, isn't it, that blood of childbirth!'

The streets pulsed at Independence with feverish passion, like the ecstasy of procreation. Those who were not in the streets were equally passionately packing their existences into containers as the election results were posted. As those who lived off the land, but did not have it, had known for months that Mr Mugabe's ZANU-PF, which had fought for fertile soil, was to win a landslide victory, the silent people who packed their property knew the victory of that same party heralded a devastating deterioration of standards. Households were hauled into aeroplanes headed for the shortly-to-be-superior standards in South Africa, Canada, Britain, Australia and New Zealand.

This more acceptable living to which the jumbo jets winged included university standards. As a result, the University of Zimbabwe now had vacant spaces and enrolled mature students whose A-Level certificates exhibited Ds and Es. However, it turned out Babamukuru's prophecy concerning my professional possibilities was correct. The only faculty I could enrol in was Social Science. My returning confidence shaken once more, I opted for the Department of Sociology.

Ntombi was in the second year of her Master of Philosophy in the French language when I went up. She was still in residence, but looked ahead, as though there was no one coming, when I met her in the corridor. In the dining room, she sat with the Ndebele girls. 'That one, she's a MuNdevere,' the other Shona speaking girls explained when I asked. 'Those ones, let them stick together! It's just that she grew up somewhere else, I think, over with those MaChangana. That's why they just speak English. That ChiNdau they speak that side!' my informant, who was also in Sociology continued, exhibiting great ignorance of other Zimbabweans' ethnicities. 'Ha, that language of theirs! They call it ChiShona, but have you ever understood a word of it? I don't think anyone at all, in all of this world, understands it!' I did not, at that time, experience shock at this student's view of group belonging. I merely nodded, considering what, if anything at all, was to be gained by revealing my ex-classmate was in fact a MuChangana. In the end, nothing was. I realised I would merely end up feeling inferior, being a newcomer while Ntombizethu was a post-graduate student. I overcame my anxieties by becoming once more aggressively studious.

Babamukuru had been struck by a stray bullet that ricocheted off a flag post during the twenty-one gun salute while they lowered the Union Jack and raised the Zimbabwean flag at the Independence celebrations. The bullet lodged in his spinal cord. When he was not supine in bed, he sat in a wheelchair, which rendered him yet more full of umbrage and more cantankerous than usual. So to the scars of war were added the complications of Independence. Neither he nor any of my family came to campus to celebrate my graduation.

I emerged from my studies to a new dispensation. I could never, after all the years at Sacred Heart and Fridays in the town hall, bring myself to believe Rhodesians had died; definitely they had not done so in sufficient quantities to cause a great blimp in the course of history. Admittedly, Mr Swanepoel had, but the twins were fluent in Afrikaans, so that even Bougainvillea at the time acknowledged the rumour that went round the convent then, that Mr Swanepoel was not a Rhodesian but an Afrikaaner. Convinced it was not the deaths of Rhodesians that had caused Mr Mugabe and Mr Smith to talk to each other with some degree of sincerity, I assured myself happily that the phenomenon was due to a bigger and better motive on both sides: a desire to desist from chopping away lips, ears, noses and genitals from the bodies of people's relatives by the elder siblings; a desire to develop a larger, kinder heart on the part of Europeans. From time to time I wondered how Nyasha was getting on with hers. Were they the same as our whites, or were they better or more notorious?

However, in this new dispensation with its new Europeans, Babamukuru's predictions were still in force. To my dismay, the only profession that accepted me with the poor lower second degree I acquired in spite of obsessive turning of textbook pages, was again the profession of teaching. So I discovered how, in spite of a degree, I was only marginally better paid than the beggars, who, fulfilling the prophecies of the whites concerning declining standards, began to strum guitars made of Olivine cooking oil cans in the central streets of the capital. My self esteem suffered another setback, for it seemed only rejects were required to shape our nation's children. And even in this profession I was on the lower rung, as I possessed only a Bachelor of Social Science degree and did not have a qualification in education. Oh dear! How disgruntling and galling it was each time I opened the doors to my class in the high density area of Mabvuku.

Oh, how low I was falling, as though I had broken a glass floor and, hurtling through, would end up splintered once more in the mess of the homestead. Even though I had not arrived there yet, but was merely slithering in that nasty, nether ward direction, my current position oppressed me as being much too low for someone who, during two entire terms, had enjoyed the distinction of being the girl who obtained the best O-Level results at the Young Ladies' College of the Sacred Heart, the country's most prestigious young women's institution. Stumbling on stones on my way to catch a *combi* to work, holding my hand to my face against the putrid evaporate from rotten pipes, I was soon petrified by intense surges of aggression. I found little respite from my desire to rage, not even when I gave up on life for the hours of the night in the wretched room I rented from a single woman in a rundown part of Greendale suburb. Mould shimmered blue, grey and green on this room's walls. On the ceiling dark whirlpools left over from last season's rain rushed round like vortices of sinister might until the murkiness sucked you in, tossed you around and drowned you. The gyp boards sagged and buckled at the marks, so that if drowning was a fancy to be shaken off, the ceiling had the last word, threatening at any minute to cave in and crush you. My grief in this house, that magnified my sense of failure and frustration, lashed out at the landlady herself. This woman had a home, a possession of her own. Insupportably, she had managed when I hadn't. Yes, I felt passionately indignant when I thought about it – why she should, when I couldn't. An impulse to perform drastic and damaging acts upon my landlady's body soon welled up whenever I caught the sound of her footsteps in the hallway.

This perpetual rage was unbearable for me. I considered myself a moral person. In fact, as a moral woman I did not intend to harbour such uncharitable, above all, angry, emotions. To ensure I did not commit any atrocity upon my landlady, I began to spend, soon after my furious urges surfaced, long hours at the school I did not want to teach at, in order to lessen the time spent in my landlady's house. In the bus, too, from the suburb, I began to chatter compulsively, pressing up close to people, to assure myself I was still, for all my failure and unfeminine passion, a normal and likeable person.

'Yes, my sister!'

'How are you, sister?'

'Have you slept well?'

'I have slept!'

'It's hot today!'

'Yes it is! Let's hope that means rain.'

'If only it would do that – rain! So we can be happy! Could we fail to raise fine ripe crops if it rains? Ah no, that we can do! People will eat if water comes down. We are expert at farming. And the land now, we are getting it!'

'Yes, if water comes it will be good for us.'

'But these roads! Ah, look at them, as they already are! If it rains, do you think. . . ah, surely no, we won't! We won't be able to walk them.'

More often than not, this last observation was mine, for in spite of striving to be enthusiastic with my companions, upon relaxing, I relapsed into a now chronic depression.

'Maybe!' came the rejoinder with mild censure. 'But does it matter if we are eating? Even if we have some trouble walking?' Silence settled uneasily as the bus lurched on, since my dejection disturbed other struggling citizens. To make amends, I pointed out I merely wished for more propitious conditions to live in, such as pavements to walk to work on and sewer pipes which, if not new, were at least regularly serviced and welded. Yet silently, I swore this was just like Mai not cleaning her latrines, and was there a good reason why this cleaning of latrines, or of anything else, was not possible? On the positive side, however, I discovered in such conversations there were accommodation options in the city which a person could take advantage of, if one possessed the money. Having the information, I was so discouraged at the thought of another failure that it took me several weeks to make a decision. Finally, however, I devised a plan. First there was to be a better job. That obtained, the second step was to make the move to better conditions. It was beneficial to plan in this way, for legitimate improvements, therefore I did not concern myself any longer with the outrage I felt against my landlady.

Now, however, my uncle's prophecies once more predicted with unfortunate precision the limits of my mobility. The job I obtained was lowly and only marginally better paid. I became a copywriter at Steers, D'Arcy and MacPedius Advertising Agency. While the position rescued me from another teaching post, I could not manage more prestigious accommodation than a room in a single ladies' hostel.

Even now you can walk past the building in the ox-span broad street which begins on Enterprise Road and runs west for several kilometres past the park, and which today's signposts, painted shortly after Independence, proclaim to be Herbert Chitepo Avenue. The institution was called Twiss Hostel, and taking up residence there was another sad disappointment, causing me to remember bitterly my former landlady who owned the home she lived in. There was not another alternative, though, but to put my head down and move on. I developed the habit, in order to avoid becoming completely dejected, as I walked towards my new home from the advertising agency, of picking out one by one and concentrating on the hostel's advantages.

There were several. At first it required an effort to remember this, but with time the practice grew easier. To begin with, the institution was a distinguished, clean, white-plastered building, built for an old colonial purpose which nobody who now lived there knew anything of, except that space and graciousness were essential. The foyer was particularly comfortable, wider than it was long, which gave it an atmosphere of extending constantly a generous welcome, and this inviting air was intensified by a teak floor that glowed gently deep in the tiles, as though it were a restful bed of velvet. A neat dining room with starched white tablecloths opened off to the left of the foyer as you entered. Here heavy wooden tables were set for six, with napkins folded to attention beside the settings, very much like sentinels to ensure we did not eat too much, thus maintaining both our figures and the hostel fees within manageable proportions – for you could not contemplate eating in any manner but daintily so as not to soil the immaculate linen. On the right of the entrance hall was another wide and generous structure, the reception desk, which suggested straight away people leaning out and, with courteous enquiries, beckoning. Ahead, the foyer ran into two corridors leading east and west, from which the bedrooms opened. These hallways turned north and then turned again to form a rectangle in the middle of which was a courtyard, open to a sky too blue in one season, swollen grey with water about to burst in another. There were no trees, but a woman could read in most months on stone benches set in the shade of bougainvillea bushes and clumps of hibiscus. The city was still tranquil in those days, and Twiss Hostel incorporated in its design some of the serene grace of the grounds of the college in Umtali.

In those days when I took a room at the hostel, a woman could still walk in Harare Gardens at any time without apprehension. The building was agreeably close to the park's gentle expanse of green, although it was sad to see the bursts of fire that flamed from beds so carefully laid out gradually, imperceptibly fading. The city of Harare, busy with other tasks, forgot how the public needed the beauty of our Gardens nurtured, and so I considered, as I walked by another bed of shrivelled cannas, it would be far more competent to have the place run by a caring team like Maiguru and Sylvester.

Another advantage of the hostel was that just beyond the park the city buzzed like a large swarming insect waiting to drink the nectar of the garden's trees. My new home was convenient for the central business district; a generous blessing for a woman who did not like the class conferred by public transport, but could not afford the one that accompanied possessing one's own vehicle. Not even my former landlady had enjoyed her own transport, I smirked to encourage myself, not concerned with the malice of it because I was impressed only with my discomforts, and was of the opinion that since I had sustained so many misfortunes, the notion of malevolence was irrelevant. Then, finally, reinforcing my new home's merit considerably, a sign which read 'right of admission reserved' was still glued above the entrance, proof that none but the most superior and exclusive had at any point in time, whether before Independence or after it, been admitted to the premises. What a satisfaction it was to know one was now included! Nor was there need to fear one's presence might cause that infamous deterioration in standards. For even though the laws were dismantled, the situation was very like school had been: there were only a few of us, the greater number of rooms being rented by white young women.

'Hi! Isabel!' one of these white girls, who was called Faye, came bustling up one morning. 'Seen Tambu, by any chance? She's got a phone call.'

It was some time after I had settled in. I was walking, as had become my habit, through the foyer softly so as not to disturb Mrs May, the elderly matron. She was silver of hair, in complexion a baby, sun-defying pink. She was a tired-looking, soft, querulous woman with dried powder – face and talc – caked permanently in her creases. Dustings drifted off when she moved or spoke, giving the impression that if she did so too vigorously she would disintegrate like an unwrapped mummy, in an avalanche of dusty particles. Supervising us, however, did not demand exertion. Mrs May spent most of her hours patrolling the few metres of curved space behind the reception desk at the side of the foyer. The watch entailed shuffling from one end of the reception area to the other, which provided sequentially a vantage view of each approach to the hostel. Thus, with practically no expenditure of energy, our matron ensured that male persons did not pass an invisible but generally accepted boundary between the foyer and the dormitories. It was, Twiss Hostels oral tradition told, only ever in repulsing trespassers that Mrs May became sufficiently impassioned to stop being tremulous. But the last occasion on which this happened was long ago, when the matron was much younger and more able-bodied, free of crevices that powder clogged in an age before collagen creams, and none of the current residents remembered it happening.

When she was not assessing the gender and intentions of residents' visitors, the elderly citizen turned her glasses to the crossword puzzle in the newspaper which was invariably spread out on her desk. She slid the former with her palm flat on its centre, over the reception desk as she shuffled up and down, executing her duties. The matron sighed heavily and despondently throughout as she sought for solutions to the crossword's cryptic phrases, as if the answer to each clue, though still undefined, was yet another terror unleashed upon her by her country's unscrupulous forces. For all her having been intimidated by life, however, our melancholy Mrs May was always concerned about the well-being of her charges. This morning she observed kindly in her thin, tremulous voice, as I was accosted by a resident, 'Oh, I do hope she hasn't left yet! That poor Tambu hardly ever gets any mail, or anyone asking for her! Dear me, I can't remember the last time, in fact I'm quite sure there's never been a letter for her!' With this the hostel matron, who unlike Miss Plato was a native of the land she now lived in, adjusted her glasses upon her nose and focused through the lenses upon me. 'You don't mind having a look do you, Isabel? It will be a treat for that Tambu, I'm sure. I do hope you'll find her, and just in case you don't dear, if I see her, I'll let her know.

'Oh, now I do hope I don't forget,' she added, fiddling with the bridge of her spectacles, anxious about something that might not in fact occur. As she attended once more to the top set of clues, she unhooked the tortoiseshell glasses from her ears and apprehensively sucked one end of the frame. Faye hurried into the dining hall where girls who worked in government departments that opened for business at a quarter to eight were busily gulping coffee, so that I was left facing Mrs May in a great deal of irritation and dread of her striking up with me one of her conversations. I was so put out by what had occurred, I scarcely remembered the telephone call that had brought me to the matron's attention.

'Good morning, Isabel!' was how the matron began when she noticed me, and at the greeting a glow gathered on her face, as though the morning was significantly better for my appearance. The poor woman's situation was that the government department girls did not have the time while we opened at half past eight at the agency, yet another of the Steers, D'Arcy and MacPedius Advertising Agency's advantages. True that a good number of residents enjoyed similar posts in other glamorous organisations, but youth had them out all night so that they were always rushing past reception late for a rendezvous or work after oversleeping. My time was not taken up like this. Indeed, as Mrs May observed, my social life was melancholic, being limited to coffee with Dick Lawson, the senior copy writer at the agency, during working hours, or occasionally the happy hour at the agency on Fridays – or rather the happy evening, as Mr Steers the major shareholder and Managing Director called it. Therefore, in the initial stages, I paused politely when she called, to pass pleasantries with the senior citizen.

Seeing how my circumstances made me pause, Mrs May progressed compulsively, quickly after my arrival, from greetings to conversation. 'And yes, it is a good morning now, but soon it's going to be hot, terribly hot, Isabel, isn't it? It has been like that these past few days! Unbearable, dear, absolutely insufferable! I always said I was too old, and perhaps I shouldn't have said that.' Having foretold discomfort, Mrs May grew rueful. 'I should have listened to my son, Mark! He always told me this would happen. I can't tell you how often he said it! That's why he wanted me to go with him. He went on and on about how bad it would be all the time before he moved to England! Come with me, Ma! You know, there wasn't a day he didn't insist on it. He still does, when he calls. He doesn't write you know. He only ever calls. At least once a week, sometimes twice if something particular's happened! Oh, dear, Isabel, I'm even older now! I'm sure I don't know!' The elderly woman paused pensively here, as though each time she told the tale she was obliged to make afresh a painful decision. 'I'll just have to bear the heat. That's what I think, and I tell him. The truth is, Isabel, my poor old bones couldn't stand those damp winters. When I think of my poor old bones, dear, I know I'm not going anywhere!'

Within a few weeks of arrival, I learnt that the bones which kept Mrs May in the land were not in fact her own, but her husband's. When she was fit enough, she travelled up to the north west of the country on a coach to visit the place where they lay. There she watered the flowers personally and pulled away the weeds. It was a border death during the war. The widow was now alone as her son, Mark, did not want to return to the country in which his father was killed so uselessly. Having found out this much in a very short time, before she issued another instalment I developed the habit of tiptoeing past the reception desk to avoid the matron. It was difficult to think of the small, soft woman grieving, hard to relive in this way the events of that old and implacable conflict so that I was in horror of receiving more details. This morning, eager to brighten a resident's day, Mrs May urged, 'Someone's still hanging on, aren't they? Off you go, then, Isabel, and see if you can find Tambu!'

I did not bother to correct her. I cannot recall whether Mrs May began to employ that name for me during our conversations, or rather her monologues, and other hostel residents followed suit, or whether she had at one time asked a girl who I was and received an incorrect answer. The real Isabel was shaking cereal into her bowl in the dining hall, and clearly Faye did not recognise her as Isabel calmly put down the Willards packet, took up a jug and poured milk onto her bran flakes as Faye passed by with a plate of bacon.

What I had done early on was smile and say, 'Actually, Mrs May, it's Tambu!'

'Of course it is!' the matron corrected herself then, and the next day reverted to Isabel. 'Tambu! Yes, dear! Tambu!

Yes, dear!' And Isabel. 'Tambu! Yes, dear!' And Isabel. So my attempts to educate Mrs May ended in reversions.

This morning, after the double dose of not being correctly identified, I vowed 'I am going to tell her again, her and Faye Morisson. I am going to say it! Now I will tell them I'm Tambu!' That was the information they needed to know. I am Tambu and that is Isabel. And there is a difference between us! I promised myself, but I did not believe it.

What I did, in fact, was smile benignly, but I was planning quickly. 'Oh, I'm sure she's already gone,' I exclaimed, to explain why I did not rush forward quickly to fetch myself. 'I'll take a message,' I came to a strategic conclusion.

Mrs May was not paying attention. Her face lit up and she wrote a series of letters quickly but neatly in their boxes in the puzzle. Relieved, I walked through the door at the side of the reception desk into the phone booth. The telephone was buzzing and crackling, the line dead. How maddening it was now, missing contact with someone who knew who I was because I had not been recognised, had not been perceived as an individual person but as a lump broken from a greater one of undifferentiated flesh! I walked out smiling, but I was terribly grieved.

'Now don't you forget to give her that message,' remarked Mrs May as I emerged from the booth. 'I'll get you a piece of paper. You can write it down.' Her glasses were hooked once more over her ears. A finger marked the clue she was working on. 'Oh, just pop into the office and get it, will you, Isabel!'

'I am Tambu. This is what you should know!' I said this to myself, noticing how oddly the voice was stronger, as if someone were actually speaking. I ignored this development and instead smiled once more, this time at the ridiculousness of the necessity of it – of me telling myself who I was. Pulling the grin towards my ears, I walked into the office, found a bit of note paper, pondered for a moment and then decided to scribble 'phone call for you, this Tuesday morning, about seven thirty'. The act made me feel I had prevailed at something. Folding the note, I walked out again to placate the matron by promising, 'I'll slip it under her door.'

'That's very kind of you to take the trouble, Isabel. I'm sure she'll be very glad.' Mrs May pushed her spectacles high onto the bridge of her nose, leaving a smudge from the ink of a classified advertisement. After surveying it, I turned to the French door through which the morning sun slanted cheerful and yellow from the courtyard.

'Hi, Mrs May!' quick voices called.

'Morning, Matron!'

'See you!'

Tic-tac, tic-tac! The words were followed by the clip of squat metallic heels, a girl's currently indispensable 'Princess Di's', on the polished wooden floor. Without waiting for the matron to answer, a trio of residents whirled through the double glass doors onto the veranda's crazy paving. Tic-tac, tic-tac! Short shiny bits of daintiness hit the stone in two-four time and the young women, with the energy of tardiness, disappeared round the hedge of yesterday, today and tomorrow.

Mrs May craned her head as the young women trooped past. 'Morning Barbara! Hello Fiona! Hello Jane! No need to dash like that, girls! You've plenty of time.' Her voice tagged along behind them wistfully, uselessly. They were gone, with the morning sun burning three golden halos off their shiny bobs. Ah, yes, that exit made it worse. I couldn't be remembered, others could. I couldn't even have my irritation in an absolute way – I had to have it in opposition.

In my room, I was still irritated with these white people. So to relieve the annoyance I shredded the note into very small pieces and flung them out into the courtyard through the window. As for the phone call, who could it be? Maiguru was the only person I had sent the Harare number to. Would she really call me, I wondered, quivering on the brink of a wretched self pity. I suspected not, for her hands were full with Babamukuru. In any case, I still felt guilty. Would a woman converse with a person whose mother had plotted to kill her husband? No wonder, I thought miserably, my uncle had disowned me. To manage my reality, I took several deep inhalations, and after that it was time to pull the smile back into place, to venture out once more and steal gently past our momentarily contented matron.

I believe, however, that communing with Mrs May did something for me as I had not bonded with anyone in Twiss Hostel, a consequence, no doubt, of my being older than the other residents; and probably of other reasons too. Mrs May made me feel a part of life, even if it was a life ignominious and incognito at best (I had after all possessed the best O-Level results at Sacred Heart for two whole terms), and at worst a life at the margins of it, at the centre of exclusion. So I became soldered into scenarios I reluctantly found myself part of.

Outside, the city meandered on more fluidly, like a

river of precious things and possibilities. For Harare was wealthy in those days. More people had it and they wore their affluence matter-of-factly, not with today's disdainful arrogance that comes from festering recesses deep inside which the glow of gold has not burnt away, so that noses must be lifted high against the putrefaction. It is true, riches at that time were sprinkled more evenly over the city's inhabitants, and everyone believed that soon they too would be caught in one of fortune's showers. Drops of noble metal glinted at women's ears, loops of it peeped from between pectoral hairs and bosoms. Set with fabulous stones, possession glittered around fingers, so that the wearers proclaimed themselves as noble as the ore the mining companies extracted. Be My Wife's purred past, Mercedes Benzs, Rolls-Royces and Jaguars, as though the parking bays under the jacarandas at Sacred Heart had migrated to colonise the capital. Those not wives who sat in those cars looked down their too pale, expensive noses, scornful with the attentions of married men and the droppings of capital.

But this elite of ours was good enough for us in those days in Harare. Their sharp but languid eyes were not yet shifty with fear of other people pacing close, a band of smiling glassy-eyed youths or malicious, morally circumcised *tsotsis*. It was the sunshine city, where patches of light danced through the fiery flamboyant trees warmly onto the pavement. The air was fresh, tainted with neither anxiety nor pollution. Shops displayed much more of what was and much less of what was not needed. In that peaceful environment, Harare's 'high lifers' could not be greedy; they simply had an affinity for affluence, an aptitude for creating cash where other citizens hadn't. Everyone envied them and buzzed with the dream of having what others didn't. If you were rich, you did not have to fear as there was nothing wrong. You were merely made; for all wealth did, as my reflections on *unhu* had predicted, was make the person. This knowledge fuelled the citizens' quest for money. Craving for the signs of possession encroached, much as my cousin Nyasha's craving for food when she was bulimic, until the city's residents craved excess, calling it comfort.

This morning I forfeited the park and crossed towards Second Street, for I was by this time late. A green Pajero hurtled past. I jumped back to avoid injury. The driver blared his horn and flung up his hand as he disappeared, in contempt rather than warning. I proceeded, dejected, knowing that was what happened if someone was driving and you were walking. But still, this was Harare, this was our Zimbabwe. One day, if I went on as was required, managed to perform what was necessary, I too might reap a reward like the driver.

In the combi, though, these daydreams of a better future position I was working to occupy could not ward off more aggravation. The vehicle's windows were jammed. The air smelt of sweating, barely-washed bodies. We were so packed we would not have fallen out if, jesting, a god had ripped off the roof, turned the vehicle upside down and shaken us. Sweat seeped out under my arm in dark noxious stains into the synthetic material of my blouse. What a terrible day I was going to have at the office pressing my elbows into my sides as I typed my copy. Other occupants gripped the seat in front, or propped elbows on the door, oblivious to the moisture and odours their armpits exuded. The warmth of body upon body, the commonality said 'we are here', and I became dejected again. It was harrowing to be part of such undistinguished humanity.

13

I disembarked at the corner of Jason Moyo where combis from the university turned to their rank. From there to Robert Mugabe Avenue where the agency was situated was two blocks, past fast food outlets populated by girls in too tight pants, and penny markets which matched imperfect foreign products to the local market perfectly and sold them for dozens of Zimbabwean dollars, past jewellery shops designed for someone else that glared at you in your office clothes forbiddingly. The morning was beginning to glare just as fiercely. Heat glittered and undulated like a reptile's skin on the paving stones and tarmac. The ground rejected such torturing heat so early in the morning and heaved up circles of it like sacred pools so that twin women walked as though upon water on the mirages. I slumped through the agency's revolving door into Steers and Associates' air conditioned reception.

'Hah-eee!' That was Pedzi, the youthful receptionist. '*Sisi Tambu, mamuka sei?* Did you get up well this morning?' she chattered on, exhibiting more *unhu* than one would have expected from one so young and modern. 'I-i-ih, your hair! It's so beautiful! Is it for the advertising awards? Who did it for you, *Sisi* Tambu?'

As she spoke, she smiled deferentially, in the way youth does when it seeks for inspiration. The fact that I was a copywriter in the biggest advertising agency in the country represented to this eager girl something she could hope for. Taking me for an elder sister figure, ignorant of my position with respect to my own sister, young Pedzi confided, soon after I came to the agency, that she had failed every single one of her O-Levels. Her teeth sparkling, she related how her one regret at the time was not taking more subjects to demonstrate how, no matter what she was taught nor by whom, she would not ever learn any part of it. Pedzi had gone so far as to laugh at her father and suggest he could take the exams himself if he found them so important. However, she continued, after I informed her of my university degree but not its lower class status, when she became a receptionist in a suspicious firm she returned to reading the requisite English and Maths, and three other subjects, in addition to taking her typing. Now she possessed pass marks on five separate pieces of cardboard and was taking her A-Levels in two of the subjects. She ended the tête-à-tête by asking me, as the workload was heavy and taxing, whether I would help her. 'Do you think you'll make it?' was my reply as she gazed on with shy but shining eyes. No, I had no desire to encourage. She was that kind of girl, having that kind of effect on another woman. A man with biceps as big as her beauty would without moving a muscle be labelled a bully. The receptionist was taller than most of us and weighed perhaps a quarter, with skin as tranquil as midnight, in spite of turquoise eye shadow. Pedzi was always neat and precise in her memory for a client's name, her inscribing of messages on the while-you-were-out pad, and in her manicures, coiffeurs and the portions she put on her plate in the cafeteria. Not one of those people who can eat a horse without a bulge, she at another time confided candidly that she had compensated for that incapacity with discipline. Pedzi and her vitality were overpowering. When she turned her admiring smile my way, I did not have the wherewithal to face it and shrank from what she was requesting. Yes, something each time closed at her adulation; a small pane slid down that had always remained raised when I spoke to colleagues in the dormitory and at university who did not exhibit this admiration. When this thing locked I believed this girl who looked like a goddess was mocking. Could a mocking person be liked? How, indeed! Besides, she was one of those children I taught in Mabvuku, a born-location.

So this morning I scowled at her upper arms that neither the adipose of age, nor of pregnancy, nor for that matter of gluttony had ever spread. Her only fault was her voice which was pitched and modulated like a siren. However, in order to maintain my disapproval, I steeled myself so that I was not softened by this weakness. Quite on the contrary, in order to maintain my disdain of the younger woman, I concentrated on her hair, which although smooth was coloured an iridescent purple. The style of her clothing was another thing that provoked both women and men and confirmed the girl was outrageous. Her appearance was proof, I believed, that the reason for her friendliness was that Pedzi planned to manipulate me into taking her on as a model for the firm's advertisements.

'Hot, isn't it!' the receptionist's friendliness exuded. She tilted a hand topped with long rectangular nails in furious fuchsia towards her cheeks and fluttered the fingers, fanning. 'At least I was here earlier,' she sighed with an engaging, but stressed grin. 'In the high densities, you wake up for your transport if you want to be on time. Those cocks, we might as well forget about them, even they sleep too much! It's a question of setting your alarm clock properly. At least I got here before the heat started killing.' She looked at me with her open face, nails still fanning.

I did not share with her my own experience of high density living, preferring my address to be in the avenues.

'Who's being killed by anything?' I snapped. Releasing some of the irritation I still carried from being interchanged with Isabel provided a momentary satisfaction. 'Who's been killed?' I became sarcastic as the quick contentment faded. 'Where d'you come from! Ethiopia, hey? Biafra, Pedzi? What about Sierra Leone? You're going to have to read that history very hard, you know. Keep going! But careful, hey! You might end up knowing something!'

She sucked her lower lip and let it droop out and sucked it in again. I was gratified to see she was sufficiently upset for her to spoil her appearance by licking off most of her lipstick. Ah, what an outrageous and despicable person I had become! Regaining confidence at Pedzi's distress, I proceeded a few paces behind the reception desk to the lifts which were secluded behind some potted elephant ear palm trees. I was preoccupied with how my day was now rescued from its disturbing beginning, and this clearly, as I look back, is why I did not take in the situation that was unfolding.

The executives' offices were on the fourth floor. The lift was stationed at this uppermost floor when I pressed the button. Four-two-one, the display counted down, carrying executives with it. The elevator clanked to a halt. Jerking to my senses, I ducked around. The bathrooms were a few metres down the corridor. But in my high heels I was obliged to walk slowly on the tiles of Italian marble. I was too late. A woman I did not want to meet, the 'Afro-Shine' executive stepped forward into the foyer.

'Hi! Howzit?' she asked of my back. At the sound of her voice I felt compelled to turn and face my former class-mate, Tracey, for that was who it was. Ms Stevenson had climbed high up in the agency hierarchy now, and may or may not have been responsible for my employment.

'Howzit going?' Tracey repeated. Before I could answer she rushed on, 'I've got a nine-thirty. I won't be back before lunch, but maybe first thing this arvy. By the way,' she flung over her shoulder, 'It's got to be read, hey! Make sure you get Belinda to type it, Tambu.'

The streaky hair was streaky still, but now in bronzed shades of blonde, a combination that was authoritative and brooked no nonsense, and this hair stood up in spikes upon the top of the head, and lay firm and trim, like a steel hel-met, at the back of it, hinting at a superficial playfulness, but an iron will behind it. Her normal healthy outdoor colour was accentuated by careful contouring with delicate brushes. Her fingernails were short and shiny, devoid of artificial colour, except for a rim of white at the tip; square-shaped and adamant, they were the fingernails of a woman who, like Sister Emmanuel, pointed at objects that should be gone, as a consequence of which action, such objects invariably went. That was the new Tracey, in the new Zimbabwe, advertising executive for Afro-Shine, a local product by young entrepreneurs in baggy suits, and also Deputy Creative Director. Her product was finally out-selling rival Pointouch Advertising's 'Bright and Lovely', following the first campaign we launched together and also because it was cheaper. Surely now, she would slap palms with me, as at school in the corridor she had slapped palms with Ntombi and Patience, on the basis of our common success! This I thought of often. But Tracey's smiles remained as cordial as on the day I first reported for work at Steers *et al*, and as distant. The most she volunteered was reading my copy before it went to the Creative Director. Neither of us could ever bring herself to mention our common schooldays.

'Morning, Tracey. I'll see what I can do,' I replied non-committally, with anger smouldering only in my eyes, ready to be doused down to a friendly light if she turned, as I stared after her. The lift door closed. I swore, hoping Pedzi had not observed the brief contact, and again pressed the elevator button.

'Hi, Belinda!' I exclaimed as I entered the creative department. It was open plan, with copy taking up one section, art and graphics another, while a third area was set aside for traffic. A colour code, orange for art, green for traffic and blue for copy, which extended to the extra large tiles, kept the divisions visual. I was not friends with Belinda. In fact it was for this very reason that I spoke to her so cheerfully. All the other workers on the floor were white so that everything had to be thought out, the smallest greetings mapped and manoeuvred. This was particularly true of Belinda who always had too much to do, and whom I was now required to prepare for extra typing.

'Low, more like it,' the copy typist returned. 'Never mind hi!' She paused to deliver a shuddering groan, her hands wilting from her wrists over her typewriter keys. 'Tambu, have you got any ideas for this bloody campaign? What is this? D'you call this copy!' She glanced at the uneven print beside her machine. It was type-written on the copywriter's jerking manual. Margins did not match. Every second word was crossed out and written over again, and scribbled through and another inscribed above it. Meanwhile arrows swept up to the body of the text from tiny paragraphs pencilled in a cramped script at the bottom of the page, to indicate where the writer's late inspirations were to be inserted. The writer was Dick Lawson, the senior copywriter.

'He probably thinks he's written a bestseller!' fumed the typist. 'And man, he's got it in for me!' Belinda's eyebrows wriggled over her forehead. 'There just can't be another explanation! D'you think I got it yesterday, hey, Tambu? Imagine him giving it to me when there's actually time to type it? N-o-o—o!' she dragged the syllable out. 'Ten to five, hey, I ask you! That's when it's chucked on my desk. He's lucky I was still effing here and he doesn't even know when he's lucky! Call this a bloody advert!' She pushed the copy towards me.

It was my policy not to read other copywriter's copy. In this way I protected myself from being accused of copying. I merely smiled at Belinda.

'Ad, my foot,' she snorted. 'It's an effing encyclopaedia! I bet you could do better than that in ten minutes, hey! I really do! How about it? Why not, hey? I'll type it. He's going to rewrite this five times. You know him. Go on, Tambu! Pretend it was a mistake. Go for it! Take this campaign off him.'

It was tempting. ZimAir. I heaved a buttock onto her lime green desk top and pulled Dick's efforts towards me.

'Brevity is the soul of wit!' encouraged Belinda. 'And all that, hey! Your concepts are always so much shorter!'

Take Dick's campaign! Make it my own! Never mind about him. I was beginning to think I could do it. 'Fly higher than your dreams and further . . . with ZimAir – because with ZimAir, the sky is not the limit!' The phrases, practically of their own account, began forming. I was, however, prevented from dictating my composition when a question concerning brevity struck me. As each of my actions required analytical planning, so other people's statements required meticulous analysis. I wished to be careful as it was not clear to me what else, beyond what she had voiced, Belinda's comment concerning precision implied. Of course, the industry required copy to be brief. But by saying what she had, was the copy typist employing a shrouded code that meant I exhibited an insufficiency of development, that my succinctness was a sign of paucity? Dick was able to quote pages of Camus, Tolstoy, Pushkin, Mann, people I'd only read without memorising a single sentence. Did it matter then, if his copy required several précis, when he had all this at his disposal? Didn't elegance require elaboration? Wasn't that why Shona poetry and homestead rituals repeated, while Mann's sentences convoluted again and again and twisted one more impossible time upon themselves?

The man in question shambled in while Belinda and I endeavoured to conspire together. 'Loser!' Belinda hissed under her breath, startling me by referring not to Dick but to me. So I missed the moment to bond with Belinda by defrauding someone else of a project.

Ta, ta-ta-ta! Ta-ta-ta! Belinda's nails beat a cross staccato into the silence. To break it, without appearing to do so in case she was offended, I grinned, 'Hi, Dick!' Ta, ta-ta-ta, Belinda's fingers continued like small missiles aiming at Dick's endless copy and my sense of failure and her grievance. Her eyes flickered from the typewriter to the sheet of scribbled paper. I slid from her desk to stand by, half hoping to hear her insist I do myself the favour of appropriation.

'MYSTERY TOURS,' the brand name appeared.

Belinda released the shift lock and reverted to lower case. The two words were the headline after the client's name, ZimAir, was inserted in a little box up in the left hand corner of the page. Next the product, Great Zimbabwe, was typed. This was followed by the names of first the advertising executive, Tracey Stevenson, and then the copywriter, Dick Lawson, in their labelled boxes. Done with headers and names, Belinda stabbed into the copy's body.

'Who were the ancient architects? How many centuries must a river run to make this magnificence? Take off your shoes – if you value your soul! Zimbabwe is an ancient land. Long, long ago, when the stones could speak, folk tales began. Air Zimbabwe brings you to the incredible places where people hear the whisper of the stones still speaking. The pearl of the British Empire is shining again! Its glow is unknown and ancient. Dare to luxuriate in the utmost of comfort, with ZimAir's Mystery Getaway! Zimbabwe, the free pearl in the body of southern Africa, is open for everybody to experience its ancient mystery,' ran the opening paragraph. 'No-one knows who built the awe-inspiring Zimbabwe Ruins,' whispered the following one mysteriously. 'These masterly turrets, tunnels and tapering walls are situated just north. . .' There followed some German names, two paragraphs of archaeological detail and several lines devoted to a Berlin museum.

Raphael came in, pushing the early morning tea trolley with his lugubrious gait towards the traffic typist's table. Belinda relished the chance to stop typing long words in endless sentences about acropolises, dentate patterns and conical towers. 'Great! Here's the tea boy!' she beamed.

Raphael passed up the office handing out mugs, and then trundled once more down it. This brought him back to me, as he refilled Belinda's tea cup.

'I'm not going back down the office. Next time be there if what you want is tea to drink!' he snarled at me in Shona. 'I'm not your boy! I'm not your servant, he! We're all workers here! You'd better hear me properly!' Lifting a pained and dignified chin, he trundled back through the office, pouring more beverages for those who wished and accepting more empty mugs from those who did not. My tea was cold when I reached my desk. There was a little puddle around the bottom, where Raphael had plonked it down. This put me into another dilemma. Should I go and throw the tea away in the bathroom? What if the cleaners complained of stains and dregs? What would Raphael do if he had to carry back a mug of cold scummy liquid? I held my breath and downed the mug's contents. He was so annoyed that I'd forgotten to ask him for sugar.

My stomach curdled at the horrible liquid and tension had it bubbling back up as heartburn. The trouble was, what had just happened with the Mystery Tours campaign occurred much too often. Dick bounced ideas off me. I bounced other ideas back. Dick let them fall and wrote his version. This, under the pretext of Dick's being engaged with an urgent new job, Tracey asked me to look over.

Now I'd have to edit the ZimAir copy, which was how Tracey, Dick and I referred to rewriting the senior copywriter's work so that his name remained legitimately in its box at the top of the form. I sighed, wishing again I'd taken up Belinda's offer to steal the text from him! Oh, was I ever going to function in the new Zimbabwe, if I couldn't go to the necessary lengths, stop letting people put their names to what in the end was mine! Another bout of misery threatened. I took out the duplicating paper we used for notes to plunge into a pool of words.

Words – you could do so much with words. You could maul them and twist them and tear them, but if you did they would not dance. Yet words were forgiving. You grappled with them and sweated and when you were tired became gentle, and the words leaped for you, streaked with healing powers from depths, as it is said of dolphins. So I loved words and attacked the Afro-Shine copy Tracey requested with a vengeance, waiting for the words to exhaust everything, including tension. In this state of readiness for work, it seemed to me all was prescribed and normal. There was a calming 'I have seen you before'-ness, a 'yes you were here yesterday'-ness 'and will be there tomorrow'-ness, an everydayness about the whole situation that was calming and tranquilising, and which enabled me to work through my concept for the Afro-Shine copy, following an obscure beginning of phrases interspersed with doodles. So I created, patiently writing draft after draft of nonsense, labouring towards inspiration. In between, to relieve the pressure, I wondered who had called that morning. If it wasn't Maiguru, then who? Maybe someone from school, or perhaps my cousin was home – it was Nyasha! What a wild, exciting mystery this was, someone spending money to engage me in a telephone conversation!

A few minutes before one, Pedzi called, shrieking that Tracey was delayed. I scribbled on through the lunch hour, waiting. When it happened, they would see how I could spin that tongue, how I could make the language leap and spin and dance, how like a soul in and out and round and round in rhythm I could twist it! I stayed in after hours to clean type on Belinda's machine, not daring to ask her for the effort. Dick, large and round-shouldered, waved as he lumbered out. In the airy recess that was partitioned off the creative floor, Mary Mallory, the Creative Director's secretary, was still calling airlines to make bookings at six o'clock that evening. The Afro-Shine copy would, she nodded in distracted stress when I waved it tiredly to attract her attention, be in the Creative Director's tray the next morning.

As mysterious as were the builders of Great Zimbabwe to the world's great historians, was the sensation of pleasure to me. The day following my aborted conspiracy with Belinda, however, a sufficiently large pleasure awaited me in the creative department to cause me to forget Mrs May, who again that day had greeted me with, 'How are you this morning, Isabel, and isn't it a shame about Tambu!' In my tray, officially, lay the Mystery Tours folder, along with Dr White toothpaste, another new local product, and Honey Valley tinned foods that Maiguru had, from time to time at the mission, brought to the table for a treat. For Dick was busy now with Mighty Dough, a new chain of bakeries. My thoughts immediately turned to work, for I could see my name in the box in the copywriter's corner. 'Down! Down!' the ideas slithered at first and then rushed on like the proverbial lemmings. 'Down in Honey Valley where the finest fresh foods grow, there's a hustling and a bustling before the cock begins to crow!' Here was something I was good at! It did not matter so much anymore that my uncle's wish for me to peer down infected throats was frustrated. It was wonderful to believe in my prowess again, particularly without the burden of memorising hundreds of pages. Perhaps I would win a prize at the advertising awards! Then Baba and Maiguru would see me on television, and Mai would have to find another laugh that was not me!

I worked late regularly thereafter, in order to complete the new jobs excellently. After I left the creative department, I strolled to the hostel through the park, giving Mrs May time to busy herself in the little office behind her desk for the end of day before I arrived. The afternoon the ZimAir copy was proofed I returned home even later than usual. Ting-ting-ting! A medium-sized bronze bell in hand, Mrs May was announcing supper.

'Oh, hello, Isabel.' The matron thrust her hand into the bell's dome to damp it.

I smiled tiredly. 'Mrs May, good evening. What's the good news? Have you heard anything else from your son?'

'There was a telephone call for you,' she said. 'Tambu went off to find you.'

I smiled at her again, proceeded to my room to wash my hands, and then returned to the dining room. Here too, as with the creative floor, you stood in the entrance, surveying the options. For deciding where to sit was a dismal, discouraging business.

The large room was almost empty, but we all knew the

patterns. The white girls, who were in the majority, took the tables at the top and front of the room, away from the door and under the windows. This left a pair of tables, awkward as afterthoughts, as the hall filled up, unoccupied in the draughts of the entrance. Here the handful of us took our seats, beginning with chairs positioned as far from the door as possible. We were, practically to a person, young Zimbabweans who had no parental backing but who had acquired the means through some sort of tenacity, however dubious, to lodge at the respectable hostel.

There were six seats to a table. We were fourteen individuals, which meant that each meal time two of us endured unfathomable dismay at the thought of turning out a remainder in the mathematics of fourteen being divided by half a dozen; and of course this fear soon became concentrated in two individuals. My habits were known, and naturally were spluttered over (with some exaggeration) behind my back by the other occupants of these designated tables. Isabel and company did not invite me to sit with them, even on days when some of them reached the dining hall before me. In fact, and I have a confidence of Isabel's to prove it, these girls on occasion went so far as to prevent my joining them by whispers as pointed as arrows, and sidelong glances. On the worst occasion, craving company, I boldly carried my plate to the table, only to be informed another resident had booked the seat, so that I was forced to sit alone at the end of a table at the opposite end of which were grouped three white girls, and although I examined the table I left carefully, the other resident did not come. However, in addition to me there was another person left over, a woman of gold, who said her name was Katherine McLaren. She did not speak of her mother's nationality, but her father, whom she mentioned frequently, was British, from Scotland.

I occasionally compared myself with this Katherine McLaren, liking to think she was even older than I, although my judgment may merely have been influenced by the preserving effects of concentrations of melanin. Katherine always sighed a lot when she entered the dining room. The girls I could not sit with laughed at this. 'Me, what Mai used to ask me,' Isabel brayed loud enough for Katherine to hear on many occasions. 'What she always said is, Isabel, why are you never closing the door! Are you telling me you've got a tail? But with this one, hm! That Katherine! Can you ask if she's got it, a tail! No! That one, she is a tail!' This was followed by gleeful guffaws, a merriment based on Katherine's flesh, as premeditated as murder. I too participated in this, hoping that by doing so I would be spared the embarrassment of being left over, and be included at one of our tables. I did, however, endeavour to be circumspect, as I did not want to upset the woman excessively since this would turn her, another person, against me. Therefore, each time, I restrained my Adam's apple from bobbing particularly obviously.

The cause of our malice was Katherine's habit of arriving for her meal in the wake of Fiona, Jane and Barbara, Mrs May's trio of haloed girls. They clicked across the hall, bumping into each other like energetic calves. They sat in an intricate little knot that precluded anyone joining them. However Katherine invariably braved the barrier to tag herself on at the end of their table. There she remained, separated from her table mates by two seats, to ingest only ever in halves what was before her: toast, egg, steak, mashed potato or porridge. For Katherine everything must be completely split. She even meted out this treatment to the dull blobs of margarine that sat squat contemplating consumption, like suspects contemplating execution, on a thick white plate in the centre of the table. Yes, Katherine cleaved every section of the spread in two before allowing it onto her side plate. I could not bear this solitary display and never so much as tried to sit next to Ms McLaren. Now, this evening, wishing to enjoy the success of completing my numerous assignments, I stood working out where everybody might go so as to find the most stress-free position. While all this was whizzing through my head, I was informed by Isabel, who had it from Fiona and hoped the latter had it right, that indeed it was Tambudzai Sigauke, myself, who had received a phone call.

In the cramped telephone booth next to Mrs May's reception, a voice close to the apparatus was speaking to another in the sibilant confidential tone one uses when addressing a person some distance away about a telephone call one is making. I could not make out what was said. When it finished the voice sighed. Influenced by this, I did too, very lengthily.

'Ah, there's somebody,' the voice exclaimed and grew louder as the speaker turned. 'Who is it?' came the anxious question. 'Tambudzai Sigauke! Can I speak to her, please?'

'She is on the line.'

'Oh, is that you, *Sisi* Tambu?'

'Maiguru!' My voice jumped with joy, but I did not have time to tell my aunt how elated her communication made me.

'Are you well, dear? But perhaps you'll tell me that later, Sister Tambu. I have to be quick now, because there's someone here for you.'

'Wait, Maiguru! Is everyone all right? Have you heard from my cousin? How is Babamukuru managing?' I called, more loudly than was necessary. Instead of an answer there was a fumbling at the other end, followed by low whispering.

'Tambudzai!' I pressed my lips together and now refused to answer. 'Tambudzai, *iwe*, Tambudzai! Don't say you don't know who is talking!' the voice commanded. 'Don't say you can't tell the voice of the woman who bore you! And don't tell me,' Mai went on sharply, for it was she, 'that you're not there! You are holding that phone, breathing! I can hear you!

'Ko!' she responded to my greeting immediately in a shrill accusing voice, without bothering to return the pleasantry, disrupting a lot of the space around the line with waves of agitation. 'Ko! So that's what you're doing now! *Kushinga makadaro*! Being that tough. *Rambai makashinga*! Well, keep on doing it!' I waited, patient with helplessness for her to finish, praying there would be time to gather my thoughts before she did that, and she did not disappoint me.

'Even if you keep on keeping quiet,' Mai hissed over the kilometres implacably, 'do you think we can't find you, child! As if we can't walk! Even if we don't have cars, our legs haven't been taken by anyone, you should know that, my daughter!'

I retracted the receiver from my ear in order to reduce the volume. Mai was at once silent, only to resume again as soon as she heard my breathing. 'Whatever else we haven't got, legs are something we have still attached to our bodies! Even those you can't bear to think of, even with one, Tambudzai, I want to tell you, people are still walking!'

I was silent, unable to think of anything to say to this, an advantage Mai took to continue, 'Since we're walking and have come to the phone, I want to ask you something, daughter. I want to ask, are you aware who gave birth to you? Can you tell me you know which stomach you came out of! Or do you think you dropped from a tree big and ripe like that! Or sprang from a well! You came from a stomach. Do you know that?' she demanded. 'Tell me!'

I decided not to be angry and conceded in a conciliatory way, 'Yes, Mai, I know it.'

'Well then!' My mother was disconcerted for a moment in the face of such compliance. However, she soon found another position for the ambush. 'So child, what are you telling me? Saying all along, ever since you know, you've been sitting there in that Harare of yours, enjoying knowing you were borne by someone!'

'Sitting in Harare!' Imitation was useful at times of uncertainty. To buy myself time, I repeated my excited mother's statement.

'No, no! Don't tell me you didn't give your number to anyone! You gave it, don't we know it! And didn't the people you gave your number to tell you we were waiting?' Mai's voice beat at my ear drum.

'Waiting?' I repeated again, my heart sliding into my bowels. 'Ah, was anything said by anyone,' I pushed myself to improvise, 'about waiting? Mai, if it was, I did not hear it. No one calls, Mai. I don't call anyone. The last time I talked to anyone. . .' I groped to prevent mentioning Maiguru by name in order to keep the atmosphere between the two, where there was sufficient hate to murder a spouse, as calm as possible. 'The last time I spoke with anyone that side, that was very long ago! And I cannot remember a thing about waiting.' Having taken this in, Mai was silent a bit too long for comfort, so that I exclaimed, 'Waiting, Mai! Surely, no. What I heard people talking of that time was coming.'

'*Iwe*, Tambudzai!' There was a sigh in my mother's voice, 'Truly, you are still a child. Your mind carries the thoughts of an infant which cannot see beyond what is shown to the essence of anything! Ko, think about it, *mwana'ngu*. Did anyone talk of money? That time that you are talking of when the coming was mentioned, did anyone say anything about money? And how could we come without that money? At the same time how could we talk of it when there was none of it! Doesn't decency say it is up to the person who has, to talk of what is there and how it can be used to help. Isn't that what we did? We had the wish to visit. That is what we told the ones you speak to! The wish that we had is what we spoke of! We expected those with money to speak of it!

'But anyway!' she took the opportunity to speak in a derogatory way of Maiguru. 'How could you have known? That is why the elders said "*Kuudza mwana upedzisira!*" Those people who have been telling you things, my child, they haven't been doing it properly!' In the time that I did not answer because I was gathering defences together once more, she commented snidely, 'No, we won't forget again. Next time we send a message, we'll know a child is receiving it! Even those white people you learnt with didn't teach you to grow up, did they? So since we'll be talking to a child, we'll know we can't be asking for anything!'

'How much is the bus fare, now?' I eventually brought out the question Mai wanted to hear, but now it only made her laugh harshly.

'Ho-ho,' she scoffed. 'Now, when we don't need it, then all of a sudden you're asking!'

'Ah, Mai! Don't say that! Don't tell me you're not coming.' I struggled to press disappointment into my expression instead of the profound relief I experienced. The resulting hollowness in my voice made Mai merry with malice. 'He-he-de daughter! Is that what you think, that we just sit around doing nothing, just sitting and waiting for things to happen? Even before you came along, long before that, I was doing!'

'I know, Mai!' I swallowed apprehensively and tried conciliation while at the same time I threw nervous glances at the door to see how much of this Mrs May, or perhaps Isabel and company were interested in, and understanding.

'Eh-eh!' Mai pretended surprise. 'So now you even know what you haven't seen! You already know how hard I have been working in the vegetable garden so that I can come and see you. That since Babamukuru put the water pipe in we've been selling vegetables to everybody, even Gambe whose fields as well as whose vegetable garden are both down by the river!' Pride expanded her voice. 'Two dozen of my tomatoes,' she went on, 'were as big as a woman's fist. And they weren't just full of water either! You know, Tambudzai, since Babamukuru refuses to give us his money,' she charged, not caring if he were listening, 'since then fertilizer has been difficult to get. But the tomatoes when they grow well, they aren't just full of water! They're sweet, so people love those sweet tomatoes. They even leave that Samhungu alone with his bags of fertilizer, coming down here! And of course I say, they are good, aren't they? And when people say yes, I charge them, and I put a bonus on top for the sweetness!'

'Tomatoes, Mai! You're charging more! For a little dish! Then how much is it you ask?' As usual, in my dealings with Mai, shame welled up. Was there any misfortune in the world as bad as being the daughter of this woman! First her habits were ill bred and intolerable, next she plotted the murder of her brother-in-law, Babamukuru, her *samusha*, who was her benefactor and without whom neither she nor her family would be anything. Then she measured her achievement by the number of tomatoes she sold at inflated prices to impoverished neighbours. How sorry for myself I felt, and how angry with my mother for making me suffer like this. For her part, Mai was not in the least disconcerted.

'Eho! Yes, Tambudzai,' she scoffed again. 'Do you think money is only for you people and your education! Me, I put my prices up! So,' she crowed in her triumph, 'I am coming down to you. I'm bringing Netsai, maybe you've forgotten you have a sister. I want you in that city of yours to see to your sister's leg! You must see what you can do to help her!'

'That took an awfully long time!' Mrs May observed, staring over her glasses, as I emerged from the stuffy booth several minutes later. 'Was it for you after all, Isabel? I was positive,' she went on, puckering her brow, 'I was positive the lady said Tambu. Well, I hope it isn't bad news you received,' the matron sighed, reflecting on her own unhappy plight. 'You look a lot sadder now than you did when you went in there.'

I began to shake. My mouth was sour with too many angers. 'It's not Isabel!' I boiled at the astonished woman,

276

shouting aggressively. 'I've got a name, Mrs May! Tambudzai Sigauke, for your information. Why can't you learn to use it!'

The trouble with making a point is that you also hear it. Immediately the words were out I recoiled from them in distress. My own voice whipped me and cowed me terribly. Surely I had not planned to say this, to contradict, as it were, this hopeless old woman, the matron! But said it had been. I could not retrieve the words, even though already that was what I desperately wanted. Oh, if only Mai had not called, I groaned to myself wretchedly, I would have remained on my guard. Yet here I was, having done the opposite, insisting on my own particularity! What was going to happen now? Mrs May could not be happy! However, there was not another way to act, therefore I bungled on plaintively. 'Actually, it isn't! What I mean is, it is me. If you don't mind, Mrs May, it's someone else, not Isabel!' Finally, coming to a tired end of my disclaimers, I declared, 'Like I said, even if I got the tone wrong, it's just me, Mrs May, Tambu.'

I waited, tremulously smiling. I was full of apprehension watching the matron, as I had not any experience of contradicting in this way and did not know what would occur as a result of it.

As the calibre of crosswords was still considerably high, Mrs May had taken to bringing a dictionary into the reception with her to help her solve the puzzle. Now the matron pressed a finger on its page to make sure she would find her spot when it was needed and, when she was certain nothing was amiss, she looked up to continue the conversation. She was marvellously benign. With her free hand, her knuckle removed an edge of pink from a lip corner and she regarded me, smiling. 'Of course not!' she conceded, examining me carefully so that I was sure she was impressing all my characteristics upon her intelligence. On she went to my great joy, 'How on earth could I have thought you were Isabel! You don't look anything like each other! What was I thinking of! How are you, dear? I do hope it wasn't bad news, er. . . er . . .' she hesitated and her cheeks quivered with discomfort, '. . . well. . . er. . . Gertrude!'

At this repetition of what had so angered me, I became once more as close to cheerful as I was capable. The situation immediately grew clearer as good taste and tolerance always told one what could or could not be undertaken, and I became pleased, in spite of my mother's opinion, with the good quality of my development. I began with great deliberateness to fade and recede, so as not to put out the matron. Of course, one couldn't continue hinting at a person's mistake. Especially not when the person was the head of the hostel! Going on and doing it would only annoy her and fortify conflict. Armed with this pacifist knowledge, I felt once more in control. I considered, as I walked to my room, if one day Mrs May remembered me, over and above my serenity, then that would be a bonus.

14

Being so magnanimous towards Mrs May delivered me into a state of gracious peace. The night was thick with the sweet soporific odours of the garden's flowering shrubs, an atmosphere in which I floated, oddly suspended between waking and sleep, feeling myself beatified and exalted, divinely, immaculately able to turn the other cheek, grandly exhibiting the supreme virtue of tolerance. That evening I felt for the first time, as I lay in bed, like a complete woman.

It was only towards dawn, when the nocturnal tranquillity turned to ashen grey behind the curtains, and night's flowers stopped their secretions and waking doves demanded an interrogation of fathers, when the day stretched out before me again, that I recalled this new day, of all days, could not be countenanced. A twig knocked on the roof, and it was as if Mai in her navy and white spotted *doek*, tapped on the glass door to the foyer. Yet, it was impossible to instruct her not to travel to the city, and so the question remained, where would I put her? How was an ageing African matron to be explained away at the hostel? The only alternative to explanation was smuggling her to my room, and again that was not possible. Mrs May had done it with men, had leant over the reception desk, her powdered nostrils flared, breathing in deeply, smelling. I was chilled to imagine what stimuli might settle upon the matron's nasal nerve endings. Wood-smoke, dust and sweat, whatever they were, natural or not, would disclose both my mother's presence, and my unmentionable origin. And if my mother resorted to coercion, bringing Netsai with her, then those aromas would be concentrated! Beyond that, an explanation to the matron concerning the absent limb would be necessary, one that did not aggravate her awful grief about her husband's passing. It was not possible to imagine a more dreadful event: Mrs May and Twiss Hostel's young women meeting a walking – or more precisely, one that went hopla-hopla – a lurching memento of their war-time tragedies! How inconsiderate of Mai! How inconvenient of that mother of mine to want to be where she was not and produce such a dilemma for her daughter! Reluctantly I realised a journey to the village, which I had not visited since Babamukuru's beating and which I had declared I would not visit again, was necessary in order to avert disaster and stave off my mother's arrival.

I began calculations immediately of the quantities of which groceries I would buy, and how much could be transported, bearing in mind the kilometres long walk from the bus stop to the homestead. Soon I was satisfied with a sense of the correctness and expediency of this strategy, and awaited my pay cheque at the month end. However, these plans were, in the end, not implemented due to a series of accelerating events at the agency.

'How'z it, Tambu!' It was shortly before pay day, which occurred on the penultimate Friday of each month, and this particular pay day fell a couple of weeks after my telephone conversation with my mother. Dick called out to me as he destroyed a piece of duplicating paper between his palms. He tossed it over his shoulder impatiently and it landed beside the blue wastepaper basket. 'Hi!' he repeated, and sauntered with his hands pressed into his pockets over the sky-coloured tiles to my desk. Here he stood peering down from his mountainous height, with his head pressed low and his shoulders permanently rounded, as though from the weight of his shaggy beard. From his pocket he withdrew a roll of papers. With one hand he banged these repetitively into the palm of the other. Appearing to consider a new idea, he selected a sheet from the roll, folded the chosen item small and wedged it into his back pocket.

The copywriter's behaviour was perplexing, but it was best to be polite. 'How'z it, Dick!' I answered.

'You got a moment?' He considered for a minute and seemed to change his mind for the second time, as though the nature of this mind of his persistently annoyed him. 'Not here. How about me buying you a coke? How about Pedro's?'

Today Dick's mind was more unsettled than usual, for he changed it once more when we stepped onto the pavement, proposing now coffee at the Double Donkey.

'I hate bouncing things in the office,' he confided, his eyes heavy with paranoia, as we scraped back cumbersome chairs at wrought iron tables striped in the red, blue and white colours of northern nations. 'You can't even *think* to yourself in that place, because if you do, you know everyone's listening.' His long, heavy face, with its depressed cheek bones from which flesh hung meatily like hams, creased with concern at this untoward circumstance. 'Before you're even sure you want to go with it, the Creative Director's heard everything. The client as well! Because Bill,' he mentioned the Creative Director's name with umbrage, 'just went ahead and proposed it. Then of course you're stuck with whatever crap it was, and you've just got to take it and pretend you like it!' I nodded sympathetically. My colleague's shoulders descended from where they were bunched up, as though seeking refuge, under his earlobes.

'Anyway, I've got this.' Dick fumbled at a cigarette with yellow fingers. When it was clamped between his teeth and trickling smoke, he extracted the fold of paper selected earlier, with finger and thumb, from his back pocket. This he examined without actually reading, before gazing up from under eyebrows like bottlebrushes, with something vastly put out in his expression. 'Hope you don't mind, hey!' His tone was surly and pained, confirming he did not like me, without volunteering a reason. I ruminated without conclusion over what this reason might be for some moments, during which Dick smoothed out his sheet of paper and started reading. 'Do you want to shine in the night? You want stars in your hair, right?' He grew excited, and started tapping out the time, first with his foot, then with his hand. Finally he was jigging and jiving in his seat, jerking in an astonishingly rhythmical way the entire weight of his cumbrous body. A smile stretched over his face and lit up his grey eyes, and a vein on the bridge of his nose pulsed to the beat of the sing-song. 'Sparkle like the disco light! No one needs the sun when you're in sight! You're hair's Afro-Shine bright. Afro-Shine, all the time! For brilliant women!'

I could not recall when I had been happier. It was not on the first occasion of indescribable joy, when I had left the homestead to live with my relatives at the mission. Nor was it on the second occasion of entry into Sacred Heart.

Nor was it either on the third occasion when I read the slip of paper that confirmed I, Tambudzai Sigauke, had obtained the best O-Level results in my year at the convent. No, none of these events compared with this moment. For now I had moved forward and been recognised as a result of my own resources. I had used what I had been given to take into the world to achieve a work of merit. The perfect peace of a few weeks before returned. Copywriting was a lowly profession! What did that matter! It was my lowly profession and I was good at it, so now I was going to own it! Doing what I was good at, I saw I was appreciated. On the opposite side of the table was the proof: the senior copywriter completely taken with reading my copy, which had been completed on schedule and handed in to the Creative Director. Other people relaxing at red, white and blue tables observed us, smiles fluttering about their faces, for we were an intriguing new Zimbabwean couple. I leant back in my chair and stared the fact in the face that I was about to become a jubilant woman. When had something good been done before, and I had received acknowledgement mingled with congratulations? That happened such a long time ago, I could not remember. Soon, though, reward would be reaped for effort. Then the trip to the homestead, that tiresome journey would take on a different character, when I went to show everybody how well I was performing, and carried evidence in plastic bags bulging with margarine, sugar, cooking oil and candles. The forest gives only to the exhausted, the elders said, and now the giving was scheduled! The coffee was served while I dreamed pleasantly like this and listened to Dick's enthusiastic droning.

283

'I didn't have a clue there was all that competition,' the senior copywriter observed, tearing the tips off three sachets of sugar at once and shaking the granules into his beverage. 'But it looks like there's hundreds out there, these hair straightening products. Bill told me all about it.' I sipped my coffee calmly and smiled encouragingly to help him to make his point, for it was clearly difficult for him to be obliged to admit how outstanding the copy I had written was. At the same time I wondered how I would take praise after such a long time with such paucity of it, and at this I admonished myself not to behave in the same self-defeating way as had been the case with Belinda. Dick examined the paper again and lit another cigarette, a prelude to suggesting, 'I think the night/bright lines might just be the right jingle, hey? What d'you think? Did you have any ideas for the music?'

'Disco!' I nodded automatically. 'The brief's fifteen to thirty-five, right? With that line in, you can't do anything except disco.'

'It's low end though,' mused Dick. 'I'm looking for a common denominator for that market. So what about rumba?'

'Rumba,' I pointed out firmly. 'Won't do.' I wondered now whom I was defending my copy and ideas for, but I did not want to dwell on this too long as it resulted in my becoming uncomfortably agitated. 'Rumba lyrics jive, they never disco, hadn't you noticed?' Dick, who could not understand the local lyrics, raised his eyebrows. 'Jiti doesn't disco either,' I instructed. 'Mbaqanga, maybe. Mbaqanga might cross, but if you're looking for a common marketing factor, it's probably too Ndebele.'

'You're not drinking your coffee,' Dick observed, apologetically rippling the surface of my coffee by tapping his teaspoon against my saucer. The sleekness of a weighty tiredness that washed over me was broken. The ripples eddied out to nothing and the liquid again grew still. I could feel people still looking at us and nurturing their smiles like hope at this reconciliatory, post-independence harmony.

Dick smiled reassuringly. 'Bill,' he resumed with the Creative Director's name, and paused before proceeding, 'Bill thinks the copy's bloody brilliant.' He hesitated again and took a gulp of coffee. His voice was low and apologetic as he spoke, as though he was sufficiently sensitive for his words to hurt him. 'Bill has asked me to present Afro-Shine to the client. Next week. The date's already set for the meeting.' A kind lover does this, speaks gently and, perhaps with a kiss, about a wedding between the lover and another person, pronouncing dates and locations so that you understood you are not to appear there. So although I did not have many love affairs behind me, I understood. I was not to meet the client. My copy was, but I was not good enough to merit that. And even that, I thought bitterly, like everything else about me was incorrect. My copy was not good enough; under someone else's name, it was.

I drank the coffee, without tasting it, while Dick, looking relieved, brought up a variety of issues, the desperate state of judging at the advertising awards and how Steers *et al* was to be commended because it created excellent campaigns for local products which, Dick observed, was good for our industry. How on earth were we to build a country if people and advertising agencies kept on promoting foreign products? A few minutes later Dick took a couple of crumpled red two dollar notes out of his pocket, one of which was mended with sticky tape, and put them on the table. We walked back to the agency. Dick's hands were pressed back in his pockets. His shoulders slumped over and his usually morose face gave not a clue to what he was thinking. His strides were long. I struggled to keep up in my high heels, my thoughts falling irregularly to the beat of our soles on the pavement.

About a week later I caught sight of the Afro-Shine copy on Belinda's desk for clean typing. Wanting to move on, I was nevertheless riveted to the spot and stood watching.

Rat-a-tat-tat, Belinda shot out from the keys, typing in the product name Afro-Shine Hair Care, and the name of the copywriter, Dick Lawson. 'Who said miracles never happen, hey?' the typist enthused. 'Old Dick! I never thought he had it in him.'

'That's right,' I agreed. 'I wish I could write like that.' I forced myself to be cheerful so as not to develop a complex.

'You will if you keep at it,' Belinda encouraged in a sisterly way. 'You've got what it takes. Don't give up. I know you'll do it!'

I then went by, passing Raphael on the way, not bothering to ask him whether he had left tea for me. He hadn't. Beyond not asking Raphael, I did not see what could be done, and therefore did nothing about my stolen copy. I calmed the twisting in my stomach by reminding myself that Dick was, on the whole, a decent colleague, otherwise he would not have informed me of what was taking place. If he had not, I might have been shocked into a moment of jumping out beyond myself on seeing what Belinda was preparing, and making a fool of myself in the office! So I felt quite grateful to Dick for being so considerate, and threw an appreciative look in his direction, but he was hunched over his typewriter, busy with Mighty Dough, and was not looking.

Having come this far in my beliefs, it was soon clear to me how Bill, the Creative Director, had thought through all aspects of the matter appropriately: what was good for Afro-Shine was good for the agency which I was a part of, thus what was good for Afro-Shine was good for me. This act that put Dick's name to my work was good for everybody; and I remembered names I'd learnt about at school: Elliot, Schumann and Bronte. Rewards did not accrue immediately, especially if, as your uncle pointed out, you had an inferior Social Science degree and A-Levels on different bits of cardboard. Contemplating this unpleasant fact, I did my best to boost my prospects at the agency by remaining agreeable.

On Fridays – every Friday and not only those associated with pay day – there was happy hour at the agency. Staff congregated in the office bar for half-price drinks, courtesy of Fortress Breweries, who were clients. In the weeks after Dick bounced the Afro-Shine copy, I began to celebrate happy hour regularly in order to be sociable. It was advisable to be early, to find an unobtrusive place, but on this particular Friday, a few days after Belinda clean typed the copy that was now Dick's, I spent time doodling question marks on a bit of scrap paper, to take my mind off what I was about to do and give myself the courage to go up. Should I, should I not, I asked myself, but knew I must. When I entered, Dick was already wedged into the angle between the bar and wall, his usual position, selected so that he could support himself from several sides as the evening developed. A couple of Fortresses were at work, levelling like a bulldozer the humps in his shoulders. Another sat before him on the bar, which he sheltered with interlocked fingers. The small space was unusually full. Raphael stood at the other end of the bar chatting to the barman, Alfonso. Pedzi was seated at a far table with two other dim forms. Light from the head-high wall lamps was gulped up by the dark wooden bar and the panelled walls. In the semi-darkness only one of Pedzi's companions could be recognised, and this only when she smiled. When she did, in the dim glow reflected from the room-wide mirror behind the bar on which was inscribed the name 'Phart and Pheasant' in curly letters, the girl's teeth, as strong and even as the grains of a perfect cob of maize, phosphoresced. It was the Dr White girl. Both she and Pedzi waved at me. I ignored the younger women and turned away.

'Oh Dick! You're a poet, although you don't know it!' Belinda, with that annoying Zimbabwean habit of repeating clichés as though they were a novel observation, made her way towards Dick bearing a gin and tonic. She set it down before the copy-writer and laughed in a surprised fashion as she stared at her colleague. After thumping him on the back, she waved me to an empty stool beside her, but I remained apprehensively motionless. Bill walked in through the door, waved at everybody, then strolled over and took the place.

'Miss Sigauke,' observed a friendly voice behind me. 'You are made not-of-air, nor-of-glass. That being the case, I am afraid I have to ask you to let me pass.'

It was Mr Steers. Behind him was Liz Wand, his

secretary, and behind both was my former classmate, Tracey Stevenson. Mr Steers nodded as he smiled and made his way past me, at the front of the little procession, moving as though by instinct to the bar's centre. Raphael shouldered over with three drinks, which he pressed into the party's hands.

Ting, ting, ting! Tracey hit her swizzle stick against her glass. Nobody paid attention. 'Hey, everybody! Be quiet a minute!' she roared, giving up niceties in the interests of atmosphere and high drama. Everyone was speechless for a startled moment, during which my former school mate tinged on her glass again and a respectable balance was restored. Mr Steers suavely inserted himself into the lacuna of silence and, with a delighted smile, announced not only a happy hour but an entire evening of subsidised imbibing. 'And if anyone would like champagne,' he now nodded at Alfonso, who popped a cork from a bottle on cue, 'I'd recommend it. Veuve Cliquot, which only bubbles in our bar here on extremely special occasions. In fact Tracey,' he turned his kindliness on the Afro-Shine executive, 'you must be one of the few who remembers.' Tracey beamed pleasurably and nodded her head as Mr Steers' face turned down remembrance road, to light up agreeably and gently at what it saw there.

'How many years ago?' our Managing Director mused deliberately, happily putting off recall.

But Dick, who was tipsy now, lumbered in plaintively, 'Thirteen! I was here too. My God, except for that stint in that fucking bloody place, I've been here forever, since before. . . before. . .' Dick could not supply the word, nor, for too many moments, could anyone else. We all became occupied with tearing at small pieces of biltong with our teeth or gulping drinks, until Alfonso, who was Mozambican and so could mention things Zimbabweans could not, volunteered calmly as he made his way round with a tray of champagne, 'Since the end of the war. The liberation struggle, the end of that. What was your name for it here in Zimbabwe? That's it,' he nodded sagely. 'People here say the *Chimurenga*. Or else they call it the *hondo*!'

Mr Steers accepted Alfonso's observations stoically, and used them to guide himself to the centre of troubled waters. 'You came here with a wealth of experience, Dick, both times you came to Steers and Associates,' he reminded the younger man, whose puffy flesh and clouded skin, due to remedies for the burden of memory in an assortment of capsules and bottles, caused him to look several years older than the elder major shareholder who was managing director. 'Dick,' Mr Steers went on kindly, 'I remember clearly, I was delighted when you came to us the first time. We all were, as we knew we had the good fortune to have amongst the team here an exceptional talent.' At this point Mr Steers looked at everybody and nodded. It was a prelude to adding yet more gently, 'Of course we were very anxious, indeed all of us were naturally very concerned at the time when it was necessary for you. . .' With this, the address faded out. It was a rare occurrence when the boss did not complete his sentence, and at this moment he did not. However, in a minute Mr Steers overcame the catch in his throat and added more animation to his tone. 'We were very anxious when you were called up to another service that very many of us were subjected to at the time!' There was a murmur for which Mr Steers paused once more, a dentist's excellent polishing job gleaming as tranquilly between his lips as the curve of the moon. This crescent expanded to half a moment later, when young Pedzi, who was practically but not quite a born free, cried into the ensuing throat clearings, sniffs and catches of breath, '*Saka, nhai*! Well then, where was everyone going?'

'No pissing where!' Dick drowned the rest of his words in a gulp of champagne that emptied his glass and Mr Steers resumed his speech kindly before the younger man had finished swallowing.

'All the management here were delighted when you returned,' Mr Steers assured Dick, who glowered until Alfonso pacified him by depositing in front of him an empty beer glass and a pint of Fortress. 'I wish I could say it was all on your behalf!' Mr Steers admitted with such an endearing mixture of jovialness and humility that relief flooded the room and everybody chuckled. 'Management,' continued Mr Steers in the same tones of apologetic appreciation, 'knew we had with us again an exceptionally special talent. That's why I am glad to see all our staff here this evening,' Mr Steers beamed, commending all of us. 'As you all know,' he informed his staff at large, 'we were particularly successful at this year's Advertising Awards. Most of that success accrued as a result of the Afro-Shine campaign taking the golden cock in print, radio and television, in every category it entered.'

Dick buried his face in his arms while everyone else broke out clapping. When the applause ebbed, Mr Steers flowed on at high tide, 'I thought you should all know that, as a result of that remarkable achievement, the Afro-Shine parent company is relocating two more brands and is introducing one new product to Steers, Darcy and MacPedius!

'As I'm not, like Dick here, a wordsmith,' Mr Steers continued to assure us, 'I'd better be brief. This year we are introducing our own internal awards. The award is to the creative department for the best concept, copy and campaign. I'm afraid to say we told Bill he's management himself as the Creative Director, and so can't very well give himself an award.' Here we all chuckled again. 'So the two awards this year,' continued the Managing Director, 'the inaugural year, for the copywriter and visual artist, go to Dick Lawson and Chris de Souza!' Tracey handed to Mr Steers a plate on which sat two envelopes. Pop! I upset my drink at the uncorking of another bottle. Pedzi struck up 'For he's a jolly good fellow!' Everyone joined in, and Alfonso, leisurely like a steeplechase champion, disbursed a victory round of champagne. 'Dick, you're a poet although you don't know it!' shouted Belinda as the copywriter went up to receive the award.

'Well, he does now!' rejoined Tracey. My mouth was dry and I wondered how much she knew. 'Or else he'd better,' Tracey laughed. 'I've got all these new accounts!' Amid the gaiety, Mr Steers proposed a toast to creativity coupled with good management and hard work. Pedzi stole the show again by shouting 'Three cheers for Dick!' and when we had all yelled hooray she capped it with, 'and one for Mr Steers!'

I downed a martini and wove through the tables holding a glass with an olive in it. When I came to Dick's table, I slipped my arms around his neck.

'She's after your money,' Belinda said, and all of us laughed.

'*Makorokoto!*' I said, resorting to quaintness. '*Amhlope*. Well done, hey, Dick. Anyone could see it was a great campaign! Congratulations!'

Dick pulled up a chair, by which movement he disengaged me. 'Sit down, Tambu, I'll buy you a drink,' he murmured, reverting to his usual strategies which this evening, because of the circumstance of happy hour, did not have any meaning. Away, away, away, was where I wanted to be. I spun from his touch on my arm, down the stairs to my typewriter. However, I still felt a sense of responsibility for Mr Steers, who might not have been told the true situation by the advertising executive and the Creative Director. I wrote: 'Dear Mr Steers, I am sorry to give you short notice. However, I am leaving your employment in order to be married. My husband does not wish me to work.' I signed my name, and this is how I left the agency. It is true, I hesitated for a while, staring at what I had set down. What would I do now being jobless? Was it not better to cultivate by tolerance my prospects at the agency? To be trodden on was discouraging admittedly, yet was it not a matter I had sufficient resources to come to terms with? But no and double no! To be crushed with Pedzi, Raphael and the Dr White girl observing it was not a matter a woman could countenance! This was a shame that precluded recovery! Besides, how much did they know? Were they also contributing to my decimation? The thought of it made me determined. I moistened the gum of an envelope with saliva. Before I walked through the revolving doors, I slid the message with my resignation under the Managing Director's door irretrievably. Balancing on toppling paving stones, I walked through the night to the hostel.

The trip, I considered with relief, could no longer take

place. Mai cannot come as I am no longer working. I contemplated the message. What if she took this news as an urgent invitation! But going home without anything to give! No oil or matches or meat or paraffin because I was looking after my finances! People would say they hadn't seen me. Besides, to say I did not have a job in spite of my degree was too much of an admission of failure. Ruminating on what should now be done, I arrived at the hostel.

The yesterday, today and tomorrow bush by the gate let off its fragrance, and I did not see today, only tomorrow glimmering softly, and yesterday gaping like dark holes in an old textile ravaged by larvae, these two extremes accentuated by too dim illumination. Half a dozen girls were at supper. Mrs May, a finger in her dictionary, the other hand holding a pen above the newspaper, looked up as I entered in order to examine me for a long time with a thoughtful gaze that did not blink behind her glasses. I coaxed a smile onto my face and Mrs May's wary demeanour relaxed instantly.

'Now, that's better,' she approved. 'You can't imagine what an improvement it is when you girls smile. And that's what I wanted to have a word with you about, my dear. You do seem particularly out of sorts in the past few weeks. If you're that unhappy here. . . um. . .' she decided not to risk specification and continued '. . . my dear, I'm sure you could find somewhere else that suits you.'

At this, my knees drained away. I stepped over to support myself on the counter. Mrs May smoothed her newspaper with a sad, nostalgic and solicitous expression. 'In fact,' she continued, 'I do believe I have some good news for you, something that should keep that smile on your face! What

do you think? Come over here and have a look at this paper.'
I did not want to approach her end of the desk, and so
remained where I was. 'There!' the matron went on, indicating. '9 Springbok Lane. That's Mabs Riley's place. I've
known her, ooh, for a long time, since we were in school
together. I used to see her regularly earlier on, although we
don't see each other much lately. It's so difficult to get out and
about and using the telephone's growing so expensive!' Mrs
May paused a while, exhausted for a moment by the intensity
of her memories. 'Oh, that Mabs!' the elderly woman shook
her grey permed head with a mixture of apprehension and
satisfaction. 'She's been threatening to leave for a long time!
Just like my son! I'm sure Mark's very happy where he is!
He's an anaesthetist in a hospital in Wales now, you know.
He's done very well. But Mabs won't be starting anything
new at her age.' Now the matron sounded so wistful that
I pulled the paper towards me and pretended to examine
it in order to give her some comfort. 'No, we're both past
new beginnings!' Mrs May nodded. 'That's why I wouldn't
go when Mark asked me to. If we'd had family over there
it would have been different. Proper family, I mean. And
Mabs is in exactly the same situation as me, you know! She
lost her husband, during the. . . during the. . .' the matron
faded out and then picked up again. 'Luckily, she owns her
house. She doesn't have to depend on her job like I do.' Mrs
May shuffled across so we could look at the daily together. In
the classified columns the elderly citizen had underscored an
advertisement with thick lines. 'I'd answer the advert myself
if it weren't for the job. Her husband passed away too,' she
repeated the inalterable fact. 'We'd be such good company
for each other! But I couldn't afford to without the job and

I'd never be able to get in and out of town. Besides there's always night duty.'

'I'm very sorry about Mr May,' I told the matron, as I had done many a time before, although I had noticed, in the weeks since the incident of the name, how Mrs May engaged with me in monologue less frequently than previously, and that she also answered in an unusually reserved manner when I greeted her spontaneously. Now she peered at me warmly.

'Mabs put an advertisement in. You see?' She pointed at the marked paragraph. 'She probably needs to, to help with expenses. It means she's staying, it definitely does.' Mrs May lifted her weight happily from foot to foot. 'My dear, I thought of you immediately! I'm sure it would be good for you, my dear, and I'm sure you'd enjoy it. It's in Borrowdale,' she named one of the city's northern suburbs. With this she became enthusiastic and her voice grew brighter. 'Wherever anyone comes from, if you're going to Borrowdale, you're going up in the world now, aren't you! You know, that's something to think of. Anyway, there's no point, Isabel,' she finished off, 'in your being here if it makes you miserable.' This last was delivered with some severity, suggesting that I did not appropriately appreciate my blessings, and hinting that I should not ignore this new chance I had been given as providence might become exhausted and cease offering me chances. 'I get dozens of applications everyday,' the matron explained, stretching her neck to see into the office where large black files sat on shelves built into the back wall. 'So all things considered, you'd be better off somewhere else and someone else who'd like it could take up residence.' She shuffled into the anteroom where she picked up a pair of scissors. 'There!' she waved when the advertisement was cut out. 'If there's any trouble, let me know. I'll put in a word for you. In fact I might just ring her up and tell her you'll be calling. It'll be lovely to get back in touch with her again.' The caked powder cracked as the matron's face creased in anticipation of a long over-due conversation with her schoolmate.

I thanked Mrs May as warmly as I could, then made a great show of picking the slip of newsprint up and stow-ing it carefully in my bag, to have the matter concluded. Miserably I sidled off down the hall. What was I going to do now? Was there any way to go back to the agency? Now that I was not wanted here, what would I do for accom-modation? There was no longer a place for me with my relatives at the mission. I could not go back to the home-stead where Netsai hopped unspeakably on a single limb, and where Mai would laugh at me daily. I had forgotten all the promises made to myself and providence while I was young concerning carrying forward with me the good and human, the *unhu* of my life. As it was, I had not considered *unhu* at all, only my own calamities, since the contested days at the convent. So this evening I walked emptily to the room I would soon vacate, wondering what future there was for me, a new Zimbabwean.

Glossary

Words:

Amhlope (Ndebele)	congratulations
Baba wenyu	your father
Babamunini	uncle
Biltong	dried meat
Bonde	reed mat
Bonga	a wild cat, which is a totem animal
Chimbwidos	female war collaborators
Chimurenga	war
Chisveru	tag
Chongololos	millipedes (corruption of zongororo)
Combi	minibus
Coup de grâce	blow of mercy, the last of a series of events or acts which brings about the end of some entity
Dagga	marijuana
Doek	head scarf
Ekani	exclamation made in greeting
Exeat	short mid-term holiday or overnight outing
Fasha-fasha	descriptive phrase for swaying movement
Fototo	onomatopoeic word meaning squashed or flattened
Ganja	marijuana

Hondo	war
Honkies	white people (derogatory word)
In flagrante	in the very act
Iwe	you
Kaffir	unbeliever
Kani	exclamation of emphasis
Koek sisters	variety of twisted doughnut
Kraal	cattle pen
Madhumbe	yams
Magrosa	grocer
Mainini	little mother (literal meaning); used as a term for a young aunt or in respect to any young woman
Makorokoto!	congratulations!
Maswera	greeting inquiring how the previous few hours have been
Matamba	fruit of mutamba tree (plural)
Matumbu	intestines
Mazikupundu!	great big spots!
Mazikuzamu!	great big tits!
Mbambaira	sweet potatoes
Mbuya	grandmother
Mealies	green maize
Mhani!	man! (exclamation)
Morari	a night time political gathering with song and dance, corruption of morale, from morale raising
Mufushwa	dried vegetables; especially spinach cooked and then dried out
Mujiba	male war collaborators
Mukoma	elder sibling

Mukuwasha	son-in-law
Mumwe wedu	one of us
Munts	African (derogatory word), corruption of *munhu*, person (Shona)
Murungu	white person
Musasa	name of tree
Musoni	dried vegetables; especially spinach cooked and then dried out
Mutamba	variety of tree
Mutengesi	betrayer
Mwana'ngu	my child
Nganga	traditional healer
Nyimo	groundnut
Nzungu	peanut
Povo	lower classes
Rigomhanya	to make it run
Rukweza	millet
Sahwira	extremely close friend
Samusha	head of the family
Sadza	staple food of stiff mealie meal porridge
Sekuru	grandfather, uncle
Sisi	sister
Sjambok	a heavy whip, usually made of animal hide
Takkies	canvas shoes
Tickey	small coin of value about two and a half cents
Tshombes	sell outs
Ubuntu	no direct translation: a philosophy of being prevalent in southern Africa based on the essence of the person

Unhu	personhood
Vakoma	the elder siblings
Vana bhuti	the brothers
Vana mukoma	the elder siblings
Vana sisi	the sisters
Vanachimbwido	the female war collaborators
Vanasekuru	the grandfathers
Vasikana	the girls
Vatengesi	the betrayers
Veld	meadow, plain
Wekuchirungu	people from European places (literal meaning)

Phrases:

Aiwa, kwete!	No, no!
Bhunu! Rova musoro rigomhanya!	The white! Hit it on the head to make it run!
Ini zvangu!	Oh, me!
Kani! Uya	Come on! Come!
Kure kure! Kure kure! Kure kwandinobva, vana mai na baba, tondo sangana, KuZimbabwe!	Far, far away! Far, far away! I come from far away, mothers and fathers, we will meet in Zimbabwe!
Kushinga makadaro!	Going on like that!
Kuudza mwana upedzisira!	You have to instruct a child down to the last detail – a proverb, equivalent to crossing the 't's and dotting the 'i's
Manheru mwana, wangu!	Good evening, my child
Manheru, shewe!	Good evening, Lord
Pamberi nerusununguko!	Forward with freedom!

Pamberi nechimurenga! Forward with the liberation
Pasi nevadzvinyiriri! war! Down with oppressors!
Rambai makashinga! Stay strong!
Saka, nhai! Well, then!
Sisi Tambu, mamuka sei? Sisi Tambu, how are you this
morning?

Tiripo, kana makadini wo! I am well, if you are well too.
Usvuukue! Usvuuke! So that you peel! So that you
peel!

Yave nyama yekugocha, This is meat for a roast, stab
baya wabaya! it, whoever can!
Zviunganidze! Pull yourself together!

Special thanks for encouragement and support to
Fatima, Megan, Viv and Julia
Chinua Achebe
The Zimbabwe Women's Word Circle
The Zimbabwe Culture Fund Trust
Swedish International Development Agency
The Civitella Ranieri Foundation

Also by Tsitsi Dangarembga

Nervous Conditions

Two decades before Zimbabwe would win independence and end white minority rule, thirteen-year-old Tambudzai Sigauke embarks on her education. On her shoulders rest the economic hopes of her parents, siblings and extended family, and within her burns the desire for independence. A timeless coming-of-age tale and a powerful exploration of cultural imperialism, *Nervous Conditions* charts Tambu's journey to personhood in a nation that is also emerging.

'A masterpiece.' Madeleine Thien

'Unforgettable.' Alice Walker

'This is the book we've been waiting for.' Doris Lessing

faber

This Mournable Body

Here we meet Tambudzai, living in a run-down youth hostel in downtown Harare and anxious about her prospects after leaving a stagnant job. At every turn in her attempt to make a life for herself, she is faced with a fresh humiliation, until the painful contrast between the future she imagined and her daily reality ultimately drives her to a breaking point.

In this tense and psychologically charged novel, Tsitsi Dangarembga channels the hope and potential of one young girl and a fledgling nation to lead us on a journey to discover where lives go after hope has departed.

'Magnificent.' *Guardian*

'Subtle and intelligent.' *Times Literary Supplement*

'Marvellous.' Sara Collins

faber

Sign up for free

Become a Faber Member and discover the best *in the arts and literature*

Sign up to the Faber Members programme and enjoy specially curated events, tailored discounts and exclusive previews of our forthcoming publications from the best novelists, poets, playwrights, thinkers, musicians and artists.

Join Faber Members for free at faber.co.uk